AN ACCURATE ACCOUNT

AN ACCURATE ACCOUNT

LINDA M. MUTTY

All characters and events in this book are fictitious. Any similarity to real persons, living or dead, is coincidental and not intended by the author.

ISBN 978-1-7323221-3-4
ISBN 978-1-7323221-4-1

Where I sit is holy,

Holy is this ground

Forest, mountain, desert, river, ocean

I listen to the sound.

Great Spirit circle

All around me.

Anonymous

Chapter 1

His count was accurate. Fifteen scratch marks. But to be sure, Quin counted once again, this time in a better light. Fifteen as of this morning. Piercing another hole in the soft leather, he tightened the belt around his shrinking waist, the excess leather having grown in length with each puncture while the scratch marked leather dangled between his legs. The desert sunrise was less than an hour old but already he felt the familiar heat of the past days with no relief in sight. In his weakening state, he considered staying where he was. Staying there until the end. With no idea where he was or which way to head, he saw no reason not to stay. He was no different than any animal in the wild who was on its last legs. Alone, open to what would naturally occur, acceptance of its ending because it had no choice. He wondered if an animal sensed finding peace or if it just perished, its brain not considering what might be beyond.

The unexpected death of Edward, his younger brother and only sibling, was the catalyst that inevitably brought him to this place as he waited for his own death. It wouldn't be long now. It occurred to him as he surveyed his final resting place that his imminent death would be different than Edward's. Not sudden, unexpected as Edward's had been but a drawn-out event that, if he chose to, would allow him time to reflect on his life. He would, to a point, experience the onset of his body failing, every one of his senses dying, one by one, until he was no longer aware of anything. He wondered if it would be a painful death or if he would just go to sleep not even aware of taking his last breath. He hoped that the latter would be the case.

"Edward never knew what hit him," the attending physician told Quin. "He died instantly upon impact." An officer who had been at the scene offered his attempt at consolation. "Edward was in the wrong place at the wrong time." This did not settle well with Quin, as if Edward were to blame. But he held his tongue. He knew that the officer was right in an existential way. Fate. Pure and simple. If it was any consolation, the speeding, running-the-red-light fool did not survive either. He lay in a hospital bed for a few days before succumbing and Quin hoped that he had suffered.

When Edward died at twenty-three, Quin had been on his own for five years. And in those five years, he had never returned to the island, his birthplace. His only attachment to it had been his brother. When Edward joined him on the mainland four years ago, their lives together were enough for them. Neither one desired to visit Whittlestone or their parents again. The separation only grew stronger the longer the sons stayed away. The mainland was their home now. Besides, their parents never asked them to come back to visit.

With Edward's death, neither Quin nor his parents came to terms with their loss as a family. Instead, his parents grew distant from one another and then from Quin. Their mourning became an individual process that blocked out everyone else. At one point, Quin questioned whether he was still considered the surviving son or was he also lost to his parents. He knew they blamed him. Edward would still be alive if he hadn't followed his brother to the mainland.

Quin's story wasn't original. In his seventy-three years on this earth, nothing he had done had been original. One of the sobering thoughts that led him to his decisions to leave relationships, not once but three different times. He knew that it was just one of the millions of others already played out or, like his, still in process but with the end imminent. He wondered if others suffered for as long as he had or if they were smarter and called it quits early on, leaving less tragedy in their wake. In any case, what was done was done.

At the time, the decisions felt good. The right ones to make. His only options. He repeatedly told himself this each time he left the familiar. With each affirmation, his anticipation for the unknown growing stronger. An intoxicating feeling overwhelming him as he left his past for the first time when he turned eighteen. He tried to name it as he watched his birthplace grow distant on the horizon as the small vessel moved through the waters carrying him to the mainland. The feeling. It suddenly hit him. Freedom. The feeling was freedom.

When he was young, he imagined many scenarios of how his life might turn out, all possibilities with great promise. Now, no longer young but old and dying as he suffered the growing heat of the desert sun, he struggled to remember if any of those imaginings had come true. Perhaps, but he wasn't really sure anymore. However, he was certain of one thing. He never imagined that his life would end this way.

The Time Before

Just twenty-eight miles from the mainland on the island of Conical, Quin and Edward Leet were born in the family home one year apart. Only when supplies ran low had they ever been off the island accompanying their father on the short boat ride to the mainland. Their mother was afraid of the sea, an unusual fear as she was born on the island as were her own parents. However, she didn't mind sending her sons and husband out into the waters. It never occurred to her that they might not come back. They always returned. Her false sense of security that this would always be the case allowed her to function in their absence. Others had lost their lives in the treacherous currents and hidden jagged outcroppings of ancient mountain tops that surrounded the island, only visible at the lowest tide. It was then that the boats left the island, and it was only then that they returned.

The air stank of dead fish. When the westerlies blew, they carried the stench from the small fishery tucked against the northwestern shoreline less than a mile from town. Windows were kept shut even though everyone was used to the intrusion. The men and women who returned home each day after working there permanently carried the stench with them. It permeated their clothes, their skin, their very being. No matter how much they cleansed themselves each evening, the residue that built up over time refused to let them forget their lot in life. They did not complain. Their earnings put food on the table, kept a roof over their families' heads, and left enough to enjoy a pint or two at the pub on the way home once or twice a week. Never more than that for there were those who kept a watchful eye on those who ignored the unspoken rule while imbibing when they knew they shouldn't. There were no secrets kept in Whittlestone and if there were, they were never kept for long.

One of three small enclaves established in the early 1700s on Conical Island, Whittlestone was located on the western side of the island, the other two on the eastern side, one in the north and one in the south. All three were sustained by fishing, although Whittlestone was the largest of the three. It wasn't unusual for young men to cross the island from Danbury in the east or Fiddlestowe in the south for more profitable work in Whittlestone. Some years, the outliers were welcomed, especially if the sea blessed the western side of the island with an abundance of fish. The help was welcomed and even more so the shared profits. But this was not so when the outliers arrived during the time when it seemed the sea ran almost dry. The fishermen of Whittlestone did not shy away from informing the outliers that they were not welcome. It was during these times that the pub was not a place of comradeship but of conflict. And it was because of these times that the brotherhood of fishermen grew farther apart, a growing dislike and distrust in one another.

Quin and Edward understood this history as told to them by their father. But neither boy experienced it, nor did they want to. The island afforded no future for the brothers. Neither one could see his life imitating his father's. That of a fisherman barely bringing in enough money to put food on the table. Other sons on the island did not question their futures. They were not allowed to any more than Quin and Edward. However, the brothers liked to break the rules, to disrupt the status quo. They did not do it out of disrespect. They never would hurt their father or mother in that way. Perhaps because they were born so close together in time, they thought as one which gave them the strength to break the mold together. Whatever the reason, Quin and Edward each, upon turning eighteen, left the island. They were a disappointment to their father, but he did not give up hope that he could persuade one of them to stay on the island and follow in his footsteps. Even as each son on the day of their departure from their birthplace proceeded to board the outgoing vessel to the mainland, his father's attempts to convince him one last time were met with failure. Quin and Edward knew that the rift created between their father and them could never be mended. The farewell was the beginning of the end, both shaken by their father's curse upon them.

As Quin attempted to remember every detail of Edward's anticipated arrival only three weeks after turning eighteen and the few years they spent together on the mainland, his heart ached for his brother. However, the incomplete memories were overwhelmed by the thought that very soon he would see him again. He only hoped that Edward would be waiting for him. Quin would tell his brother about his life, his failures and successes, and he wondered if Edward would care. After all, almost fifty years had passed since Edward's death. Fifty years that were needlessly denied Edward. Fifty years in which Quin had, for the most part, screwed up his life, maybe even wasted it. His thoughts came one after the other as he fought for breath and it occurred to him that he had nothing to complain about, not in light of his brother's fate.

The rising heat of the morning inhibited his movements, and his breathing was labored. He slowly shifted his body to lean against the outcropping of smooth stone that was to be his deathbed. He tried to think of "happy thoughts" as Peter Pan suggested but he knew that he would not suddenly fly. He quietly laughed. If he could fly, he could escape this place. Besides, he didn't have any happy thoughts. He couldn't remember the last time he did.

Chapter 2

Upon his arrival on the mainland, Quin purposely traveled inland leaving the ocean far behind him. He crossed one coastal mountain range and then another until he settled in the town of Crosswood. Lacking any worthwhile skill, he was hired on as an apprentice to an electrician who was grateful for the help and eager to teach the young man. The town's steady growth for the last year provided him with more business than he could handle. The fortuitous arrival of Quin was a blessing. "Just in the nick of time," he would always tell his customer.

On his way to acquiring the necessary qualifications to become a licensed electrician, Quin understood payback and he owed it to Gary Sunderlind. Comfortably situated in his home with food on his plate and pocket money to spend, Quin did not let a day go by without saying a silent thank you to Gary for taking a chance on him. He was eager for Edward to meet Gary not that he presumed that his brother would follow in his and Gary's footsteps but that he knew Gary would welcome him warmly into the community. There was no guarantee that Edward would be as lucky as Quin had been procuring a job so quickly. Quin was aware of this and even told Edward this in a phone call about the arranged meeting spot for Edward's arrival. Having turned eighteen less than three weeks ago, Edward was eager to join Quin whether a job came quickly or not. The only thing on his mind was to leave Conical Island behind him and to start a new life with his brother.

The trip over the two mountain ranges to the coast took four hours by car. Quin looked forward to the time by himself, stopping along the way to take in the glorious views that, on this clear late October day seemed to go on forever. Everything felt so right as he took in the seasonal changes that struck every one of his senses. He had seen nothing like it on the island. His memories landed on the storm times, the destructive nature of the sea's angry waters and the wind's intensity. The dismally dark and dank days that took possession of the island. The depressed fishermen who openly cursed the skies, the ocean, and God because they could not go to sea. It was during these times that the pub filled to capacity as wives insisted their fishermen husbands leave the house until they could be civil. Quin remembered these times, never the better times. As he breathed in the warm fall day's dry air, he allowed himself to relax as his body absorbed the sun's rays. He wondered if this was what heaven was like. He hoped so.

He hadn't been back to the coast since his arrival on the mainland a year ago. As he walked to the dock, Quin was struck by the stark differences in environment. Not that he had forgotten his eighteen years surrounded by ocean but after only one year inland, the comparisons were few. He had left Crosswood wearing shorts and a tee-shirt remembering at the last minute to throw in a hoodie. The chill he felt as he made his way to the water's edge, surprised him. His hoodie left in the car, his lack of preparedness identified him as a tourist.

Edward waved from the bow of the small vessel whose sole purpose was to transport people and goods between the mainland and Conical Island. A proposal to build a ferry system years ago came to nothing. Change did not come easily on the island. As the vessel docked, Quin waved back anticipating the imminent reunion.

It was as if no time had passed between the brothers. Little was said about their parents. Only that their mother, in the presence of her husband, begged Edward not to go, not to leave her behind like his brother did, alone and unhappy. All Quin could do was shake his head in affirmation that his mother had not changed, that nothing would ever change in that place. Before heading back to Crosswood, the brothers spent time catching up over a couple of beers in an establishment that was one step up from the pub on the island, another fisherman's holdup. However, the cliental were not all men of the sea. The place appeared to be a crossroads where seamen and land lovers came together.

Edward did not know what he wanted to do for work, a statement that struck Quin as immature. After all, Quin had told Edward about the many opportunities for work in Crosswood and of his experience with Gary Sunderlind. Even though it was fate that brought Quin to Gary, Quin was sure that the same would happen for Edward if it wanted it to. But his words fell on deaf ears, and it occurred to Quin that Edward had no need to seek independence, not when a warm house and food awaited him.

As close as the brothers had been while still under their parents' roof, Quin sensed the beginnings of a rift between Edward and him. He was sure it was one-sided brought on by his own disappointment in Edward. Perhaps he was expecting too much of his brother too soon. He would give him time to settle in. Quin's expectations, however, would not change. Fair is fair. Edward needed to make his own way.

"You two are as different as night and day," their mother used to say about her sons. "Hard to believe you both came out of me."

There was a time in which Quinn and Edward found comfort in their mother's words. Never said in anger or frustration but in awe of whom she had birthed, she'd break into laughter, shaking her head as if she still couldn't believe it, and without another word spoken, she'd walk away from them. It was her laughter that signaled to them that they had nothing to worry about. As long as she laughed, it made no difference what she said about them. A far cry from their stoic father.

Neither boy could remember ever hearing him laugh. For that matter, they would be hard pressed to remember his speaking voice, so little of it did they hear. But when they did, it was loud, demanding, angry, and saturated in weariness. Whatever he said to them was not meant to be responded to. It was his way of blowing off steam, his sons being easy targets of his dissatisfaction with his life. He never hurt them, never laid a hand on them. That much could be said about him. Quin spent many quiet hours on his own before Edward's arrival searching his mind for just one memory of his father's kinder voice, one that he was sure he must have heard at some point, but no memory existed. Instead, his father's words of anger were the last words he recalled as Quin boarded the vessel to the mainland.

Quin and Edward shared four years together in Crosswood. Edward found work in construction and, much like Quin, learned on the job. The rift that Quin sensed at the beginning never materialized. Edward did his fair share to keep the roof over both of their heads and food on the table. Both exhausted by the end of a workday, they collapsed every evening in front of the television until they called it a night. A comfortable pattern of coexistence developed. Neither brother missed the island or their parents. And when spoken of, neither subject elicited much interest in continuing the conversation.

The news of Edward's death shattered everything. The eighteen years of life before Crosswood meant nothing any longer to Quin and the brothers' four years together on their own had gone by too quickly for Quin to appreciate Edward. His brother's death left him teetering on the edge of an endlessly deep and inviting crevice of blessed forgetfulness. All he had to do was take the final step forward. As close as he came on numerous occasions, Quin could never go through with it, never take his own life. And each time he failed, his belief that he was and always had been a coward was reaffirmed. It was no way to exist, just as it had been unthinkable to stay on the island and stink of fish for the rest of his life.

His decision was made almost six months to the day of his brother's death. Gary understood and wished him well, reminding him that he could do electrical work anywhere he landed. A good fall-back, if needed. Quin told him he'd keep in touch, but he knew he wouldn't, any more than he kept in touch with his own blood who, for all he knew by now might be dead or close to it. No one mattered to him, and he sensed in his deepest depression that no one ever would. He was entirely alone, and he willingly accepted it.

Chapter 3

"I've got an idea."

"Another? It's only been an hour since the last one." Quin sipped on his morning coffee.

"Okay, but this one's good. Hear me out, okay?" Edward sat across from Quin.

Lately, Edward's positive outlook on life had intensified, as Quin saw it, and he wondered what had gotten into his little brother.

"So, we find some land in the mountains and you and me, we build a cabin." Edward leaned back in his chair, a smug appearance of having solved all the world's problems. Before Quin could respond, Edward lunged forward again. "Between the two of us, it could happen."

"It could but I don't think it will. You going to commute into the valley every day for work? We need income and you won't make it in the woods. Maybe when we retire. That is if we are still hanging out together, single, and oddballs." Quin wasn't kidding about his oddball remark. He was aware of some of the guys talking. Two young men living together. The rumors that came out of it. There wasn't much out there yet, but the longer the brothers chose this lifestyle, more talk would circulate. It was just the way things went.

"Why do you have to be so negative?"

"Not being negative. Just being practical. Don't let me stop you. If you want to build a cabin, go for it."

Edward did not immediately respond. "Maybe I will." He got up and shuffled over to the kitchen. "Maybe I will do just that, big brother." He slammed his fist on the counter, keeping his back turned to conceal his pain.

Quin glanced over, unconcerned having witnessed Edward's frustrations numerous times before. For someone who seemed nonchalant about everything upon his arrival a year ago, Edward's outlook had done a 180 so that everything that occurred required an overblown reaction from him. If

Quin allowed himself to dwell on this, it disturbed him. Better just to let him blow off steam as if nothing had happened.

Edward did not see it that way. He was not aware that the growing frequencies of his outwardly displayed frustrations were silently wearing on Quin. It never entered Edward's thinking. However, Quin's disinterest in his brother's emotional outbursts was wearing on Edward. But neither brother shared this with the other while the once imagined rift between them was becoming a shared reality.

Edward and Quin lived under the same roof for three more years. As time passed, the brotherly companionship that they had shared when younger and that both anticipated surviving while dreaming of their freedom at eighteen was vanishing and neither attempted hold on to it. There were no love interests to get in the way, no friendships that might threatened the security of a brotherly bond, nothing that could be identified as the catalyst for their separation. Yet, the separation was real, even as they sat across from one another while sharing a meal. Cordial conversation passed between them but nothing of substance. The important issues, assured paychecks, bills paid on time, maintenance of cars, and shared output for food and household needs appeared to be safe topics if not necessary ones. Nothing more.

As the fourth year neared its completion, the brothers finally came to accept that it was time to part ways. Neither one was happy with how his life was turning out. They could easily have blamed the other for this, but they didn't because it wasn't true. Both knew, without saying it aloud, that each was to blame. The failure of their relationship was the result of their own inability to deal with themselves. Who they had been and were becoming. As if nothing mattered in life other than waking up, enduring the day, and falling asleep at the end of it. Where a sadness for this failure should have been, there was nothing but relief as the brothers parted ways just before Thanksgiving. Edward had been ready to move out for weeks and when the day came, he tried to hide his excitement.

"I'll let you know where I land up north. But don't expect to hear from me for a while." Putting down his bags just inside the door, Edward spoke without looking at Quin who stood to the side.

"That's fine. I can wait. Just try to stay safe, Edward. I'll just continue to believe no news is good news." Quin forced his words into the space between them. He was having trouble finding anything to say.

"Right. I intend to." He extended his hand.

Quin searched for the words that would end this time together as brothers but remained silent. He gripped Edward's hand, an unintended length of time, until Edward pulled away. Slinging his backpack over his shoulder, Edward grabbed the two small bags that held everything he owned and walked away.

Not months, weeks, or days passed. Less than three hours after Edward's departure, the news of his death abruptly ended Quin's expectations of ever hearing from his brother again.

Chapter 4

The late spring in Crosswood was its most beautiful time. At least, according to Quin. It held promise of better things to come, a hope that was inevitably shattered with the first heatwave of the summer. But still. Perhaps he related to spring's last gasp of breath before it died each year. Its last attempt for him to understand what hope was, what it could mean to him. But like everything else in his life that he did not bother to appreciate, it appeared giving him ample time to connect, but disappeared before he could. He never could. It was not within him, a character flaw that he accepted.

That he found himself involved with a woman was the awakening of an unknown part of him. That he heard himself ask her to marry him and then heard her "yes", was further evidence to him that, perhaps, he did have something to live for. That attempting to sustain hope had not been a waste of time. That what he thought was a character flaw was nothing of the sort. It had just not been his time. As he walked back down the aisle with his new wife on his arm, the happiness he felt overwhelmed him and any thought of life going forward being anything but joyous bliss was far from his thoughts. His only regret was that Edward was not here to share this moment with him.

Edward would have liked Amelia Turner. She was just as spontaneous as he had been before he wasn't. It was what drew Quin to her, the opposite of whom he knew he was. It wasn't long before this quality, however, turned against him so that he grew tired of her. Quin often considered the irony of his situation. If Edward had lived, Amelia and he would have hit it off. Would have married, had a slew of children, and found their way to the cabin in the woods that Edward had built. He had been cheated out of what should have been his. Instead, Quin was ruining yet another relationship by doing nothing but being himself. He thought little of sneaking away in the middle of the night. The divorce papers, the only communication between them since leaving his marriage, he signed with no regrets. A clean break. A gift from Amelia that escaped Quin.

He turned forty the day after Christmas. A year out from the divorce, and almost seventeen years since Edward's death, Quin did not take stock of his life. What was the point? What was done was done. Even when he moved out of Crosswood and finally settled farther inland, he didn't bother to plan his life any more than the next move considering how quickly it could be taken from him.

He settled in Benton, a city four hundred and fifty miles northeast of Crosswood and far enough away from the current past and even farther from the past that should have mattered. He had no trouble finding a job thanks to Gary Sunderlind. The company that hired him also managed a construction group who could not keep up with the demand for new housing, new office construction, and anything that required skilled workers. Quin knew what he had signed up for, had signed the contract, and understood that he could keep another roof over his head. However, when the first paycheck arrived, he could not believe his luck. All the overtime added to his salary was more than he could ever make in six months if he had stayed in Crosswood. It occurred to him that maybe his life was taking a positive turn, that there was nowhere to go but up. He tried to recall if he ever felt as good as he felt now and he couldn't.

In his early fifties, he rose to a management position, his salary doubling, his former peers now those he managed. At first, the rush of power in his position was a good feeling. He savored it and, gradually, he gave little thought to the people under him who had worked right next to him day in and day out as equals. Taking on his new responsibilities was the only thing that mattered. Initially, his former peers accepted his new status, but it wasn't long before they turned on him. His own doing to be sure as he let his power go to his head. Unjust decisions, ignoring legitimate requests, favoring those he liked and shunning those he didn't. This went on until he was called in by his supervisors who gave him one chance to correct his many missteps if he wanted to stay employed.

Had it been anyone else but Quin, he would have attempted to right his errant ways if for no other reason than not to lose a good paycheck. But it was Quin, and the power he enjoyed for once in his life was not meant to last. He was sure of this. One more example, as far as he was concerned, that nothing lasts. It never occurred to him that it could have if he had seen it differently. With no attempt made to save his job, he was not surprised to find himself at fifty-three out on the sidewalk in the middle of the day with nowhere to go and nothing to do.

The realization that he could no longer afford the accumulation of "things" that he had come to take for granted as rightfully his and easily afforded, struck him hard. He would have to start over again as though he was the eighteen-year-old kid who had once been so sure of himself.

One more time, he made the move. With the limited proceeds from the sale of his house, he paid off his cards, the car, and left it all behind him. In his quiet moments, he almost delved deeply enough into his thoughts to see his predicament clearly and to chart the path of his life thus far. But he never went far enough. Never charting his path going forward from the present point. Never considering going deeper into his psyche because he didn't want to know. No reminders, no regrets. Nothing to bind him to the past. Nothing to obstruct his future. It was so simple, he realized, and he wondered why people even allowed themselves to fall into the trap of having a conscience. All that did was confuse and hold you back, was his thinking. His way was so easy, so simple.

In a perverse way, he envied Edward's premature death. But even Quin had sense enough to know that the alternative was probably better. The thought of never having to encounter any more setbacks in his life was attractive to him, but he was a coward. Besides, if he really thought about it, he was gaining on Edward by accumulating life experiences. A point in his plus column.

In the fifteen years after leaving Benton, now sixty-eight, Quin lived a modern hobo's life. He initially headed west but not far enough to smell the ocean, to even sense its presence. He moved to the northwest, a little at a time, finding odd jobs to keep him fed and, infrequently, a temporary roof over his head. From the northwest, he headed northeast never settling anywhere for longer than a few days. He never made any acquaintances that could clutter his life somewhere down the road unexpectedly, uninvited. His self-imposed isolation was all that sustained him. Drawing him farther from unnecessary human contact while insolating him in his own myth, he was untouchable. He was solely in charge of himself. He was completely alone, and he was the happiest he had ever been.

Chapter 5

Twisted tendrils. That's how he would recall his first sight of her. Honey-soaked strands flowing through a mound of midnight black braid that balanced on her right shoulder before heavily dropping just below her waist. He had never seen anything like it. She caught him staring at her, knowing full well that she attracted his attention because of it. How many times had others commented on her locks? Never seeing her first. Her face an afterthought. She held no resentment, however. It was her choice to flaunt her natural gift from her mother and grandmother. One day, maybe, she might cut it.

She was placed in his path, directly and squarely. He had no options but one. When he engaged with her, who she could be to him was immediately apparent. A soulmate. A partner. The love of his life. As if she had been placed in front of him on purpose by the gods who were fed up with his meanderings, a life without any purpose, a life wasting away with nothing to show for it. One last chance. They had better things to do.

Matilda allowed Quin into her world, a world overflowing with the vibrancy of life. She never questioned his past or his current circumstances. She appeared to accept him in the moment, but she did not presume to have a hold on him. Her life remained intact. Quin's was fraying. He struggled to keep up with her. A struggle born out of love and commitment, something so foreign to him that he was surprised by his willingness to try. She was an artist whose canvases filled her small studio that was attached to a home that she owned outright. She purposely bought the land, built the house and then the studio when she came into her first real sale of her work. More money than she ever dreamed of possessing. He asked her why she lived alone so far north in the mountains less than ten miles from the Canadian border. Her answer was simple. "It is where I am meant to be." And he wondered if he was finally where he was meant to be, even though she did not include him in her answer.

When she worked, she allowed him to watch but not always. Today, she had invited him to the studio but only if he remained silent. He knew her demands well and had never gone against them. Many times he had observed her process, something he did not understand, and when asked was told that she didn't understand it either. Although enthralled by her creativity, he never stayed long for fear of her asking him to leave having overstayed his welcome. He would creep out of the studio avoiding any interruption in her concentration. Some days he would not see her at all, not until she came back to the house, darkness long fallen and he already deep in sleep. Other times, she would surprise him by her early arrival having spent less than a few hours at her work and ready to "do something spontaneous" with him. And he was always compliant. As time passed, their relationship was maintained because of the unexpected. The idea that they were equally unencumbered by any restraints brought happiness to their relationship where love should have been.

"Have I ever asked anything from you, Quin?" She looked up from her work as he sat behind her always admiring. She did not turn to him, standing still as she balanced the brush between her fingers. She waited.

"No." He hesitated before responding sensing an unease as he tried to remember if she ever had.

Placing her brush in the narrow wooden groove at the base of her easel, she kept her back to him as she spoke. She took a step back and admired her progress.

"No, I haven't. But I am going to ask you now. Only one thing and only one time. And I want you to respond to me now. Here, where we are at this very moment. Okay?" She turned the upper half of her body as if looking at him over her shoulder.

"That's a bit unfair, you asking me to agree to respond before I know if I can, don't you think?"

She turned back to the unfinished canvas. "Oh, I think you can."

He rose from the stool, his observation post, and moved to her side. "What's all the mystery about?" He turned to her.

"There's no mystery, Quin. Not really. I'm asking you to leave." She remained still as if frozen.

"Leave? You mean here? From the studio?" She was making no sense.

"Yes and no."

Confused, he moved to stand between her and the canvas.

"You're going to have to be clearer than that. What's going on?"

"I'm asking you to leave. To leave me, Quin."

Clarity was not helping him even though she could not have been clearer. Unable to accept her words, to absorb their meaning, he simply asked, "Why?"

"It's simple. It's time for you to go. Can't you see that?" The words came, one at a time as if in exaggerated slow motion, as if he were incapable of understanding.

It had been almost five years, their time together. He was content and he would swear that she was as well. Their arrangement was unspoken but worked so well that he woke up each day amazed that he was still with her. Had she ever given him reason to believe that it was otherwise? Had she?

"No, I can't see that. I don't get why you are even saying this to me."

"Because I need to. Because if I don't, neither one of us can move on. It's just time, Quin. That's all." They were less than a foot apart but for her, it felt a million miles.

Her communication was clear and final. He considered attempting to convince her otherwise, but the effort was too much work. A fleeting memory of his father appeared and vanished. What would he accomplish if he tried? Nothing but unnecessary stress and anger on his part that he knew would be one-sided. Matilda had her own world to escape to. What did he have?

Had he considered anything beyond his hurt feelings and confusion, he might have related this with the previous departures he had experienced. Leaving his parents, Edward's departure, Gary Sunderlind, Amelia, and now Matilda were all part of a pattern that was his life. It never changed, the pattern, even as each event occurred. Instead, each departure wove one more layer into the fabric that was his life, a collection of failures that, standing alone meant nothing but intertwined were all there was of Quin. It was just a matter of time before the fabric faded, its many weaves unraveling as if in concert with one another. Just a matter of time. He closed the door behind him. A last glance in the direction of the studio and then he was gone.

Chapter 6

The morning was crisp. The northwest was deep within the fall season. It was not the best time to be without shelter but not as bad as the winter months that were approaching rapidly. The freezing cold mornings, the shortened lukewarm days that faded too soon into darkness and cold once again, were wake-up calls for Quin. Since leaving Matilda's home, nothing was permanent for him. Moving from one homeless encampment to another, depending on strangers to save him from himself, he struggled to find direction. Unless he contributed something to the outcast communities he came to depend on, he was not welcomed to stay. Fair was fair. For him, it was easier to leave.

He made his way to Canada, the crossing at the Washington border into British Columbia. His passport and documents were in order, a surprising feat considering the chaos of the rest of his life. In the last encampment, he borrowed a razor, scissors, and soap attempting to appear presentable. Watching Quin's efforts from a distance, an old man in the camp gave him a clean jacket, almost too small but much better than what he had been wearing for months. "Got no use for it anymore." A younger man offered him a pair of jeans, not new but again, better than what he owned. "Might as well take them. You look half-dressed if you don't. Won't get into Canada looking like that." For a fleeting moment, Quin felt grateful to the strangers, but it passed. A grunt of thanks was all he could manage.

He convinced the border patrol, a middle-aged woman who stood in her booth fully prepared to turn him back to the states if she deemed it necessary, by stating his reason for entering Canada. A lie but one that was convincing enough. He was visiting family for a month. A brother and sister in Vancouver and cousins on Nanaimo Island. The woman's demeanor was friendly as she carefully looked through his passport. Nothing in it to indicate he traveled much other than one Mexican stamp of entry. She flipped through the small blue booklet twice and once more. Handing it back to Quin, her words sent a wave of relief through him. "Welcome to Canada. Hope you have a good visit with family."

As he entered the visitor's center, a building set deep within a broad lawn whose flower gardens, even at this time of year, were almost too much to take in, the warmth of the building overwhelmed him. There were more people gathered there than he had seen in many months. He sat down on a long bench that bordered the large space between him and the welcome desk. People from all over the world moved in front of him, small clusters of families, couples young and old, and solitary figures, all with a direction, unlike him. He debated whether to go to the counter and ask for information. But to do that, he needed to have questions. What could he possibly request that they would gladly answer? Where is the nearest homeless camp? The nearest shelter where he could get a hot meal every day? Maybe shelter at night from the cold?

For a moment, he wondered if he could stay in this country. Observing the visitors moving on with their lives, eager to see the sights, to greet their relatives, or to pass through the country on their way elsewhere, he could not have felt more alone. And briefly, his lie and the truth melded into one so that he anticipated seeing loved ones again. He leaned back against the wall shifting his weight so that his backpack served as a cushion and then closed his eyes. Undisturbed, he slipped into a deep sleep, the afternoon kind that blocks everything out. He dreamt of a reality that did not exist, not for him. An aunt and uncle welcoming him into their warm home, a hot meal waiting for him, and a warm fire glowing in the fireplace. He heard laughter but did not know why they laughed. He dreamt of crossing the frigid waters from the mainland to an island and his cousins waiting at the ferry landing to take him home with them. He saw in his dreaming what the lie could have been like if it were true.

"Excuse me, sir."

The deep male voice woke him, and Quin struggled to come to. His body reacted but his brain did not, still drenched in the comfort and security that was not real.

"Sir? There is no loitering in this building. If you have business you need to attend to, please do so. If not, I am asking you to move on, please."

The officer stood in front of Quin waiting for him to respond. He blocked Quin's view of anything directly in front of him. Regaining consciousness as he tried to focus on the man standing over him, Quin swallowed and then coughed.

"Do you have any need to be here, sir? There are people right over there who can answer any of your questions." The officer turned and pointed to the long counter where numerous lines of visitors formed.

What had Quin wondered about when he walked in? Questions? Did he have any questions? Homeless shelter? Food? Nothing he could ask without being thrown back over the border, he was sure.

"No. Nothing. I'll be on my way." He leaned forward forgetting the weight of the backpack and feeling encumbered by it and so many things.

"Very good. Welcome to Canada and we hope you enjoy your stay." The officer did not wait for a response but turned and wove his way through the crowds. Quin lost sight of him but only after the man turned toward Quin, his expression conveying that Quin needed to move now. He was watching.

Within a day, Quin left the United States and returned to it. His brief stay in Canada drew the attention of the American border patrol, pulling him in, searching his belongings, and lodging questions at him. All reasonable suspicions, Quin acknowledged, but he had no reason for the turn around other than he had changed his mind. No, he was not carrying any contraband. No, he had no criminal record, although they knew the answer before asking it, and no, he had no permanent address currently. But as a U.S. citizen, he was finally released to go about his business.

He caught a bus that took him into Seattle and then another that continued south to Portland, Oregon. He had no plans to stay any longer in either city than the time it took to move on. From Portland, he made his way to Eugene, Oregon, a late afternoon run that dropped him off at the Greyhound Station after dark. The cold air of the Willamette Valley saturated his clothing so that a chill set in his bones and stayed with him throughout the night and into the next morning. He had not gone far from the bus station when he found a group of homeless people under a freeway overhang. Ragged tents nestled together, some in better condition than others, but not a soul in sight. He knew that they were hunkered down inside. The remains of a barrel fire, its charred wood and coals emitting remnants of what had been a blazing source of heat, drew him to it. Extending his hands below the rim of the barrel and just above the embers, he tried to draw in the heat from his open palms to every part of his body. He imagined his blood warming, flowing, reviving his frozen being. Until he, too, could find shelter from the elements, his imaginings were momentary. It was too dangerous to disturb those he could not see both for him and for them. One last effort to draw in the heat from the embers was all he could do. Shoving his fists into his jacket's pockets, preserving what little heat he could capture, he quietly left the encampment and walked the town's streets throughout the night until the blackness hinted at the dawn.

In the early light, he tried to adjust to what had gone unseen in the hours before. He realized that he was not alone in his impermanence, his wanderings. Nestled in doorways, huddled in narrow alleys between store fronts, discarded beings stayed under cover until they could no longer. When the town woke up, they would abandon their resting places, disappearing from the site, not their choice, but the expectation of others. Quin understood this as he wandered during this in between time. For a moment, he felt a sense of importance, an identity that existed in neither place, having this world to himself.

The money he had left on him would see him through the end of the year, another three months. He had made sure of this. Having chosen the life he was currently leading, he had kept his checking and savings accounts opened with the bank, monies that could not be accessed by Matilda or anyone else for that matter. Appearing to be without means was purposely done. He was not foolish when it came to his own safety and welfare. With a nest egg to fall back on, he allowed himself the luxury of temporarily experiencing what other poor souls endured daily. And he did it not to nurture empathy for those less fortunate, not to end this experience with a promise to help make their lives better, not to make change happen in any sense, or to become a better person. He was doing it because he had nothing else to do with his life.

Seventy-three years had disappeared in a moment. What he had left of his life, he had no idea. At times, he liked to think that he could live into his nineties. Not that he consciously looked forward to twenty or so more years. But what harm was there in wondering?

He never saw it coming. Oblivious to his surroundings when he chose to be, he never suspected. Even when it could not be avoided any longer, demanding every bit of his attention, unwilling to depart, to let him go on his way until he had, he fought against it. At one point, he would have sworn that Edward was pressing him to see it, so vivid was his brother's presence that Quin was afraid to open his eyes in broad daylight. Darkness was welcoming and allowed him to hide from it. But even then, he knew he was weakening, giving himself over to it and fully aware that he would never be able to return to the way he had been before it arrived.

Chapter 7

The In Between Time

Dawn did not arrive. The subtle hint of first light made no impression on the still darkened skies. Where the sun was to rise, it did not. Nor did the musky dark skies give way. If anything, to Quin they seemed to darken above him. Perhaps the weather was changing, a cloud cover undetectable was building during the night and its oppressing thickness was not allowing anything to break through. But even then, even in the worst of storms, many of which he had experienced, there was always a demarcation between the light of day and the darkness of night. So he waited, huddled in an available store front entrance, like the others who still slept. It would be only a matter of time. The sun always rose.

The quiet stillness woke him. His eyes slowly opened while the rest of him refused. Velvety fog suppressed his senses. He could not distinguish between sleep and an awakened state. But as his body slowly began to complain of its unnaturally cramped position, Quin gingerly began to unwrap his appendages that had been drawn up around him for warmth. As he did, his fog dissipated, now conscious of his surroundings. He rubbed his eyes with the back of his hand. The prickly sensation that started in his fingertips and worked down to his knuckles was familiar. It was then that he knew he was awake and, more importantly, alive.

He had no idea of the time or how long he had been asleep. He tried to remember how he got here, huddled against the cold in the corner of a storefront. Where was he? Why was he here? As he recalled walking the streets of Eugene hours ago, it seemed, he felt centered again. He was fully awake now and knew that the morning would soon be upon him and the others. It was time to move.

He understood that time was passing. It always did. Nothing remained still. He told himself this repeatedly as he walked the empty sidewalks of the town. But if time was passing, there appeared to be no indication of it. Not a soul in sight, no cars carrying workers to their jobs, no stores opening as the morning hours indicated on the signs fastened to their front doors. He strained to hear anything fearing that, somehow, he was losing his hearing when nothing disturbed the silence surrounding him. Even those whom he had passed seeking shelter in the recesses of the storefronts could not be found as he retraced his path from the night before.

The night before. It was still with him, all around him. Long past sunrise by his reckoning. He stopped and looked up surveying the space above him. He wondered if he could still call it the sky. The heavy curtain of semi darkness teased somewhere by an unsuccessful light source frightened him. This was no storm approaching, no darkening clouds heavy with moisture building over time until they could no longer hold their contents. He had no words for what he was seeing and desperately looked around him for someone, anyone, to share his confusion. He saw no one and startled himself when he heard his own voice calling out. The deafening silence shook him to his core, and he collapsed on the sidewalk unable to understand. In his weakened state, he let his fear take over as he felt the bite of cold air against his tear-stained face.

Whether it was common sense or animal instinct kicking in, Quin understood only one thing. He could not stay here. Whatever here had become. There had to be a way out. There was an explanation, he was sure of that, as he shifted his body into a standing position. It made sense to him to make his way back to the bus station for no other reason than that was the last place he could hold onto that was real. He had been with other people on the bus, had disembarked with some of them, had thanked the driver, and had asked directions into town. He had walked the streets after dark and had seen others. There had to be an explanation.

As he made his way back, his memory guiding him, he was surprised to see a bridge up ahead. Had he walked on that bridge last night? If he had, he didn't remember it. The darkness, the unfamiliar territory, his fatigue all could have been reasons for his inattentiveness. He had no choice but to cross it as the road he remembered he had traveled led nowhere but over the bridge.

It was old. A style of bridge he had seen before built in the 1930s. With only one sidewalk, the rest of the surface a two-lane road, he kept to the barrier side of the walk. He reached his hand out to the cold iron railing using it as a crutch as he made his way across in the semi darkness engulfing him. Stopping midway, he turned and placed both hands on the barrier's railing so that he was facing the river flowing below and in front of him. It was hard to determine its current driven movements in the little light offered, but he could hear it and knew that the waters below him were running high and its currents were unwelcoming. Grey black liquid churned below him, as he tried to decipher anything else. He saw no outcroppings along what he assumed were the embankments that supported the beginning and end of the bridge's expanse. The darkness of the waters seemed to rise on either side of the river, meeting and then blending in with the dense undergrowth that disappeared into the wall of tall trees whose naked limbs reminded him of a multitude of minute fractures on the surface of shattered glass. Letting go of the cold iron with one hand while the other firmly kept its grasp, he turned and moved forward. Still unsure of his orientation, he was aware of his body quivering as he stepped gingerly ahead. He could not see where the bridge ended even as he knew he was moving closer to it. The embankment, although in the distance as he gauged it moments ago while standing on the bridge, would certainly be upon him at any moment. But he began to question what he had seen, or at least thought he had seen, as reality. He had been walking toward the end of the bridge far too long. He should be over it and on the other side by now.

His thinking was logical to him even as he fought off the possibility that, perhaps, there was no logic to ground him anymore. That there was no answer for what he was experiencing. Where absolute fear should have taken over, he suddenly felt none. Instead, he continued forward in a state of confusion but also of anticipation. Everything about him suddenly felt light, free, and strangely eager. It was comforting and familiar. When had he felt like this before? He let his mind wander searching for answers. When and with whom?

Edward stood in the center of the roadway. Quin sensed his presence before seeing him. He was not fearful nor surprised by his younger brother's sudden appearance, just as he had last seen him before Edward left Quin in Crosswood. Quin smiled and waved, the memory of his brother's tragic death never entering his mind. Edward did not respond but stood quietly still. No matter how close Quin moved towards Edward, the distance between them neither grew nor shortened. What had a moment ago felt so wonderful to Quin was replaced by frustration. He tried to run to Edward but even this awkward attempt to rush fate was unsuccessful. He was no closer than he had been before. In a last desperate effort to make a connection with Edward, Quin yelled out his brother's name repeatedly not waiting to hear his brother's acknowledgement that what Quin saw in front of him actually existed.

Even as he yelled, Edward slowly disappeared into the darkness. Quin dropped to his knees, his brother's name barely a whisper now. What had he seen? A ghost? He did not believe in ghosts or any of that paranormal stuff. Edward was not a ghost. But what was that? He struggled to rationalize it all. He knew he was not well, in a weakened state not having eaten in over twenty-four hours. He hadn't slept well, almost freezing to death. And he was in a strange place never having been in this town before. He was sure that his rational for everything he was experiencing was because of his depleted state. He needed to find help. He needed to see one other person, to touch him, and to be reassured that he wasn't losing his mind.

Once again, he pulled himself up and reached for the bridge's railing. He stretched his arm farther but made no contact with the barrier. Taking a step closer to the railing, although he could not see it, he reached again but his hand grasped air and nothing else. He froze, afraid to take another step. What he had come to depend upon was no longer there. Was he even still on the bridge? Where was the light of day to illuminate what was all around him but remained in the dark? Where had Edward gone? Had he even been there?

Something compelled him to move forward on the sidewalk, solid ground leading him somewhere. He had no choice but to follow it. Before he realized it, he had crossed the bridge. He turned to take one last look before going on. Straining to see any distinguishing markers of the structure he had just crossed, he could not make out anything that even remotely looked like the bridge. Where it had been, where he had been just moments ago, was nothing but black space. Even as he listened for the waters' currents, the river's anger, he heard nothing. Again, a deafening stillness surrounded him. It was familiar, the stillness, so he was not frightened by it, not like before. A strange calmness filled him so that any fear he still harbored was absent now. Only more questions rising to the surface but not voiced aloud.

The one that spoke the loudest to him in the silence of his thoughts calmed him even more. Am I dead? If so, Quin rationalized once again, then all of this makes perfect sense. He felt his face relax and allowed a smile to form, something he couldn't remember doing for a long time. Of course, I'm dead. If I were sleeping, I'd be awake by now. I'm dead. But I haven't left this world yet. I'm dead. My physical body is dead. No good to me any longer. But my mind is unwilling to die yet. Why? Where does it want to take me before it accepts the inevitable? I have no choice in the matter, do I? Of course not. So relax. It's so simple. You're no longer in the picture, Quin Leet, no longer in control. Any more than Edward is. Any more than billions upon billions before you. And that thought was comforting for Quin. Finally, he realized, he was no longer alone.

They came towards him, hand in hand, moving slowly. Matilda and Amelia. But this time, Quin was not disturbed by their presence. They were not real. Mere figments of his imagination. At one time they held a place in his heart, or at least he thought they had. But now they were nothing more than memories that were appearing before him. He did not bother to call out to them as he had to Edward. Instead, he willed his legs to carry him to them and then beyond them, never acknowledging their existence if they existed at all. As he came closer, the women dropped hands and stepped apart so that, as he intended, he moved easily between them. When he turned back, he saw no one, just as he expected. If he was dead, which he was fairly certain was the case, then anyone or anything that appeared before him was not real. He felt confident in his reasoning. And this confidence made him unafraid. He was moving on until he could not.

No longer concerned that the sun had not risen, Quin traveled on with little care. Not in control, he allowed himself to be led. Miles of back roads never took him to the bus station but beyond the town and into open fields that stretched in front of him for miles. Yet, he moved across them with ease, his body carrying what was left of him so that he felt nothing but movement forward. At the end of the fields, the foothills rose, one after another as his legs climbed to the crests and then back down into a valley only to repeat the motion numerous times. How many of these ranges he crossed he had no idea. The last range was the highest and as he climbed it, unable to see its summit in the continuing darkness, he felt nothing. No fear, no pain, no relief upon reaching the top, no anticipation of what might come next. Not until he summited it. As he paused on the crest and strained to see below and beyond him, the darkness became velvet black, palpable, and suffocating.

When it appeared, he shielded his eyes from the harshness of its illumination. A sunset that sliced through the darkness filled the space in front of him so brilliant and intense that it hurt to look at it. He stood on the mountain top feeling the waves of warmth penetrating his body, enough that he was aware of his body's uncontrolled rocking as if caught in the currents of a river. He knew it was just a matter of time before the sun set as he forced himself to endure the strangeness of the moment. Nothing was real, he reminded himself.

When the sun dropped below the horizon, a sudden chill ran through his body, a shock to him for he was sure he no longer existed. He wrapped his jacket tightly around his front and pulled up the collar. The cold did not abate but only grew in its intensity. What had moments ago been a generous bath of relief and warmth had turned on him leaving him shivering and miserable. He needed to move on, to descend the mountain to the valley below. He was sure there was a valley below. There was always a valley below.

It took no longer than the thought of doing it before he was standing in a forest among the sequoia redwoods, the tallest trees in the world. He remembered learning about them in school. Looking up, he could see no end to their blackened silhouettes in the continuing darkness that had not left him. But he knew they towered above him, and he found comfort in this. The land he moved forward on was almost flat, a small incline here and there, as he grabbed onto the ancient trunks around him for support. Somewhere, deeper in his memory, he thought he could smell these ancients, their distinct aroma, but he could not bring it forward. As his hands touched the bark, he felt nothing, but he remembered their rough fibrous skin against his young flesh.

No sooner had he found himself in their midst, was he long gone from them as he detected a familiar smell. He was aware of a curtain of damp mist enveloping him as he continued walking. Or was he floating? He couldn't tell anymore. The chill he had endured at sunset revisited him but in the form of cold droplets of ocean mist. For a moment, he welcomed its freshness on his skin. He welcomed a memory of being in the middle of the ocean with his father and Edward as they waited for the casted lines to jerk with life from the depths of the waters that their small boat floated upon. Another memory overwhelmed him as he felt the nausea rise from the sight of a gutted fish whose life's essence laid injuriously open to the young sons. The guilt of ending a creature's life that he did not understand when a boy now consumed him as he moved towards the unknown.

One last image appeared as he fought through the sickening reminders of his childhood. Somehow, he knew it would appear, even now when nothing was real. His father's face. He heard his voice, but his words did not come from his mouth. A rigidly closed opening that should have moved. But there was no need. The words Quin heard reminded him why he had left his father so long ago. Why he had never returned to him. Why he needed to prove that his father was wrong, and with the passage of time, why he eventually didn't care if his parents were ever a part of his life again. "If you leave, I will blame you for breaking your mother's heart. For abandoning Edward who would never think of doing such a thing. You are a fool if you believe you will be better off on the mainland. This is your home, where you belong. Where your family is. You will forever be sorry for leaving us and this place, Quin. Forever sorry."

The guilt lay deep below the surface. At times like this, Quin sensed its attempted uprising, but he did not panic for what he sensed was no threat to him now. Once, it had ruled his life. Forced him to go against his common sense, his ability to reason and rationalize away any circumstance in his path. His immediate actions left a trail of hurt, dismay, and disappointment in their wake. His father's words had pricked its sleeping state but not enough to linger, an unsuccessful reminder to him.

The ocean's waters below the hull of his father's boat gasped aloud, an earth-shattering guttural intake of water, swallowing itself so that nothing remained but what appeared to be a dry seabed. The boat lay on its side. Neither Edward nor his father were anywhere to be seen. Quin crawled from the boat, surprised that his hands were sinking into the quicksand of the seabed and then his knees doing the same. He struggled to stand but the deceptive soil would not release him. In a strange way, he welcomed the earth's pull on him, wanting him to sink below her surface, to leave this place. As he relaxed, he watched hundreds of tiny creatures scurrying away from the weight of his body on what had moments ago been their homes. He marveled at their agility to overcome the collapsing grains all around them, clamoring a bit higher than before only to drop down to the bottom of the depression and then to start up once again. He wondered if he was as alive as they fought to remain so.

No longer able to keep his head above the engulfing surface that refused to release him, he tilted his head back so that the last of him to descend would sense the acrid stink of the dying ocean life that surrounded him, a reminder that he was not alone, once again, in what was certainly his own death. He kept his eyes open knowing that the darkness above him would not change. But some bit of hope lingered. Hope that a sliver of light would penetrate what he had endured for days now, ever since his first night in Eugene. A warmth that would smother his face in comfort as if being nestled against his mother's breast when he was too small to understand that gift. But there was no warmth as he felt the last of him being sucked under. The tiny creatures, in their struggle to survive, were the only signs of recent agitation on the surface of the sand as they burrowed themselves under the surface once again but this time on their own terms with no thought of the cause of their disruption in the first place.

Chapter 8

Its weight did not linger as it moved across his chest, a continual narrow, undulating movement forward, almost an imperceptible vibration that began on one side of his body and traveled to the other only to cease when the last of the weight had crossed him. He felt the last of it drop to his side and then begin again across his lower arm brushing against the exposed skin of his hand. As before, its forward motion continued until it was no more. But Quin was conscious enough to understand that if he moved, it could strike so he lay still, eyes closed as if to fool it, and waited.

He strained to hear its movement across the ground, any indication that it wanted nothing to do with him having endured the obstruction in its path and was now free of it. Time meant nothing now. He didn't know how to calculate it anymore. It might have been a few minutes, or it might have been an hour before he dared to open his eyes. Afraid to move even enough to turn his head in the direction that he imagined it had gone, he forced what was left of his peripheral vision to detect any sign of it. Nothing appeared but a faint trail of gently displaced dirt that began within an inch of his hand.

It could be behind him, nestled against the warmth of the rock that supported his back. It may have slivered into the dry brush that he recalled dotted the dry desert lands in which he now found himself. He tried to imagine where he would have gone if he were the snake. A waste of his dangerously diminished energy, but he couldn't shake the fear of its presence, possibly so close that one small movement of his body might frighten it to commit its deadly strike.

When he awoke next, the air was frigid. It hurt to breathe even as his intake of air was shallow and barely enough. The darkness that had fallen marked another passage of time for Quin. When next light, a new day to be scratched into the leather remains of his belt. As he attempted to shift his weight, to free his body of its paralyzed form, he remembered. He had already moved his hand to join the other in pushing his body up further against the rock. His vision, not yet cleared of its dormant film, could not focus on where his hand had just rested. He blinked rapidly and then lifted his hands to wipe away his dry, unfocused vision. He saw it as he had seen it before but this time, he turned his head and saw that the disturbed earth continued into the dried brush no more than a yard from him. If it still lingered, maybe curled around itself in a deep sleep as he had been, it might have been alerted by his recent movements. He watched. No movement. No sound. It had gone on its way.

Quin wondered if he had been visited by the last of the living he was to encounter before he died. His thoughts wound about him, through him and out again, until he could think no longer. Well beyond hunger, his body did not insist that he feed it. Instead, he felt nothing other than the dying machinations of his brain fighting to exist just a bit longer urging him to remember before he could not.

Chapter 9

In the thirteen years since Quin left Amelia, he spent little time thinking about her. Wondering how she was. Where she was. He made no effort to move beyond wondering. It never occurred to him that he should attempt to connect with her. He had no reason to. What was done was done. His doing, his decision, and his unfinished business. The distance created by the unknown was his saving grace. He had no intention of shortening that distance between his present and his past.

His only intention was to live his life as he saw fit. Matilda being the only person whom he had ever met with the same intention. And she proved to be the stronger one. He often thought that he should find a way to thank her for telling him to leave. He would never have done it on his own, happy to be in her company, sheltered, and unencumbered by responsibilities. Besides, he had loved her. He was almost sure of this. Without her ending what they had together, he would never have ventured any farther than the front porch. An exaggeration but not far from the truth.

Playing the part of a nomad who had plenty of resources to fall back on was an attractive choice. After all, if he grew weary of his new lifestyle, he could end it. He could go back to the world he had left behind with one swipe of his bank card. He might even pay Matilda a visit. He imagined her surprise upon seeing him again. Standing in front of her in an exquisitely tailored three-piece suit, a bouquet of lilacs, her favorite, resting in his arms. All for her. What would she say? What could she say? He had the freedom to imagine her possible responses. And because imagination was all he wanted, all he had to rely on, his nomad life seemed to have no clear ending. Even so, he told himself, he was still in control. A matter of making the decision to end it when he chose to do so. It was simple yet, ironically, he could not imagine doing so.

If it was truly gone, well beyond where its trail disappeared into the brush, then Quin could close his eyes. But he couldn't be sure. Even as his brain strained to reason away his fear, it was fatigued so that his thinking was muddled, unable to focus on anything for more than what seemed a second. Willy, Matilda, Amelia, Edward, his parents, scattered bits and pieces of their shared history with him so that, strangely, a kaleidoscope of fragmented images of his life appeared before him. He wasn't meant to understand what he was experiencing. Somehow, he knew this. But he attempted to do so only to give in to his own imminent demise. He dropped his arms to his sides, his fingers splayed on the dry cold sand with no thought of the snake, his last visitor, or of anyone else for that matter. He welcomed the sensation of dropping, unencumbered, into the blackness of a void that closed behind him rapidly as his descent continued. No fear, no wondering, no imagining, no longing. The void that enclosed him also filled every part of his being until nothing mattered any longer.

Chapter 10

"Ever been out of the country?"

It was a simple question deserving of a simple yes or no. But Quin could not decide between the two. Did Canada count, the couple of hours he spent there? If so, yes. But that response would imply something completely different. If a no, then he'd be lying. Had he been anywhere else? Did crossing the border into Mexico from southern California count? Again, a day trip in Tijuana only to say that he had been there.

"Yes."

"Where?"

"Canada and Mexico."

"Where?"

"I just told you."

"I mean where in Canada and Mexico?"

"Only just over the border in both."

"Why?"

"Had no reason to go any farther."

"If I could leave, I'd go to as many places as I could and stay in each one for as long as I could. I might never come back home."

"Is this your home?"

"I mean this country."

"Where is your home then?"

"I don't remember. It's been too long."

"How can you forget where your home is?"

"Don't know. Just have. Do you know where yours is?"

"Yes."

"Are you going to tell me?"

"What difference does it make to you?"

"None."

"Right. That's what I thought."

Quin figured that the man questioning him was not much older than him. Maybe in his mid-seventies, but his appearance identified him as much older. The result of being homeless most of his life, as Quin was to learn. He went by the name of Willy. No last name. Not necessary, he told Quin. Besides, if he ever had one, he couldn't remember it. Not originally from Eugene, he migrated up north from central California in the sixties, found work in a lumber yard somewhere between Eugene and the coast, until he fell off a log in the log pond and was almost crushed to death by it and the other water saturated floating trunks. No longer able to work, he went on disability, but it wasn't enough to survive on. He told Quin that the world turned on him, through no fault of his own, so he turned his back on the world. It wasn't an easy life, but he was the happiest he had ever been. The only regret he had was that he had never traveled.

The soup kitchen was open for breakfast and dinner and for only two hours each meal. Quin stumbled upon the place as he followed others in need, his recent dream state dissolved into his subconscious. Leaving their doorways, their under-highway nests, their alleys, their lean-tos down along the river hidden by the dogwoods and brush, all temporary shelters that might be available to them the following night or might not, first come first served, Quin joined the migrating group. This is where he met Willy.

Neither one foresaw the companionship that was to develop between them. Neither one of them needed it but it wasn't up to them. Quin was the first to resist and he did not mince words with Willy as the man attempted to follow Quin out of the soup kitchen the first day of their meeting. But Quin's words had no impact on Willy. In fact, the more Quin resisted, the more Willy persisted.

"You don't even know where I'm going, Willy."

"Does it matter?"

"What if I was to go far away from here?"

"What if you did?"

"You couldn't keep up with me."

"Possibly. But what if I could?"

"Well, then…"

"Well then, we would go there together and arrive at the same time."

Conversations like this convinced Quin that he had no say in the matter. Willy was going to do what he wanted to do as was Quin.

"I can't be responsible for you, you know."

"I don't want you to be, Quin."

"As long as you understand, Willy. And you can't be responsible for me."

"I don't want that either."

"So, no hard feelings if I leave you in my dust, so to speak?"

"No hard feelings. You? In my dust? No hard feelings?"

Resigned that Willy was to be his new-found companion, Quin shook his head as if in disbelief, chuckled, and headed down the sidewalk, Willy one step behind him. They maneuvered their way through the daytime people that populated the streets of Eugene now. It was their territory in the daylight, not Willy's nor Quin's. People made obvious efforts to move far around the two homeless men as they approached them. Their disdain did not need words. Their actions communicated clearly to both men.

"Got any money?" Quin did not stop but spoke over his shoulder.

"Some."

"Enough for a bus ticket?"

"Maybe. Where?"

"How does anywhere but here sound to you?"

"It depends."

"Okay. Understood. Save your money. My treat."

"No. Remember our agreement?"

"Right. Okay, then."

The Greyhound station was not bustling. Quin counted three people in the building not including the two clerks behind the counter. He and Willy made seven.

"Two tickets to Bakersfield, California."

Willy stepped forward about to say something, but Quin stood in his way.

"You wanted to travel. So, that's where you and I are going."

"Our agreement?"

"Making an exception. Can't stay here the rest of our lives."

"Okay," was all Willy felt like saying. He knew that sometimes in life he was meant to keep quiet. To accept what came to him. It was not his decision nor was it ever in his control. And he also knew that it wasn't in Quin's either. There was a reason beyond either of their understandings why they met in the soup kitchen just a couple of hours ago and now were about to travel south together.

As he stepped onto the bus right behind Quin, a peace overwhelmed him. A feeling that was faintly familiar but suddenly felt brand new. As he sat down next to Quin, he realized that he was the happiest he had been in a long time.

When they reached Bakersfield, Quin did not hesitate.

"I don't expect you to come with me, Willy, considering I have no idea where I'm going next."

"Is that your way of saying that I'm free to roam?"

"Yes, if that suits you."

"And if I say that I'm going with you, what then?"

Quin shifted his weight, adjusting his backpack. "I can't stop you, can I?"

Willy started to walk ahead of Quin as they exited the bus depot. "Oh, I'm sure you could but do you want to?"

Quin couldn't help but smile. There was something about this guy that was engaging, and Quin realized that maybe having Willy's companionship might not be all that bad. He tried to remember the last time he shared his life with someone. Too long ago to care. Besides, if he grew weary of Willy, he had no problem leaving him in the dust. Whatever that really meant. More like sneaking away in the middle of the night, Quin mused. That was more his style.

"Let's get our bearings and then figure out where we want to go from here. Sound good to you?"

Willy gave Quin a thumbs up as he slowed down long enough for Quin to come to his side.

They made their way through the streets of Bakersfield until they came to a city park. Numerous tall trees bordered the grass area so that their shade gave relief on a hot day. The two men found a spot under one of the trees, lowered themselves onto the cool grass, their backs supported by the massive trunk. Quin opened a map of California that he had tucked in his backpack. Willy watched as Quin traveled the map with his index finger from the northern border with Oregon until his finger stopped its travels in Bakersfield. About to say something, Willy held back as the finger began to move southeast. Intrigued, Willy waited.

"What do you think?" Quin did not look up from the map and kept his finger on the spot where it had stopped.

"What do I think about what?" Willy knew where Quin had landed. He knew the area well. Information he chose to keep to himself.

"Right here." Quin moved his finger off the spot to reveal Death Valley. "Never been, have you?"

"Nope, can't say I have. What makes you want to go to the desert, Quin?"

Quin leaned forward and laid the map flat on the ground in front of them. "Like I said, I've never been. It's not that far from here. I've never seen a desert. Curious, I guess."

"Well, if that's where you want to go, then that's where you'll go." Willy remained leaning against the trunk as he spoke to Quin's back.

"Yeah, I think that's where my next stop is." Quin leaned in closer to the map, his index finger beginning its travels once again. "No, not that far. Another bus ride. Looks like to a place called Lone Pine. Maybe rent a car from there? Maybe there's a bus."

Willy, his eyes now closed, listened to Quin's meanderings, a half-smile forming while fragmented memories floated in and out of his consciousness.

'Willy?"

"Hmm?"

"If you want to, why don't you come with me?" Quin did not hesitate in his offer. It felt right.

"Oh, I don't think you need me to tag along on your adventure. I'd only slow you down. You got me this far. Maybe I'll just stay put here for a while. See what there is to see. You know."

"You won't slow me down, Willy. We'll take it easy. See this place together. Anyway, I didn't bring you this far to abandoned you."

"You didn't bring me, Quin. It was my decision to accept your generous offer. You don't owe me anything. And you certainly wouldn't be abandoning me, as you say. I can take care of myself."

Quin was surprised by his disappointment as he listened to Willy. How quickly he had attached himself to Quin or was it the other way around? It didn't matter, as Quin tried once again to convince him.

"Understood. But what if I told you that I would like you to come with me. That your companionship would be welcomed. It's been a while since I've even considered the idea of including someone else in my life. But I really think that we could have a good time."

Willy did not immediately respond. The last thing he wanted to do was lead Quin on by believing that this newfound companionship was lasting. Nothing was lasting. He knew this all too well. But what harm could there be in continuing his travels with Quin? He was a good guy, a generous soul, and seemingly harmless. Besides, what else was he going to do day in and day out if he stayed under this tree in a place called Bakersfield?

"Okay. I'll go with you, Quin. What's the desert called again?"

"Death Valley."

Willy chuckled. "Death Valley, eh? Hope that's not an indication of what's to come for either one of us." He leaned forward and nudged Quin's back.

Quin folded the map and slipped it back into his pack. "Right. Hadn't occurred to me until you just said it." He stood up. "Hungry? Let's get something and we can make our plans over a hot meal."

He reached down to help Willy up, but Willy held up his hand to stop Quin, shaking his head. "If you need to help me get up from here, then there is no way I'm going with you. Each man for himself, or something like that."

Quin stood back and observed Willy slowly pushing himself up while reaching for the tree for balance. Standing erect, he let go of the trunk, brushed whatever debris from his pants that he thought he had accumulated while sitting on the grass, and turned to face Quin. "After you, my good man."

Even though the men's homelessness still accompanied them, to an observer they appeared to be just two old friends enjoying an afternoon together walking side by side as they made their way across the park.

Chapter 11

"You've picked a good time to visit the valley. Haven't seen a bloom like this in thirty years. Ever been here before?" The park ranger leaned on the long counter with both palms resting on an enlarged map of Death Valley permanently sealed under a clear varnish. More maps covered the counter's surface, one after another, all captured in this permanent state. The information center was busy and energized with tourists from all over the world, as far as Quin could tell.

"No, can't say as I have."

Willy nodded in agreement. The shock he was feeling rendered him speechless, but his memories were many. The most important one being that this place was not here the last time he came to the valley. He silently took offense at its existence.

"Are you staying at the ranch or the inn?"

"Neither." Quin did not volunteer where they were going to spend the night. They hadn't planned that far ahead.

"Oh, well then, depending on where you are staying out of the park will determine how much daylight time you have here."

He wasn't sure if it was just his own paranoia or if the ranger could tell, but Quin sensed that the ranger knew perfectly well both his and Willy's circumstances. Probably had their hands filled with folks like them and there was nothing the rangers could do about them unless they broke the law while in the park. He was sure that they favored the well-dressed tourists that kept their coffers filled. But he still paid his taxes. He had a right to be here.

"So, what do you suggest we take in while we're here?" Quin, letting go of the negativity, focused on the map under the ranger's hands.

"Okay, do you like views?"

Quin almost didn't respond to such a ridiculous question. "Depends on what it is."

The ranger forced a polite laugh. "Well, then. I'm going to tell you that every view you take in while here is worth it."

"Great. Where do we start?"

The ranger proceeded to lay out a day route to the most popular spots. From the highest peaks to the lowest elevation in the United States and all the places in between.

"You just have to be aware of the time. You won't get it all in in one day. Not unless you drive by or stop to get a shot and then jump back into your vehicle. I guess there are folks that do just that, but what they are missing by not going on foot and spending time with her, the valley I mean, makes me wonder why they came here at all." He stood straight, hands now resting on his waist belt, indicating that he was done. "Anything else I can help you with?"

Willy stepped up to the counter having kept just behind Quin the whole time. "Just a map or whatever you have back there that will add to the experience."

He speaks, thought Quin. And he's funny. Quin smiled and moved to one side as Willy took his place.

"Sure. Here you go." After shoving his hands under the countertop and emerging with three different maps, the ranger slid them over to Willy. "Not pushing it, but if you're interested, there are a lot of good publications over there," he pointed to his right, "in the gift shop. Makes for good reading and understanding this place."

Willy turned his head in the direction indicated by the ranger. "Why, thank you. I will take you up on your suggestion."

Quin had looked to his left as well only to see a sea of people among the displays. The last place he wanted to spend his time. But he kept this to himself. He was no longer traveling alone, at least for the time being. Strangely, he found comfort in this thought.

"Do you mind if I meander over there for a bit?"

They moved away from the counter and maneuvered their way among the crowds that were waiting for their turn with a ranger.

"No. Go ahead. I'll wait for you outside. I'll study the maps while you find your reading material. But watch the time, Willy, like he said. It's already eleven leaving us with a half day here. And we don't know where we're staying tonight."

"All very good points and understood. Give me twenty, maybe thirty minutes. No more."

"Right. Okay. Happy hunting."

Willy had already started to make his way into the gift shop crowd not waiting to hear Quin's confirmation.

He found a bench away from the main entrance. Trying to recall what itinerary the ranger had given them, Quin grew confused. Never one good at listening or recalling when in school, these weaknesses had haunted him throughout his life. He should have written it down or asked the ranger to highlight a route on one of the maps. The best he could do now was focus on place names and if they sounded familiar. With only a few that rang a bell, Quin grew impatient. He checked his watch. Only ten minutes since he left Willy. He'd be no help anyway. What could he have possibly heard in the din of that place? Resigned that he needed to take the lead, he opened the second and then the third map and tried to focus again.

"There you are."

Quin jumped. "Holy crap! Don't sneak up on a person like that!"

"Sorry. Been looking for you."

Quin shoved over on the bench as Willy moved closer to him.

"Success!" Willy patted a pile of books he had balanced on his lap.

"Good grief. You bought all those or stuff some under your jacket?" He meant to be sarcastic but wondered if he was speaking the truth.

"What do you take me for? I may be a few things that should not be spoken aloud, but I can assure you that I am not now nor ever have been a thief. I will ask you to apologize for such a slanderous remark."

Quin did not hear any humor in Willy's voice. He had made a mistake. Possibly. But he had no interest in making this an issue. Besides, he did not know this man regretting that he bothered to ask the question in the first place.

"I apologize, Willy. Sorry."

Willy looked straight ahead. "Thank you. I accept your apology."

"I've been studying the maps," Quin offered as he changed the subject.

"I see. And?"

Quin didn't know how to proceed. He felt his dependency on Willy growing by the second.

"I should have had the ranger show us the places. You know, highlight the route. I'm having trouble remembering what he said."

"I see. Do you mind?" He pointed to one of the maps half folded on Quin's lap.

Setting the books on the ground to one side of his feet, Willy proceeded to open the map in its entirety. He reached into his jacket pocket and pulled from it a pen. "Is it okay if I mark the map?"

Quin, relieved and a bit humiliated, spoke softly. "Sure." He was about to ask Willy if he knew what he was doing but knew not to. Something told him that Willy knew exactly.

"I suggest that we start here." He pointed his pen at Zabriskie Point. "It is a view that the ranger said we must not miss. From there, we can go to Artists Drive, depending on the time. They are within the same area. I expect that we should call it a day after that. Still need to find a place to stay."

"You said you've never been here before. Right?"

"That's correct. I am only going by what the ranger told us and this map."

He had been wrong about Willy. "Okay. Sounds like a plan. Probably should head back to Lone Pine after. Bound to be some place to stay the night."

"I agree. Shall we?" Willy folded the map and handed it back to Quin. Leaning down and with some effort, he lifted his books, careful not to let them fall.

"You going to stay up all night reading those?" Quin tried to lighten the mood.

"I very well may, Quin. I very well may."

Chapter 12

They never brought Edward home even though the Leet family plot was the final resting place for four generations of his family. The news of Edward's death came with little emotional impact on either one of the elders. Since leaving home and following his brother's rebellious path, Edward's parents had not written off their sons as lost, but they intentionally forgot, as best they could, that their children ever existed. It was Quin who sought them out about bringing Edward back to Conical Island for burial, an assumption that he did not question at the time. To his surprise and dismay, his parents, in no uncertain terms, told him to keep Edward on the mainland. He was no longer a member of the island community any more than Quin was.

Instead, Edward was buried in Crosswood Memorial Park Cemetery, one of two cemeteries in the town. It was the newer of the two and welcomed Quin's inquiry about any "vacancies". There was no service. Edward did not believe in anything. His ashes were placed in a simple box whose composition was not natural. Quin would like to have served his brother better; perhaps one of the fancy metal urns or the rosewood box or maybe the custom-made urn of his choice to symbolize who his brother had been.

As he lowered the box with Edward inside, it occurred to him that the simple box was fitting. That Edward didn't care one way or the other. Quin could not keep from grinning as the attendant stood by at a respectable distance and at the ready, shovel in hand, uninterested in the mourning brother's visage. He had seen it all before. Every emotional display, every gut-wrenching vocalization by a mourner. Everything. None of it penetrated the attendant.

As Quin walked back to his car, he passed what appeared to be several freshly dug grave sites, a disturbing fact that made little sense to him. Certainly there hadn't been that many deaths occurring in Crosswood at one time? He turned around to see the attendant still working on Edward's site and curiosity got the best of him.

The attendant didn't look up from his final touches when Quin approached. Quin waited patiently until he did.

"I'll be done in just a minute, sir." The attendant shifted his shovel so that its head was inverted as he patted the ground smooth.

"Oh, that's fine. Thank you." Quin pointed to the newly exposed dirt's smoothed surface.

"You're welcome." The attendant turned to walk away.

"Excuse me, sir?" Quin took a few steps closer.

The attendant stopped, turned to Quin, his expression communicating surprise. No one ever talked to him, especially in a moment like this. He had one job to do. Period. And he had done it.

"I just had a question for you?" Quin was aware of the attendant's unease.

"Yes, sir?"

"Those grave sites over there," Quin turned to point out the location. "Are they all new?"

The attendant looked beyond Quin. "Yes. Dug yesterday."

"That just seems like an unusual number of folks all at one time. I counted seven sites."

"Yes, sir. Seven."

"Did I miss something? What kind of tragedy would be the reason for that many at one time? I haven't heard anything."

The attendant looked back at the main building about four hundred yards away. Turning back to Quin, he motioned for him to come closer. Quin, surprised, did so while carefully avoiding stepping on Edward's fresh resting place.

"I'm not supposed to share private information with strangers about our guests."

Quin held back his reaction to the attendant's remark. Guests? All these dead people are guests? The more he played this over in his mind, the funnier it became. The attendant obviously did not think so. Quin regained his composure.

"I understand and I don't want to put you in an awkward position. It's just that it's darn unusual especially since it hasn't been in the local news. Everything's in the local news."

Shifting his weight onto his shovel that seemed to serve as a crutch now, the attendant smiled.

"Isn't that the truth. Well, no harm done if I say. Appreciate it, though, if you keep this to yourself."

"Of course."

"Only one of those is for a newly deceased. The others are for the relatives that are being disinterred and moved here from other places." The attendant stood straight and lifted his shovel just a bit to indicate that he was finished. That he had said all he was going to say.

"Oh. I see. Like a new family plot?"

The attendant half smiled, nodded to Quin, and headed back to the main building.

As Quin drove away, he made a promise to himself to visit Edward every week. Edward would not care if he did or didn't, but Quin would. Every week without fail. That was his commitment to his little brother. And for a fleeting moment, he felt his stomach turn as he realized that his brother was all alone in that cemetery. That all around Edward, members of families were laid to rest next to each other. His throat tightened and his eyes stung. That would never be the case for Edward. Never. Quin would make sure of that.

One week had passed since laying Edward in the ground, the hardest week of his life. But he had made it, keeping his promise to his brother. Quin tried not to think this way as he passed the seven sites, but the new family plot was intrusive and offensive. Only one site had been filled in and finished. No gravestone had appeared, however. Maybe the family was waiting for it to be completed. It would have to be one of those big ones to hold seven dead people's names and dates, he figured. He wondered when the dead would arrive.

He brought nothing with him, no flowers, or some symbolic trinket to lay on his brother's stone. It was enough to be here and lay his hand on Edward's name. "Next week, brother," he whispered as he stood back up. It never entered his mind that there might come a time when his commitment to Edward would be broken. Nor did he consider arranging for his final resting place to be next to Edward, still too young to consider his own mortality.

The same attendant was on his hands and knees weeding around what looked like older headstones. He looked up as Quin walked by.

"Hello there," Quin slowed down but did not stop.

"Hello." The attendant did not stop weeding.

"Looks like your job is never done, huh?"

The attendant stopped and focused on the man walking by. "Nope. Someone's got to do it. If people bothered to remember, I'd be out of a job. But people don't. I expect no one's been here to visit these for years. And I don't mind. Gives me someone to talk to." He turned back to his weeding, ignoring Quin as if he had never spoken to him.

Quin wanted to say something but thought better of it. Besides, nothing appropriate came to mind. The attendant had said it all.

Chapter 13

The first afternoon in Death Valley left both Willy and Quin speechless as they each attempted to understand the history of the place and its awesome beauty. The first full day began before sunrise and ended when they were dead tired. As the sunset faded into darkness, the men knew that they still had more to see. Deciding to extend their stay at least two more days, they drove back to Lone Pine barely able to stay awake. Willy was much better prepared to guide them as he had, indeed, spent a good part of the first night reading his newly purchased books. He brought them with him taking only the ones in his pack that pertained to the places they would explore each day. He would read aloud to Quin important facts as they struggled to take in everything. It was magical, the days they spent together in Death Valley. Like two schoolboys discovering the world for the first time, not a minute was wasted. Sunrise to sunset, every day.

Their sense of adventure only increased even as their aging bodies complained. They knew enough not to push too hard, but they were determined that they would not leave this place until they had seen all there was to see. Both, without voicing it, knew they would never return. Not in this lifetime.

During dinner one night in the Ranch's restaurant, they sat next to three men who quickly invited them to join in their conversation. Quin and Willy were introduced to the men who had traveled to Death Valley every spring for over thirty years. One by one, the men regaled them with their experiences, not only in the valley but in the mountain ranges that surrounded it. Recalling their near-death experiences, only two in the thirty years of their adventures, but memorable enough to have made them believers in the power of mother nature and of their own mortality, the men took turns playing out their adventures as Quin and Willy sat captivated and inspired. Younger men by far, their age advantage did not interfere with Quin's and Willy's imaginings. They could venture farther than they had.

Keeping their outings within the safety of the tourists' views and the recommendations of the rangers, the trip had been fairly easy. Very few challenges presented themselves and when they did it was because they had pushed themselves more than they should, feeling the results at the end of a long day. No, they still had room for challenges beyond the safe, tried, and true.

The men did not hesitate to fill them in on off the beaten track areas of the park that were worth seeing. They admitted that, in some cases, they were fool hardy to have gone into more desolate areas but the pay-off was indescribable. It was a matter of being prepared. Simple. But anything could happen, and all the preparedness in the world might not be enough. It would be up to Willy and Quin to make the decision. Just be prepared, they stressed repeatedly.

Neither one could sleep that night. Although their bodies were screaming for rest, their brains were in overdrive. Surprisingly, it was Willy who led the way as their late-night conversation about the three men gradually developed into a plan whose details were vague. When they did collapse where they sat, neither woke until well after sunrise the next morning.

With most of the morning gone, Willy used the rest of it to start his research. Nose deep in page after page, book after book, he barely came up for air when Quin informed him that he was going to explore Lone Pine having only really seen it from the confines of the motel. Willy showed no interest in accompanying him. Quin wanted some time to himself anyway. He would make sure they did not waste their day. Later, they could go into the valley. Maybe visit the information center again, especially if Willy had researched their adventure. He was bound to have questions.

"I won't be long, Willy. What do you say to heading back into the valley in a couple of hours? Check with the rangers with any of your questions." Quin pointed to the book that Willy held up to his eyes.

"Good idea. Give me a couple of hours. Good idea." Willy did not lower the book when he spoke.

A couple of hours was more time than Quin needed, he realized as he turned the corner, the motel across the street. He had explored as much as he wanted to. A good town, he thought, but definitely a stopover for tourists heading north or south on Route 395. Or, like Willy and him, visiting Death Valley.

"Hey there! Hold up!"

Quin, about to cross the street, stopped and turned in the direction of the male voice. Recognizing the three men from the night before at the ranch, he waited for them to catch up to him.

"We thought that was you. Quin, right? Staying in town?" The taller of the three, he was also the talker, it appeared to Quin.

"Yeah. Just across the street." Quin indicated the motel with a glance in its direction. "You?" he couldn't recall the tall one's name.

"Nope. Just passing through on our way up to Yosemite. Stayed the night at the ranch."

"Right. Well, hope the rest of your trip goes well. Good to see you again." Quin could think of little else to say to them. If Willy were here, he'd be grilling them with questions.

"Thanks. You heading back to the valley or somewhere else?" The tall one stepped a bit closer.

"Not sure. Making plans as we speak."

"Not following." Again, the tall one.

"My friend is figuring it out." Less said to this stranger, the better. It was a feeling that Quin couldn't shake.

"Well, we'll be around for another hour before we hit the road. That café back there is supposed to serve killer lunches. Just saying. If you have any questions, that's where we'll be. I mean, based on our conversation last night, I figure maybe you and your friend are considering trekking in the valley?"

"It's a possibility."

"Travel safe then. But like I said, for about an hour. Happy to help you guys out if we can, Quin."

Quin nodded and extended his hand to the tall one who did the same.

"If we don't see you two, take care. Maybe our paths will cross on the next go around."

Willy was right where Quin had left him. The only indication that there had been any activity in the room was that most of the books had moved from their pile and were strewn on the floor surrounding Willy. Not one of them was closed. They all were opened to pages, some dogeared while others were splayed out with their content pages facing down. Obviously, Willy had a method of organizing and Quin knew better than to interrupt him.

"A couple of hours up already?" This time Willy looked up from the book he was holding.

"No, not exactly. Not much to see." Quin moved carefully through the books on his way to the bathroom. "But the day is passing and if you want to head back in, we probably should be heading out soon."

Willy, checking his watch for the first time since Quin left, nodded. "Yup. How about in fifteen?"

"Sure. Fifteen then." He was just inside the small bathroom when he remembered. "By the way, I ran into those three fellows we shared dinner with last night."

"Oh?" Willy was flipping through one of the last two books in the diminished pile.

"They're on their way to Yosemite. Said that if we had any questions, they would be in town for about an hour at the café."

"That's mighty kind of them."

"Do you? I mean, have questions?" Quin gestured to the sea of books at Willy's feet.

"I might. Maybe," Willy mumbled as he submerged himself in the current book.

Quin, about to close the bathroom door, felt the need to remind him. "Willy? Fifteen."

"Fifteen," Willy mumbled.

Chapter 14

His name was Jeremy Redmond. He was twenty-nine when he died. His family had lived in Crosswood, where he was born, for less than three years before moving to some other small town in Montana when Jeremy was two. They were not the first Redmonds to leave Crosswood. They followed in the nomadic footprint of three previous generations. All found their way to like places or smaller. However, the Redmond family had been one of the original families to settle in Crosswood in the 1800s. Unlike those families who stayed, who would never abandon their beginnings, the most recent Redmonds had no interest in preserving family history nor felt any obligation to the long departed.

Jeremy moved with his family so many times that he lost count. His father could not hold down a job, his mother threatened to leave his father and the family if he didn't shape up, and all the while Jeremy held onto the thin hope that one day everything would be okay. Paul, his older brother by two years, ran away when he was thirteen leaving Jeremy behind. With no word of his whereabouts or what happened to him, Jeremy made plans to do the same when he turned thirteen. Neither his mother nor his father seemed to care one way or the other anyway. They never reported their eldest son's disappearance and never spoke of him again.

True to her word, his mother left Jeremy with his father shortly after moving again, this time to Utah. The mining job held promise, his mother announced, as they unpacked their few belongings and settled into the small shack owned by the mining company. However, in less than a month, his father lost his job. "Unfit and unreliable" were the words printed on the crumpled paper thrown onto the kitchen table one night before dinner, the only words that stood out to Jeremy as his heart sank. He understood what was coming next. When he woke the next morning, his mother was gone.

When he turned fourteen, he did not hesitate. Turning his back on his father was easy. He felt no obligation to stay even though his father's health was killing him. It wouldn't be long before he died and that brought comfort to Jeremy. He would make sure that he was not around to see it.

He surprised himself with his resiliency. Even though underage, he was able to stay alive by picking up temporary jobs as he moved south. He worked in the fields and the orchards during the harvests, did odd jobs for folks who hired him for a day or two at a time. On occasion, he got lucky and was hired for weeks in a row, always picking up new skills from the men working with him who, if he was even more lucky, took him under their wings temporarily. His life was tolerable, nomadic, and without any lasting human connection. Much like the first fourteen years of his life. And this was okay with him.

Jeremy never had any intention of returning to Crosswood. There was nothing there for him. Only a smattering of memories that he refused to entertain and with the passage of time were dimming. Now, just shy of turning twenty-six, he had worked for the last five years building houses. When his fellow workers started talking about greener pastures in central California, he listened to them. And when they started disappearing from the work sites only to be told they had headed southwest where things were booming, Jeremy was not about to be left behind.

One of those places was not far from Crosswood. About a day's drive heading southwest. A place called Wilmington. A new car factory had opened and was drawing workers from the more expensive places in the state. New, cheaper housing, job opportunities, and half-way good schools, were too good to ignore. Houses were going up within two months and the work kept coming. Jeremy would tell anyone who would listen that it was one of the best moves he had ever made. During the three years he worked in Wilmington, the fact that he was the closest he had ever been to where he was born since leaving it never entered his mind.

Paul Redmond returned to Crosswood for only one reason. His father was dying. Someone who knew his father tracked him down on social media thinking that it was an act of compassion and surely his children would want to know. When Paul read about his father, his first inclination was to trash it. There was no way he would pay his respects to the man who ruined his family. His father could die alone and rot in hell. The emails that followed he trashed but only after reading them. His father was near death and was asking for his sons. "Please make the effort to see him." This someone turned out to be the only friend his father had and who, even though not knowing the sons, knew that his friend was asking forgiveness from them. "No man should die alone without being given the chance to ask for forgiveness," the man consistently added to his emails.

It was a matter of opinion, Paul kept telling himself. At some point, he felt himself giving in. What harm could it possibly do to see him? He didn't owe his father a thing but was he becoming his father by not responding to his wishes? Was he perpetuating the division that his father and he had nurtured so well? What was the point of any of it? And his mother? He assumed that she was dead. He couldn't say why. It was just a feeling. But if she wasn't? Suddenly, he felt very alone, on the precipice of such solitude and regret for what could have been, that he broke down. He hadn't cried in years. He couldn't remember the last time he cried. It was then that it became clear to him. He needed to go back, just this last time. He needed to resolve for once what had been unattended to for years.

Having made the decision, he thought about Jeremy. Would he want to know? Would he care? Was he even alive? Paul stopped short as he asked this last question. What kind of family did he come from where he needed to ask this question about both his mother and his brother? It was almost too much, so close to being irreverently humorous. He searched for Jeremy online only to come up empty handed having no idea where to go from there.

On the morning he was to leave for Crosswood, he rose before sunrise. Sleep evaded him most of the night. A catnap here and there but not enough. He stumbled into the kitchen, made his coffee, and filled the thermos with it. Grabbing a bagel, he locked the front door behind him. At the foot of the driveway, the tossed newspaper waited. It had come earlier than usual. A bit of luck as it would give him something to read later.

He was feeling better with his decision to visit his dying father. He just wished that he did not have to do it on his own. Jeremy remained in his thoughts, almost as though he was sitting right next him as Paul entered the freeway heading southwest.

Chapter 15

A thousand stings. He longed to lift his hand and wipe his face clean, but he wasn't aware of where his hands might be. He had no sense that they were still a part of his body. He ignored a weak internal command to turn his head so that he might see them. He wasn't sure he could open his eyes anyway. The sandpapering did not let up as Quin gave in to its abuse. He had no choice, no longer having any control over his body. However, his imagination, seemingly not affected by the desert's current environmental change, wreaked havoc on him. He could not close the images down. He saw the sands that were his resting place rise against him, each swell of sand in the distance growing in size and intensity and heading straight for him. Just as suddenly, the swells became dark, angry, and unforgiving waters crossing the expanse of ocean that he once floated upon in the safety of his father's fishing boat.

He told himself to brace for the coming onslaught, but he was not sure his brain heard him. Just as the waters towered over him, suspended in time as he gazed upon them in awe, they became minute granules of sand painfully raining down upon his body.

The sandstorm passed, its damage unknown to Quin. The desert was familiar with the event. He was not. The weight of the sand that had accumulated on and around his body, holding him snuggly in place, was comforting and frightening. He knew that he was suffocating, his breathing limited by his clogged nasal passages no longer free to welcome air. When he opened his mouth to breath, he drew in sand-soaked air and started to choke as it tried to make its way down his throat and into his lungs.

When the spasm passed, he felt his heart pounding against his chest, a sign to him that he was still alive. If only he could react. Move his body, feel his body. But even the thought of expending that much energy died as quickly as it appeared. It was all he could do to slowly open his eyes enough to take in his limited view. About to close them again, a futile attempt to begin with, he saw it slowly slithering across the sand towards him no more than a foot away now. He felt no fear but only admiration and envy of the creature who had come through the storm in one piece, unharmed, and unchanged. Within inches of his face, its forward motion came to a stop. Its body, instead, coiled so that its head and constantly flickering black slivered tongue were all that moved.

It would be a matter of seconds, Quin knew, before its strike. He silently begged for it to do it. To end his existence. It was all he longed for as he and the reptile faced off. But the snake did not strike, nor did it move in any direction. Rather, it stayed in place, so close that Quin imagined he felt the touch of a snake's tongue, a soft tickle, gentle but probing.

Somewhere very deep within, Quin suddenly understood. If he could have, he would have taken the snake into his arms, gently caressing it, holding it to his chest, while shedding tears of regret, of forgiveness never asked for, never given, of loved never truly shared. If he could have, he would shed tears that washed away all that he had been, cleansing him, purifying him. And the snake? It needed nothing from Quin. As Quin lost consciousness, the snake stayed with him until it chose not to. If Quin ever opened his eyes again, he would see the thin curving groove in the sand that disappeared from his peripheral vision, the only indication that reality still existed.

Chapter 16

There was no mistake. He recognized him immediately. The last time he saw his little brother was eighteen years ago. His eleven-year-old cock-eyed grin gave him away. Quickly figuring, Paul stared at his twenty-nine-year-old brother's face. Jeremy's colored photo sprung from the black and white pages of this morning's newspaper, the center of an advertisement for new homes in Wilmington. He was not alone. Surrounded by other young men's faces, he was one of many "highly skilled craftsmen" recognized for their contributions in building new homes in the town. And "you, too, could join the Brindle team and be a part of making someone's dream home come true."

Their dying father was not anticipating his sons' arrivals at his deathbed any more than he wasted time over the years expecting them to return home one day. Much the same was true for both Paul and Jeremy. Never expecting to see their father again in this lifetime, and certainly not as temporarily reunited long lost brothers, the Redmond family men moved through the next two days as if in a surreal story not of their own making. Their father was close to death when Paul arrived first. Jeremy arrived later that day. Had it not been for their father's friend who was responsible for contacting Paul in the first place, the estranged brothers' meeting at their father's bedside might not have been as civil as it falsely played out to be in front of the stranger. Both brothers harbored bad feelings, mostly because of their own shame for ignoring each other. It was easier to blame the other then to blame themselves. Besides, if they could endure what lay ahead concerning their father, they would not have to maintain the reunification a minute longer than necessary. This thought was comforting.

"You boys…you came…home." Their father's voice was barely a whisper as they each leaned in to hear him.

"It's okay. We're here now." Paul did not look at Jeremy as he spoke.

Paul took his father's right hand and gently gripped it in his. Jeremy did not touch his father.

"Can you..." Their father gasped for air and then continued. "Can you boys... forgive me?"

This time Paul held back. He didn't dare look at Jeremy and prayed that his father's dying eyesight would not let him see their faces. Maybe only a blur but not the pain, anger, and hatred that Paul knew they both could not hide.

It was Jeremy who spoke first. "I don't forgive you."

It was simple and came from a place so deeply established within Jeremy that Paul understood but still was taken by surprise. How could he follow that? Two against one even in the hour of their father's death? But Jeremy spoke his truth. For that, Paul silently admired his little brother. Could he say the same thing? Was he brave enough?

Paul felt his father's hand go limp in his, as if his life had suddenly withdrawn from him as Jeremy's words were spoken. He kept his eyes on his father's face, now no longer questioning but resigned as if in confirmation of what he knew would be the truth. It just needed to be said. Jeremy took a few steps back from the bed and said nothing more.

Paul's sense of loyalty to his brother was the only reason he gained the courage to answer his father. However, before he could speak the words aloud, his father's gasp for more air was cutoff as his chest rose ever so slightly. Paul watched as his father succumbed to the disease whose source was the culmination of his entire life.

Paul was cheated out of his opportunity to give his father the forgiveness he asked of his sons. His father died with nothing offered from his eldest and everything said by his youngest. The words that would go to his father's grave with him were not the words he would have said. Should have said and maybe long before now. It was all too late.

Jeremy waited long enough before leaving for Paul to speak with the doctor. He wanted nothing to do with anything that needed to be done for his father. Paul could take care of it. Besides, he had taken care of his obligation and had said what needed to be said. He couldn't care less what Paul thought of him for doing so.

Paul knew that Jeremy wanted no part of it. It had been hard enough convincing him to see his father as it was. Frankly, he was surprised to see him turn up. But he had and the opportunity to make amends with his brother could not be ignored. He had to at least try, forced or not. He wasn't sure how he really felt towards him.

"I expect you want to be heading back?" Paul sat down next to his brother in the waiting area of the ICU.

Jeremy looked straight ahead. "The sooner, the better."

"Well, there's nothing here for you to do so…" Paul felt completely inept. He was talking to a stranger. A stranger who didn't care about him or their father's passing. "Okay, guess that's it. You have my number if you want to get in touch."

Jeremy stood up and without facing his brother, threw his last words to him over his shoulder as he walked away. If Paul heard him or not, it didn't matter. Just a parting blow that might hit the mark.

"Thanks for nothing."

Paul sat frozen as he watched Jeremy head toward the elevator. What had only moments ago been one of the most difficult things he had ever faced now seemed infinitesimal in light of his brother's flippant remark. An anger raged inside him now as he felt himself run after Jeremy, catching the elevator door just before it closed.

"What the hell was that supposed to mean?" Paul stepped inside keeping his back to the closing door as Jeremy, surprised by his brother's reaction, moved closer to the backwall railing.

"Give me a break. It was a sham. I came because you told me to. I knew better but I came, and I said what you didn't have the guts to say. But I didn't do it for me. It was for you, big brother."

The doors opened before Paul could respond. He turned and moved into the hospital lobby, a rush of people going every which way. Jeremy had not followed him but purposely headed in the opposite direction. For a moment, Paul considered going after him to finish what they had started. But he thought better of it. There was no point. Besides, Jeremy was right. He didn't have the guts.

They were so far apart in every way that the idea of never having a brother in his life again was stronger than it had ever been. He had not only lost his father today but, finally, his brother. He should have felt sadness or regret for both men, but he didn't. Strangely, he felt an undeniable peace descend and wrap him gently in its protective coating. Freedom accompanied him as he left the hospital grounds, driving slowly through the parking lot, through the town of Crosswood, and then out to the highway. He had not felt this unencumbered in years. Turning on the car radio, the melody was familiar, and he started to hum along until he couldn't hold back any longer, his voice now at the top of his lungs, filling the empty spaces.

Jeremy had wasted no time in heading back. His anger only growing as he replayed everything that had taken place since he answered his brother's call. His bad luck being in the newspaper and Paul finding him because of it. His surprise to hear his brother's voice after eighteen years and his disgust when he understood his brother's reason for calling. His buried hatred of his father and the childhood that he never experienced. Not like the other kids he met along the way. His hatred for his brother who betrayed him by leaving him on his own. The idea of having to go to his father's bedside as he lay dying repelled him, and he still could not come to grips with why he agreed to his brother's request in the first place. None of what he had chosen to do in the last forty-eight hours made any sense to him and that angered him even more. That wasn't entirely true, he realized, as he accelerated feeling the vibrations of the ton of metal under his foot as it carried him away from this place. He hadn't forgiven his father. He said it so that not only his father heard it but also his brother. That was the best decision he had ever made in his life.

As he lay dying in the same hospital less than five hours after his father's death, whose body rested in the morgue two floors below him, Jeremy's unconscious state prevented him from understanding why he was there. But if he had, his last memory would be of the sickening collision of metal upon metal, his body thrown like a rag doll as it sacrificed itself to the gravitational pull of the forces beyond his control, of his resting place pinned under the front carriage of his car. And he would understand that he would not be the only fatality because of his rage.

Paul had forgotten to turn his phone back on after leaving the hospital, all concerns lifted as he got closer and closer to home. It wasn't until he arrived there that he remembered. The voicemails were one after the other, all from the same number, all with the urgent message to contact the hospital.

He released the hospital to transfer his brother's body to Crosswood Mortuary where his father's remains would also be cremated and arranged for both his father and brother to be buried in Crosswood Memorial Cemetery.

Paul had done his part. What little he had left of family was gone. There was no need to mourn. They had both brought it upon themselves. He didn't even try to feel their loss. Far better to focus on his own life now. Unencumbered by his past, he conveniently forgot with each passing year until he couldn't remember their faces, their names. For that matter, anything about a family. There was no need that he could see for contemplating how he wanted to spend the rest of his life. Welcomed freedom was his only companion now. And he would let it take the lead.

Chapter 17

"You can drive in only so far. After that you have to trek on foot. And unless you're experienced hikers in areas like these, you shouldn't be considering it."

The same ranger who had welcomed them to the valley a day ago was telling Willy and Quin not to even think about it. It didn't take a genius to know that these two men who were not spring chickens were foolish and inexperienced. The ranger took them both in without asking questions. He had seen this before. And he and his buddies were the ones who had to find them or whatever remained of the fools.

"There are plenty of places you can hike within the park where we are comfortable with visitors doing some exploration but out there," he pointed to a spot on the map that Willy had spread out on the counter, "you'll be on your own. Not in our jurisdiction."

Willy listened but Quin could tell that the ranger was not convincing him.

"But if we got in trouble in the park, you'll be there to help? Right?"

Quin was beginning to worry about Willy.

The ranger's expression did not change. Still dead serious, he leaned over the counter within inches of Willy's face. "That's correct. However, if you follow the park's rules and guidelines and are prepared, our job is a whole lot easier. I expect you understand that. Am I right?"

Willy did not budge, seemingly enjoying his minor confrontation with the ranger.

"Understand that completely. But if we're out of the park's jurisdiction, you can't stop us from going where we want to go. Am I understanding *you* correctly, sir?"

About to shut Willy down, but thinking the better of it, the ranger shifted back to a standing position and stared Willy down.

"As long as you're out of the park, you are correct. But I should warn you that anywhere you go in the area, the deserts or the ranges, you are putting yourself in grave jeopardy. Plenty of the land that surrounds us is privately owned but you can travel off road for miles and see no sign that tells you that. See no one for days on end. But private property gives a man the right to shoot before asking." The ranger looked at both men now. "Like I said, if anything happens to you out there, you're on your own. No one's going to come looking for you. Don't bother taking your phone."

Quin could stand it no longer. "Thanks. We got the message." He nudged Willy who pulled away from Quin.

"So, after all that, are you going to tell us a good place to explore? We won't tell anyone you told us." Willy gave the ranger a wink. "Just between you and us."

"Willy. We're done here." Quin folded the map. "We appreciate your time, sir." He turned and headed to the back of the room knowing that Willy was not following him. Had he had all his wits about him, he would have kept on going. Getting in his car and leaving Willy to fend for himself. It wouldn't be the first time. The man was not all there, Quin realized. What was he thinking making this guy a companion? All he needed to know about Willy he had just observed with the ranger.

He was halfway to the car, almost convinced that he should leave Willy behind, when he heard Willy call his name. Quin turned to see him heading towards him, waving his arm in the air.

"You move when you want to!" Willy was out of breath. "You've got my map there." He pointed to Quin's hand. "Not going to do you any good so give it back."

Quin, forgetting that he had taken it, did not hesitate. "Sorry."

"Going to need that."

"What for?" Quin knew.

"It's no never-mind to you. You just need to drive me to the place, and I'll head out from there. Leave you in peace to go about your life while I go about mine."

"Come on. You can't be serious. Didn't any of what that ranger told us sink in?" Quin struggled to find the balance between gentle persuasion and complete frustration with the man.

"It doesn't matter what you think, Quin. And yes. I am quite serious."

"If you go out there on your own, you're going to die, Willy. You're not thinking clearly."

Willy took off his backpack and slid his map into a side pocket. "I disagree, Quin. I am thinking more clearly than I've been thinking in a very long time. I have considered the consequences, believe me."

"Do you have a death wish? Is that it?" Quin did not hide his frustration any longer.

Willy gestured for Quin to follow him. Finding a bench outside in a shaded portion of the center's courtyard, Willy dropped his pack at his feet as he sat down heavily. He patted the space next to him. Quin took a seat.

"I never considered it a death wish, as you call it, Quin. You and I have a different outlook on life, I think." Willy looked straight ahead as he spoke. "We're about the same age, I'd guess. Maybe I'm older?"

"We're close." Quin knew it didn't matter.

"Yes, well, then maybe you have experienced a moment of clarity when you see before you very little of what is left of your life that you, at one time, thought would go on forever. The ranger was right. I'm no spring chicken."

Quin interrupted him. "He never said that, Willy."

"He didn't have to, Quin. But he was thinking it. Given his line of work, he's probably had more than a few moments of clarity himself. He and I have that in common."

Quin wondered if he shared in their commonality. He couldn't remember.

"Willy, I'm begging you. If you are seriously considering heading out on your own, don't do it."

As the words left his mouth, he wanted to pull them back in. No, he didn't want Willy to risk his life, but he also knew that he had no right to try and stop him. Any more than Willy had when it came to whatever Quin wanted to do. He was not his brother's keeper and that was the way Willy wanted it to be.

"You know, we haven't known each other very long. Not in the scope of things. But I have enjoyed your companionship. You are a good man, Quin. And for that, I am grateful to have made your acquaintance. Sometimes, you meet a person who it seems has been with you all your life or a good part of it. A comfortable relationship, you know?"

Quin did not know, nor did he try to remember. "Sure," he lied.

"But nothing lasts, Quin. Everything has its ending and maybe today, this is where we end. Go our separate ways. No hard feelings one way or the other." Willy patted Quin's thigh, a gesture to seal his decision. He reached down for his pack, shifting it to the side of his legs and stood.

"Wait. Wait a minute, Willy. Is there anything I can say to convince you not to do this? What if we head out somewhere else together? What about heading up to Yosemite? Ever been there? I haven't." His voice was strained, almost desperate sounding. He didn't care.

"Oh, yes. A place you should see, Quin. That sounds like a good idea."

"Right. So, let's make our plans to do that. You can show me around." For a moment, the relief he felt buoyed him above his desperation to save Willy from himself, but as he spoke, he saw in Willy's face that there would be no trip together to Yosemite.

"Willy, come on. Please don't do this. Please." Quin stood and gently held onto Willy's arm.

"You're a good man and I can see that you care about what happens to me. But I am trying to tell you that you cannot care. You must care for yourself as I must do as well. I will be okay.

So will you. And if our paths should cross again, well, think of all that we will have to share. Our adventures."

Willy's smile slowly appeared. Quin thought that Willy's eyes were twinkling but saw the faint beginning of a tear ready to fall.

"Can I at least give you a lift out of the park? Take you where you want to go?" He didn't want to do this. The last thing that he wanted to do. Send this man off to his death. But Quin was unwilling to let him go just yet. And he didn't know why.

Willy lifted his pack and slung it over his right shoulder. "I could use the lift. Thank you."

Other than Willy giving him directions, the two men did not speak to each other as they drove out of the park and headed east into the Amargosa Mountain range that bordered the eastern side of Death Valley. Both men were too deep in thought to be interrupted any more than necessary. There was still time to talk Willy out of this craziness that he was determined to follow, Quin thought, but he couldn't find the words. And Willy? He knew that Quin was struggling, and he appreciated the effort, but nothing could be said that would convince him otherwise. The more he thought about it, the more he understood that it wasn't a matter of persuasion. He had no choice. He knew where he would start his next adventure and he knew how it would end. What happened in between was the adventure. Something he knew his companion did not understand. Not yet.

Chapter 18

"This is far enough. Pull over up there." Willy pointed to a turnout just ahead.

"There's nothing up there, Willy."

"Just pull off, Quin."

There had been little traffic in either direction as they traveled on Willy's chosen route out of the park. A high mountain pass at an elevation of 4,317 feet above sea level, Daylight Pass Road cut through the Amargosa Range eventually descending into the northern Amargosa Desert. Had they kept going east, they would have reached the town of Beatty but that wasn't Willy's plan.

Quin did not turn off the engine but let it idle as he struggled to find the words that would keep this man from leaving him. As far as he could tell, Willy had chosen a desolate spot to begin his journey.

"You're not thinking of getting out here, are you?"

"That's exactly what I'm thinking. And you will go on your way." Willy reached for the door handle.

"I can't let you do this. It's insanity." Quin pulled away and was back on the road.

"So, is your plan to kidnap me? You are going against my will. We had an agreement."

Quin was shocked not only by Willy's question but by the calmness with which he spoke it. There was no fight in his voice, no anger, or disappointment. A mere question and statements of fact.

"No, of course not. But you can't put me in this position. If you really want to head into God only knows where on your own, be my guest but you'll have to do it where I say. I'm driving straight to Beatty and leaving you there. At least I'll have the satisfaction of knowing I didn't leave you in the middle of nowhere."

Willy laughed loudly, a rolling laugh that usually was the result of a good joke. Quin tried to ignore it as he wondered if he had made a mistake. Maybe he should have left him back there.

"You could never leave me in the middle of nowhere. Don't you know that? Everywhere is somewhere, Quin. Pull over."

"I can't, Willy."

"You can. Pull over."

As far as Quin could tell, there was no safe place to pull over as they continued their descent into the desert below them.

"When you can, pull over." Willy remained calm, his voice confidently redirecting Quin.

Quin suddenly felt defeated by this man. Maybe Willy knew better than him, knew something that he didn't know. Or maybe he was deathly afraid to be on his own, a thought that ate at Quin now.

The turnout was narrow with barely enough room for the car to be safely off the road. This time, Quin turned off the engine. He sat staring ahead, silently preparing himself for his companion's departure.

Willy opened his door but did not step outside. "Quin, it's all going to be just fine," his voice almost a whisper. Shifting his weight off the seat, he stepped out of the car and closed the door. Opening the back door, he grabbed his pack from the backseat. He tapped on the roof of the car, an indication that Quin was good to go.

As he slowly drove off, Quin watched Willy in his rearview mirror. He had not moved but stood, backpack secured, looking off into the desert below. It was all Quin could do not to stop and go back after him. He would use force, if necessary. But when he looked up again, Willy was nowhere in sight. It was as if he had just dropped off the edge of the mountain. Maybe he had, Quin thought. Maybe that was what Willy had planned all along. To drop to his death. Had he wanted to do it earlier when they were even higher in elevation? Quin panicked at the thought. What had he done? He knew he could not go on.

When he returned to the spot, he searched for any sign of Willy, but found none. It was as if he had disappeared into thin air. The edge of the turn off was not a clean drop but a challenging downward slope with no clear path. Strewn with rubble, large and small boulders, there was no clear indication that Willy could have made his way safely beyond and out of Quin's vision. It just wasn't possible. But what other explanation was there? It appeared to Quin that he knew nothing about the man. Was he capable of surviving the descent if that was his intention?

He wasn't sure when he made the decision to go after Willy, but he did not hesitate as he gathered his gear. He had brought extra water that he stored in the trunk along with a box of nutrition bars and dried fruit that he picked up on their way out of the park. He left nothing behind that could be lifesaving if the time ever came. Locking the rented car, he noted the time. Just after one in the afternoon. The heat of the day was still building, and he knew that he was a fool to turn his back on his guaranteed safety only to step off the edge of uncertainty. All in the pursuit of a man who, crazy as he seemed, inexplicably drew Quin to him.

Concentrating on his foothold, he slowly made his way, all the while straining to hear any indication that Willy was not far below him. Quin called out his name numerous times only to be greeted with silence, the deafening kind that only the loneliest places can provide. He fought against the growing fear that Willy had fallen to his death and that it was only a matter of time before he would come upon his lifeless body. A sobering thought as he reminded himself to focus, or he would do the same.

As he came to the final few yards before he would feel safe again, at least from his descent, he heard what sounded like a songbird. Stopping to rest, his legs ready to buckle under the strain of the relentless downward movement on his muscles, he heard it again. This time a bit closer, its song short and repetitive. He looked around for any place where it might perch but all he saw were more rocks and then the stretch of desert whose horizon he could not see. One more time, its song was clear and Quin, determined to find its source, stood still, his vision focused on his surroundings.

"How nice of you to join me." Willy's voice jingled, bouncing off the rocky terrain.

Quin turned to his right, reaching out to a boulder for support as his pack lagged behind his sudden movement throwing him off balance. All he could see was Willy's head just beyond and below him. He was speechless as he tried to understand.

"Willy?"

"There was no need for you to come, but now that you are here, I could do with the help."

Quin followed his voice with his eyes, all the while wondering how he could get to Willy. There seemed to be no easy way to him.

"Are you okay?"

"Well, in a manner of speaking."

He was infuriating, even in what seemed to be a distressed situation and it was all Quin could do not to let Willy know his frustration with him.

"Stay there. I'm coming to you." He had no idea how he would manage it, but he knew he had no choice. He had left him once before. Not this time.

"Go over to your left and then to your right. Hang on. It's a bit of a drop."

For someone who it appeared had fallen, Quin was intrigued by the calmness and strength of Willy's voice. Maybe he wasn't in such bad shape as Quin feared.

Willy was right. It was at least an eight-foot drop from the last safe edge to where Willy lay sprawled on the desert floor. Quin noted that Willy was lucky that he landed where he had. Rocks of all shapes and angles protruded from the last of the hillside and did not give way until farther out into the sand. It appeared that Willy had narrowly escaped real damage had he hit any one of them in the wrong place. But he couldn't be sure until he reached him.

Quin took off his pack and let it drop just beyond where Willy lay. Searching for hand holds and gingerly finding secure foot holds, he slowly made his way downward until he was within safe jumping distance onto the desert's surface. He was surprised as the repercussion of his heavy landing sent a shockwave through his body. He couldn't remember the last time he had attempted such a thing. It took him a minute to let his body's internal structure settle and balance. Another odd sensation that took him by surprise. He grabbed his pack.

Willy tried to sit up as Quin came over to him but gave it up.

"Where are you hurt?" Quin did not touch Willy.

"Well, I think it's internal."

"Oh, God, no Willy."

"No, not that kind of internal. My inners are still intact as are my bones, by the feel of it. It's my pride." He smiled as his eyes met Quin's. "Boy, does that hurt."

Quin, squatting by Willy's side, relaxed and sat down next to him. "Your pride? You just had me risk my life to rescue your pride?" Quin wanted to laugh but didn't want to give Willy the satisfaction.

"I didn't ask you to come back if you recall. And I certainly didn't ask you to crawl down the mountain to be by my side." Willy was enjoying all of this. "Why did you?"

Quin had no clear answer. How could he explain what was inexplicable?

"I just missed your ugly old face."

"You haven't changed much either."

Both men laughed, releasing the stress that had accompanied them all the way out of Death Valley. And they both felt the weight of it going. The weightlessness that followed allowed them to breath evenly and deeply in the silence of their surroundings. A momentary gift.

"Seriously, can you get up? Can we walk out of here together?" Quin prayed that Willy had not been lying.

Willy pushed himself up to a sitting position. "So far, so good. Give me a hand, will you?" He reached for Quin's hand as Quin, already standing, reached down and pulled Willy up. He did not let go.

"How does that feel?" Quin held on.

"I'm okay. How about that?" Willy straightened out his body as best as he could, visibly growing taller in front of Quin, but he couldn't maintain the extra half inch as his spine slumped into its aged structure.

"Can you walk?"

Willy took a few steps forward, turned, and came back to Quin. "I can, it seems. How about that?"

Quin was not reassured but took Willy's word for it. What else could he do?

"Well, we can't go back the way we came, so I say we head northeast back out to the highway." Quin turned in the direction that he assumed held their lifeline.

"You are assuming that I am heading back with you?"

Not again, Quin thought. Please. Enough is enough. "Willy, you came this close to losing your life and if I hadn't bothered to come back who knows how you'd end up. As it is, we're not in the best of situations if you happened to notice. Yes, we, you and me, are heading back to the highway. End of discussion."

"What do you have in that pack of yours?" Willy did not seem to hear Quin's decree.

"Got what we need to get us out of here."

"Got enough to get us somewhere else?"

"Willy, what the hell are you talking about? We're not going somewhere else. We're going northeast, out of here to safety, and nowhere else. What don't you understand about all this?" Quin did not bother to hide his frustration. His voice, now raised, had no visible impact on Willy.

"What if I tell you that I know where we are and where we are going, and not in the direction you have in mind? What if I tell you that not far from here, there's a place that you've always wanted to go to?"

Quin was shocked. Willy was not okay. He was sure of it now.

"What are you talking about? You're making no sense, Willy."

"Oh, that's where you are very wrong, my friend. I'm afraid that that is all we have to rely on right now, sense. Don't assume you are right, Quin, and that I am wrong. I know what you're thinking. I have lost it. I'm a crazy person." Willy danced in front of Quin, a crazy person's antics.

"Stop it. Just stop." Quin was yelling now. "You follow me out of here or you go to hell!"

Willy slowed his dance and came to a stop. "I can't follow you, Quin. I told you that a while back. If you want to get out of here, go. We're back to square one, it seems to me, and I, for one, am weary of the repetition."

He was at a loss. Willy was not going to be convinced. It was clear as daylight. Even so, the thought of walking away from him again was inconceivable. He had walked away from so many others in his lifetime, and this thought further confused him. What was it about this man that would not release Quin to go his own way? He was frightened by him while wanting to draw closer to him. Maybe it wasn't Willy who was crazy?

"Willy, if I go with you, you realize that we are committing suicide. Is that what you want?"

"You have no faith, Quin. Besides, there is no such thing as suicide. It is not something that you choose. However you lose your life, it is because of the path you're on. You have no choice but to follow it no matter where it leads you. There might be a brighter outcome if you have faith in the path you are following. Don't question it. That is the key."

His words were hypnotic. That's what the hold was, Quin suddenly realized. He was being hypnotized and he was allowing it to happen. The words had no meaning to him, but the melody of Willy's intonation penetrated deeply, and Quin had no choice.

They did not walk side by side, at first. Quin let Willy take the lead. Slowly, they made their way through the last of the rocky debris that disappeared into the surface of the Amargosa

Desert. The sun would not set for another few hours, Quin figured, as he longed for relief from the heat. Stopping to drink, he shared his water with Willy who reminded him not to drink quickly or too much.

Soon, they were walking side by side in silence. Neither one had anything to say. Besides, the energy expended was wasteful. Instead, they walked, not northeast as Quin had wanted, but southeast, a slow trek whose destination would only be reached if they had faith. That is what Willy told him and that is all that Quin had left to believe in.

Chapter 19

For as long as Aaron could remember, he wanted to live far away from people when he grew up. Responses were usually the same when he told others this. "You'll change your mind." "You're still too young to decide such a thing." "Humans aren't meant to be solitary creatures." He would politely listen and then silently dismiss them. On occasion, the question was asked, deep in its intent and gave him pause before he answered. "Why?" However, he never changed his response, not even as he meditated about it numerous times in the privacy of his own mind. "I don't need them, and they don't need me."

It was tiring, listening to their reasoning when it came to needing people in his life. No manner of convincing changed his mind. He didn't know how but, somehow, he knew he was right. That the path he was to follow for the rest of his life was one of solitude, owing nothing to anyone. His mother's death accompanied him, deeply imbedded in his sub conscience, and only awakened in times of stress. He didn't blame her for his strange life path. If there was any blame to be cast, it would be at a man whom he had never known but who was part of who he was. He wondered what part.

The foster care that consumed his teenage years could not be blamed. He had tried but failed miserably. The blame did not stand up to the facts. He was taken care of, all his needs met for survival and then some. He recalled the brother and sister act that played with his psyche, but he recognized their game and could always rise above it and them. If anything, his experiences in foster care just made him stronger and even more sure of his direction.

When he turned eighteen, he turned his back on his last temporary home as he had promised himself that he would. He wasn't afraid or worried about his next steps. How to make a living. Find shelter. Feed himself. He realized that he appeared to others as a fool, ignorant, and naïve. That he might be sorry for his decision, but he knew better. He just couldn't say why.

Aaron hitched rides that took him as far away from Crosswood as he wanted to go. Into the mountains where he met other like souls who took him under their wings. Not all of them had good intentions, as he was to find out, but he learned from them. He began to understand that not everyone thought the way he did about life. That they would as soon take advantage of him if he let them, and sometimes when he wasn't aware that he had given them permission to do so. It was an awakening that stung with betrayal but that strengthened him. He did not go to college but the education he received in human nature was more than enough for him, reinforcing his initial decision to live a life of solitude.

At twenty-three, and perfectly happy to live his life as he had for the last five years, he met Tim and everything that he had assumed about himself and about others no longer held water. Looking back on his time with Tim, he couldn't say when everything changed. It just had. He wondered how the shift in his thinking came about, always returning to Tim. The guy had a way about him that never interfered, never criticized, never questioned anything that Aaron said or did. Aaron struggled to find a moment when Tim had, if for no other reason than to convince himself that Tim was just like everyone else. He longed for Tim to slip up just once, but he didn't. It didn't take Aaron long to realize that his new friend was different and, he didn't like to use the term but found no other way to express his feelings about the guy, special.

Tim was the one who led him away from the people who would, unknowingly, keep him from ever moving forward with his life. Even though, when Aaron met him, he assumed that Tim was part of this group. It was true, Tim told him, that he hung with them on occasion for the company but that was as far as it went. His thinking and theirs were miles apart and that was okay. He knew enough where and when to draw the line.

Tim made it clear. He did not depend on human contact but on his connection with the land. Admitting that he had much to learn about mother earth, he added that she was constantly mentoring him if he paid attention. Captivated, Aaron listened for hours as Tim related his experiences with her. And not just with her but with the creatures that depended on her just as he was beginning to comprehend the same dependency.

It occurred to Aaron that there was nothing holding him back. That he could easily follow in Tim's footsteps. It was just a matter of paying attention to his words and acting on them. But he soon realized that there was more to it than that. That Tim, once again, was proving to be special and in a way that Aaron had no way of explaining.

"You and I are not alike, Aaron." Tim pushed the larger piece of word upwards to let oxygen reach the smoldering kindling below. The campfire had served its initial purpose as they prepared their evening meal over its flames. But now, even more essential, it would need to keep them warm as the sun's setting invited the cooler night temperatures to fall.

Relaxed and full, Tim's words did not penetrate at first. Aaron was fighting off the urge to close his eyes and sleep. They had hiked farther into the back country, at least twenty miles since this morning's start well before sunrise.

"That's not to say we don't get along. I think that we get along just fine." Tim did not look up from his maneuvering the fire's structure.

"Yeah, I agree," was all that Aaron could manage. It didn't occur to him to question why Tim would make the comment to begin with.

"Do you ever wonder what you want to do with the rest of your life?"

"Sometimes." Aaron readjusted his position to keep awake. Now sitting up and leaning into the warmth of the fire, he was aware of Tim's eyes upon him.

"Have any thoughts you want to share?"

Did he? If he really had given it much thought, he probably wouldn't be here with Tim in the middle of somewhere in the back country heading to somewhere else tomorrow. He'd probably have found a job and hung in there with it. Made something of himself. But he was still young, he figured. There was time for that trap.

"Not really. I mean, I guess I haven't needed to, so far. Been lucky, I guess."

Tim propped the piece of word in the fire whose new-found heat warmed both men.

"I don't believe in luck."

"Why not?"

"Luck is just a word fabricated by humans to explain the natural coincidences in our lives that work to our benefit and that we have absolutely no power over."

Aaron thought about this. This wasn't the first time Tim had begun a topic of conversation and had drawn Aaron in on its winding and, most of the time, revealing path. It felt like an intellectually challenging game to Aaron, one that he was learning to enjoy.

"Like superstition? Stuff we make up because we don't get it?" He longed for the vocabulary that Tim employed.

"I suppose it might very well fall into that category. I like to think of those words as feel-good words. Words that make us comfortable and secure when we think about the unknown. They fill the need for our need to always have an answer. To assume there is an answer."

"Is there anything wrong with filling that gap?"

Tim did not respond immediately. It was obvious to Aaron that his question had been a challenge. He smiled, waiting for Tim's answer.

"I believe there is no wrong or right but that the truth resides within each one of us. We decide what is wrong and what is right. And because we are individuals with our own conscience, our determinations will assuredly disagree with another's. Right and wrong are not universally consistent terms, you see. Therefore, to accept them is not possible."

"You lost me."

Now Tim smiled. "It's simple, really. I have no right to tell you that you are wrong or that you are right. I am not your conscience any more than you are mine. For us to get along, to live in harmony with the earth and all her creatures, we must accept this."

"But surely there are absolute actions that go against our beliefs and our society? That are obviously wrong and harmful to all? What about taking someone's life? That action is not wrong or right?" Aaron was confused. "What is it then?"

"If someone takes another's life, I cannot say it is wrong or that it is right. I am not the person who made the decision. My reason for taking a life may not be acceptable to someone else but the decision to do it rests in my conscience and my conscience alone."

"I don't think that makes sense, Tim. We need to have rules in society that everyone must follow. I mean, we would have chaos if we didn't." It seemed so obvious to Aaron that he was right.

"I see. What if we did have rules but those rules were generated not by others but by ourselves? I believe that no one wants to live a life of chaos, destruction, and in fear. We long to move through each day without strife, without conflict. Those who seek that kind of life have had little control nurturing their own lives. They are the product of others' damaging behavior. We are born a blank slate, Aaron. With our first breath, however, the imprinting begins."

"So, you are talking about the what ifs? What if the world was a perfect place? What if every individual from day one was the perfect human being? What if, in that perfection, we never reacted to just living? Wouldn't we be without any emotions, anything that is remotely human behavior?"

"Interesting, Aaron. I understand what you are asking. Perhaps, we would need to understand that there is no perfection as there is no luck or superstition. Again, we depend on a word, a label, to support our thinking. I see it as simply existing while understanding and accepting that as an individual I am solely responsible for my actions, my thoughts, my beliefs, my understanding of my own existence. That I cannot presume or project any of these on another individual. It is so simple, in my thinking."

Aaron watched as Tim closed his eyes and gently rocked to and froe as if in meditation. He knew not to respond. The conversation was evaporating into the night air mingling with the flames, the embers, and the smoke of the fire between them. It was meant to. It was his choice and only his to find a place in his conscience for Tim's messages to be absorbed or to be forgotten. Just as he had decided so many times before.

As he quietly left the fire and Tim to let sleep have its way, it struck him that the original question had never been discussed. What did he want to do with the rest of his life? How had he been sidetracked? His answer? Luck. That had been his excuse for his life so far not imploding. As he pulled the sleeping bag higher around his shoulders, he wondered if it was luck and if it was, how much more of it did he have left?

Chapter 20

Tim had a destination in mind. In the weeks that followed their fireside chat, Aaron had not forgotten. Not all the details stayed with him, but Tim's kernel of an idea had found its resting place deep within Aaron's conscience. He was sure that Tim understood this. They did not return to the topic but filled their evening with random ramblings, all part of the game they both enjoyed.

"Have you ever been to a fire tower?" Tim led the way on their ascent up the dormant volcano's western front. ,

"No, can't say I have." Aaron felt good other than the oppressing heat. He was in the best shape he'd ever been in, thanks to Tim who only on rare occasions took a day off from their trek to somewhere. When asked where they were headed, Tim would simply say, "Don't really know. Does it matter?" Aaron accepted the answer without any fear or argument. He trusted him. Something that was foreign to him during his life before Tim.

The terrain was beyond his imaginings. Nothing but volcanic scree lay underfoot, lethal if he wasn't paying attention. It was slow going, and the afternoon heat reflected from the volcanic debris was almost unbearable. There were no places to hide from it. No shade that he could see. He wondered, after all the miles behind them without mishap, if their luck had run out or were they just stupid to attempt the ascent without considering the time of day. Remembering their discussion many campfires ago, he chose the latter.

"It's not far. I'd say a couple of miles. You doing okay?" Tim did not stop as he spoke, but his words were crystal clear in the desolate and quiet atmosphere. There was no wind to carry them away.

"Been better. I've got to say, this is not one of my favorite days. No other way to get there but hike up a volcano?" His attempt at humor was futile. Nothing was funny about this.

"I suppose there is. But we are here and, unless you want to turn back and waste all the energy you've already expended with less than two miles now to go, I suggest we keep going."

There was no comeback. Tim was right. Again, the conversation about right and wrong occupied his thoughts as he put one foot in front of the other.

The summit skirted the dormant vent and both men steered clear of getting too close. They took the time, though, to rest at its peak and to digest what they had just accomplished. It was evident that they were not the only ones who had been here. Imprinted by the soles of heavy boots, footprints marked the presence of others upon this earth. A few scattered stakes precariously penetrated the scree each one decorated with a piece of cloth that seemed to signify claimed territory. Others had fallen from their dominant placement by the winds that had the final say about their permanence.

Aaron thought twice before speaking, shutting down his choice of words before they escaped his lips. "Glad we made it to the top, Tim. I had my doubts a time or two." Even though he did not speak it, he knew it was luck that brought him safely here.

"Thought you might enjoy this. Worth the struggle."

"So you said something about a fire tower? Certainly not here." Aaron surveyed the landscape beyond them and saw nothing manmade.

"No, it's not here. Not right here. I'd say we're about a day out from reaching it. Maybe two."

"Maybe two? Are you kidding me? Why on earth did we climb this mountain then?" He held back what he could of his frustration but not enough.

"Because if we hadn't, you would have missed the experience." Tim casually rummaged through his pack, his words spoken calmly and with no indication that he heard Aaron's frustration.

"I don't believe it," Aaron mumbled to himself.

The descent was worse than the ascent. Aaron's bad mood did not help his outlook. His companion's, on the other hand, was just the opposite. As Aaron struggled to keep his footing, slipping numerous times only to struggle to his feet once again, he was accompanied by Tim's singing and whistling. A continuous repertoire of Tim's own making and nothing that Aaron recognized. At one point, Tim yelled back to him to join in.

"I don't believe it." Aaron realized that he had repeated this statement numerous times since they departed the summit as he tried to block out Tim's voice. He wondered how many times Tim had passed this way before. It appeared that he knew exactly what lay ahead and moved through the most difficult terrain as if an animal born in the habitat. And if he had not been here before, how did he do it? How did he not take precautions, not understand the seriousness of the situation, not seem to have a care in the world?

Moving away from the volcano, Aaron was relieved to leave the unforgiving volcanic debris behind him as they entered more rocky terrain, dry and unwelcoming. In the distance, Aaron could see greenery, trees of some kind that began crawling up a hillside. Scattered with little underbrush, the trees urged him forward but always he stayed behind Tim. If there was a fire tower within those hills, Aaron still could not see it. About to ask Tim what the thing looked like and when would it come into sight, he thought better of it. It was a tower. It would stand out when they were close enough to see it. He let his imagination play at creating his vision of a fire tower rising far above the tree line with a 360-degree view of all the land surrounding it. He imagined that someone must be in the tower watching for fires. That that someone would see them approaching and maybe have something ready for them when they arrived. A good meal. Maybe some cold beers. His spirits began to lift as he rehearsed his greeting, his gratitude for another human being in this wilderness.

Tim interrupted his daydreaming. "The tower is just beyond those hills over there." He pointed in the direction of the scattered trees. "Now, we can try to go as far as we can before sunset, or we can go another few miles and make camp. Any thoughts?"

The idea of going on indefinitely did not sit well with Aaron. "Another few miles, meaning three, right?"

Tim laughed. "Okay then. Three. We're almost there. The worst is behind us." Tim, already in the lead after the brief stop, was sure that Aaron didn't believe him, and that was perfectly okay with him.

Aaron didn't believe him, but he knew it didn't matter. Not as long as he chose to travel with Tim. And he understood that he could part ways with him at any time and there would be no hard feelings. He could go back the way they came or make his own tracks. Tim wouldn't care. He might die somewhere along the trek. It would not trouble Tim. It suddenly became apparent to Aaron that even though he didn't travel alone, he was alone. Alone in every way other than occasionally hearing another man's voice, sharing with another man his food, warming himself with a fire another man shared with him. Surprisingly, this thought did not frighten him. Instead, he recognized something akin to the freedom he thought he felt when he left Crosswood, but this feeling was much stronger, palpable.

Tim did not know that Aaron had stopped. A fleeting thought crossed Aaron's mind. Tim didn't need to know. He didn't need to turn around and ask if everything was okay. He didn't need to wait for Aaron to catch up with him. Nothing mattered. Only what he decided to do, to say, to think. It was so simple a concept and so freeing. Further surprising himself, Aaron realized that he was weeping. Still Tim had not turned around.

It was easy now. One foot in front of the other. Following a man named Tim who, if Aaron could see his face, was grinning, his teeth exposed between his lips, his thoughts composing another round of song to be sung to anyone or thing that chose to listen.

Chapter 21

The mystery that accompanied Quin into the desert played on his mind. He had nothing to guide his thinking in formulating an answer. Willy had kept it to himself. It wasn't that Quin hadn't pressed Willy to tell him, to reveal even a hint. He had but Willy was having no part of it. Quin would know it when they got there. If Quin heard Willy say one more time, "Have faith," he wasn't sure he could contain his frustration a minute longer. Besides, as he walked behind and, at times, by Willy's side, he was worried. Willy had faltered a few times, seemingly losing his balance, so that Quin needed to rush up to him or reach out to him to steady his companion. Stopping to rest, drinking the luke-warm water sparingly, Willy would be revived as if nothing had happened, and they would be on their way again. He was not willing to hear Quin's concerns. He made that clear.

Since they began their trek into the unknown, Quin kept track of the passing days. He had seen it in a movie about a prisoner in a dark, dank cell who scratched a mark on the wall's surface each time the sliver of light from the narrow opening in the ceiling faded away into darkness. The prisoner kept it up until he was taken away to his death, three hundred days after his initial imprisonment. The image left such an impression on Quin that it occurred to him that he might be in a similar plight. Certainly not for three hundred days but as far as he could tell based on what appeared to be Willy's wanderings, an indefinite time. Quin could not say what day it was but, as he undid his belt to scratch yet another passage of time, he could say how many. Twelve. Almost two weeks and still Willy wandered on.

Why they hadn't crossed anyone's path was its own mystery to Quin. He had taken a brief look at the topo map that Willy carried, and it appeared that the likelihood of seeing another human was good. One of the reasons that he stayed with Willy. They weren't that far off the beaten track. Plenty of four-wheel drive routes crisscrossed the desert floor. At the time, it was comforting. But with each passing day, Quin recognized that they were in trouble. Willy had no idea where he was going. And with each passing day, Quin's fear grew. He was torn. If he couldn't convince Willy to stop and to agree to find help, then he would have to leave him. But could he? Could he abandoned Willy in his condition that Willy refused to acknowledge, leaving him to die alone? For surely that would be the outcome. Could he bear the guilt? But to stay with him was suicide. He no longer cared what Willy thought about that. They had been on their way to suicide from the moment they stepped onto the desert's floor.

Quin buckled his belt. Willy was already asleep having eaten little and drinking even less. The sun was well below the mountains in the distance and the day's heat was quickly giving way to the cold of night. Tomorrow he would confront Willy. It was decided. Willy no longer had any choice in the matter. If it meant leaving him here, as much as he prayed that he wouldn't need to, he would do it. To find help. To come back to Willy. To rescue him from himself. Quin knew he was right. He could see nothing that was wrong with saving Willy and himself. Wherever Willy wanted Quin to go, whatever he wanted Quin to see, it could all wait. He closed his eyes, never more certain of anything in his entire life. He wasn't aware of sleep overtaking him, rescuing him from what he thought was their reality.

Willy had quickly fallen fast asleep, his mind a blank slate.

Chapter 22

True to his word, as the late afternoon of the second day closed in upon them, Tim and Aaron had the fire tower in sight. It sat at the top of a rise of pine trees whose numbers had steadily increased as they left the scattered green landscape behind them. The forest that surrounded them was pungent, the afternoon's heat releasing the familiar pine scent that blended with the earth's own emittance. No longer hard, unforgiving ground under foot, they walked on softer earth, shaded, and nurtured by the undergrowth that flourished, benefitted by the trees that towered over it. Aaron said a silent prayer of thanks.

"This is the last pull. We climb to the tower. No other way to get there." Tim had stopped, taken off his pack, and sat down next to it as he got comfortable leaning against the trunk of a tall pine. Aaron did the same.

"Looks darn steep. Is it?" Initially, upon sighting the tower, Aaron had tried to gauge just how tall the mountain was but, at a distance, he had been fooled. His estimation was proven wrong the closer they came to it. He knew the answer. Anyone could see the answer.

"Guess that's in how you look at it. It's not a romp in the hills."

Tim was digging in his pack and pulled out a candy bar whose distorted shape was testament to its inability to withstand the heat of the past days. Aaron was surprised it hadn't completely melted into a lump. Tim did not seem to notice or care as he unwrapped, somewhat unsuccessfully, the melded paper from the chocolate.

"Care to join me?" He held the misshapen bar out to Aaron.

"No thanks. You enjoy." Aaron was hungry but not that hungry.

"You need your energy. Put something in your body." Tim nodded in the direction of Aaron's pack that lay by his side.

"Right." He knew exactly where his food was, careful to have wrapped it in a plastic bag. Even so, the granola peanut chocolate chip bar hadn't withstood the heat much better than Tim's candy bar. He held back a smile that he knew Tim would not when he saw Aaron's bar.

"Looks yummy," Tim's words slipping through his grin as Aaron lifted it to his mouth. "Bon appetite." He held what was left of his candy bar up in a toast. Aaron did the same.

Not completely satisfied but remembering that there would probably be a meal waiting for them once they reached the tower, Aaron did not hesitate to ask.

"How long will it take us?"

"You mean to the tower?" Tim wiped his mouth with his shirt sleeve, the remnants of melted chocolate gone.

"Yeah. You said one to two days to reach it. But we're not there yet and it's been two days."

"You are one for specifics, aren't you? It all depends."

"Depends on what?" Aaron wished, just once, that Tim would answer his questions directly. Specifics were still important to him.

"How fast you want to go. What may stall our progress along the way. Getting off trail and wandering until we find it again. Meeting up with a creature that we startled and who doesn't want us here. Doing bodily injury to ourselves by not paying attention. Mother nature suddenly changing her mind about her weather. There are a number of scenarios, Aaron, to answer your question." Tim slid down a bit against the trunk while shoving his pack behind his back, his head now resting back on the pack and looking up to the sky.

Aaron would play the game, but he was growing tired of it. "If we don't experience any of those scenarios or any not mentioned, how long until we get to the tower. That's all I want to know. Best case scenario, Tim, please."

"Best case? By midafternoon tomorrow if we get a start before sunrise." Tim kept his focus on the sky, his eyes lids now at half-mast.

Not the words that Aaron was hoping to hear but at least he now had specific information that, for the time being, put his mind at ease.

"Okay. Good. Before sunrise. Are we camping here then?"

Tim did not respond. He was sound asleep, the beginnings of a snore here and there the only sound Aaron could hear in the forest. Not yet dark, the sun only an hour or so from setting, Aaron's second wind kicked in. He quietly left Tim to his dreaming and headed into the forest collecting what he could find to start a fire for their evening meal. It dawned on him, however, that a fire might not be a good idea in this area as he looked up at the lower hanging branches of the pines and their density. No viable clearing anywhere to start a fire. Not tonight. Dropping his armful of kindling and branches, he headed back to Tim.

Still sound asleep, Tim had not moved from his position, head still facing the sky. Aaron sat back down, enjoying the quiet and being alone even as Tim sat within feet of him. Tim was elsewhere in Aaron's thinking, oblivious to his surroundings and to Aaron. It was a moment that Aaron relished and the more he thought about it, the harder he prayed for Tim to stay asleep. He wanted desperately to experience the forest and the quiet by himself. His thoughts wandered from the present to the recent past, meeting Tim for the first time and what had transpired between them since then. But his thoughts did not stay there. Suddenly drawn to his past before Tim, to his years of growing up, to his time surviving on his own, his time before Tim. He wondered if Tim had had a normal childhood. Had parents somewhere who loved him and missed him. Maybe even had a brother or sister. The longer his daydreaming lasted, the further Aaron explored his imagined life of Tim.

Neither one heard the movement somewhere behind them not far from where they sat. Hardly perceptible but if alert and conscious, could be detected and defense mechanisms would kick in. As Tim slept on and Aaron's daydreaming drew him farther under, the bear rose its snout to the air current and sniffed. It did not move as it calculated the source of the scent that met its large, moist, nostrils. It was not hungry. Its food sources were many in this forest. Only once had it eaten something unnatural to its environment, but it was enough for it to remember its enticing taste as it slid down its throat. Long ago, it had paid for its rummaging through the human's garbage. As a younger bear having followed the foreign scents on the wind, it had come to an opening that it had never seen before. But it was here that the scents were overwhelming and impossible for it to ignore. Of all the human garbage it had consumed, the sweetness that it tasted, and its scent left an indelible memory as did the trauma that followed.

Naïve, if a wild animal can be this, the bear did not understand the consequences of coming so close to humans whom it had never seen. It did not understand that it was considered a threat to them. It still didn't understand. But it did know the pain of a tranquilizer's hit into its thick skin, and it did know the fear of containment until it was set free again into a place in the forest it did not know. It did survive and it did forget, until now. But the trauma was not what it remembered. It was the reason for the trauma in the first place and now it was the only thing on the bear's mind. The scent was on the wind, and the memories of its satisfaction on its tongue directed its behavior now, as unnatural as it was.

It made its way to the two men, both still unaware of its approach. It would make itself known only if it needed to defend itself but until then, it stealthily came up behind them, its nose directing its course. It stopped within yards of Tim, for that was where the scent was the strongest. Lifting its head again to verify that it was almost to its prize, its own body's odor escaped into the air and reached the site where the two men sat. Still not close enough for either to detect.

Tim knew better. Why he didn't put the candy bar's wrappings in his pack, Aaron would never know. It was a stupid mistake, one that Aaron had made as well but the bear was not interested in his trash. It happened in a flash and all

Aaron could do was watch in shock and horror as the bear appeared next to Tim who opened his eyes for the last time.

Tim did not freeze in place but yelled and shoved his body to an upright position, his legs beneath him an unsteady support. His instinct was to throw his arms up in the air, yell at the top of his lungs to frighten the animal but none of his antics seemed to be working. Aaron had done the same, but the bear paid no attention to him. It and Tim were engaged in their own confrontation and Aaron could do nothing about it.

The bear reared, growling, and shaking its head and neck back and forth as if to say, "Oh, no you don't." Threatening the defenseless human below him, it suddenly lashed out, its giant paw and claws catching the side of Tim's head and throwing him to the ground. It did not advance but remained in its threatening position, its body not willing to surrender yet.

Tim was not moving. Frozen in place, Aaron prayed that the bear had had enough. His focus remained on the bear's aggression, however, and if need be Aaron would turn and run for his life. Suddenly, the bear dropped to all fours, its vocalizations silent now as it sniffed the ground where Tim had rested just moments before. Aaron could not move and watched as the bear, still sniffing the ground, came upon the empty candy wrapper. It was then that Aaron understood. It was then that he detected what the bear had detected from so far away but that Aaron, a mere human, who was less than three feet away from it could not. The remnants of dried melted chocolate coated portions of the wrapper, enough that the bear's desires were finally met.

As Tim's blood seeped beneath his head onto the dirt, the bear's large paw played with the wrapper attempting to bring it to its mouth. It succeeded as Aaron, mesmerized by the wild animal's agility considering its size, could not stop watching. The bear held the wrapper in its paw and gently licked the chocolate until the wrapper was completely wiped of its sweet temptation. And then it dropped it on the ground. It turned toward Aaron seemingly deciding if it should continue but thought better of it. Turning to leave, it stopped and turned its head one last time. Its eyes met Aaron's, a silent communication between the two that Aaron did not understand but that the bear did. And then it was gone.

He had no idea how long he stood frozen in place while Tim lay bleeding, still and unconscious. The air's rapid cooling jarred Aaron from his stupor, a shiver running up his spine. It was only then that he was aware that the sun was setting. Still traumatized by the event, he forced himself to move to Tim, slowly comprehending that his friend needed his help. As he knelt next to Tim, he saw what he couldn't see minutes ago. Multiple parallel gashes extended from the back of his head to his right eye that was bloodied and swollen shut. The amount of blood loss should have been enough for Aaron to understand that he was now truly alone. But it was only after he tried to find a pulse that he understood. He stood up, pacing back and forth, completely at a loss as to what to do next.

It was a simple task. One that he could accomplish immediately and that gave him a fragment of satisfaction. He leaned down and picked up the candy wrapper, moist with the bear's saliva, and crushed it into a small ball in his fist. He moved to his own wrapper and did the same. Satisfied, he shoved both paper balls into his backpack making a note to get rid of them as soon as he reached the fire tower. He gave no thought as to how he managed to separate himself from the reality that his companion lay dead on the ground while he was left unscathed as he prepared for the night before him.

Mechanically moving through the motions, he took off his companion's jacket and covered the upper half of his body with it, hiding from his sight Tim' fatal wound. With daylight rapidly dwindling and no fire to give him further light, Aaron worked quickly as he went through Tim's pack confiscating only the items that would come in handy, including extra food. It didn't occur to him to retrieve any form of identification Tim might have carried with him. His thinking was far from clear as he stuffed his own pack with Tim's no longer needed essentials. Slinging it onto his back, he noted the extra weight. It didn't matter. All that mattered now was to get away from this place and the bear, convinced that it was just within the trees watching his every move. He needed to find somewhere to sleep and, in the morning, start up the mountainside to the tower. Whoever was up there would know what to do next. Tim would be safe until then.

In the twilight, he stumbled through the trees moving upwards as he put distance between him, the bear, and Tim. He didn't go far before he gave in to the dark. In much the same way he and Tim had stopped to rest, leaning against the trees, Aaron did the same again. He longed to close his eyes and drift into a deep sleep, but his mind was running wild. The least sound startled him as he peered through the darkness for its source. It felt like hours were passing as he unwillingly remained on alert, all the while fighting his fatigue both physically and mentally. He could not recall when he finally fell asleep.

The warmth of the midmorning's sun on his face pulled him from unconsciousness. He did not feel rested, and it didn't take long for him to remember. The immediate urgency was to move, to find his way to the tower. The realization that he had slept well past sunrise angered him. What had Tim said? Leave before sunrise? Get there by midafternoon? Now it would be more like nighttime, and he wasn't even sure how to get there. All he understood was that the tower was at the top of the mountain, and he was nowhere near it. Remembering a map he had taken from Tim's pack, now relieved, he searched for it in his own. A trail map would be all he needed, certain that Tim carried one.

He carefully began to unfold the well-used paper until he saw the faded print in the bottom corner of one side. *Trail Hikes of Hawaii.* As he opened the map further, his frustration and sudden anger with Tim escaped him and he threw the map on the ground cursing until he exhausted himself. He wanted to cry like a baby, but he didn't. Instead, he sat back on his haunches, a sudden image of Tim doing the same across from him, smiling that innocent way of his, communicating to Aaron that it was no big deal. It stunned him, this thought, as if Tim had never left him. He was right here with him climbing up to the tower together.

Aaron understood. Folding the paper carelessly so that it fit into his pack, he stood up and surveyed his surroundings in the daylight. Where he stood provided him no view of the tower, only treetops scattered against the blue sky. Had he paid better attention earlier, he would have noted at the first sighting of the tower the sun's location. Something to help him navigate the climb. At this point, he had no idea which way to go. He tried to remember. Suddenly, Tim was with him again and was pointing towards the hills. Aaron recalled shading his eyes against the sun's light blinding his view. And he recalled the time of day. That was it. Head toward the sun. He had no idea how sound his makeshift navigation was, but it was better than nothing.

Why he hadn't remembered packing it until now escaped him but the compass he purposely included still lay safely in one of the side pockets of his pack. He had never used it and wasn't even sure he knew how. Its silver case was no more than two inches in diameter, a small item but an essential one. As he placed it in his palm and lifted the thick cover, he stood still watching the red needle. He slowly turned his body and continued to focus on the needle. Where the sun was to set, Aaron stopped, adjusted his footing enough for the compass to show him a westward direction. With renewed confidence, he started out keeping the compass in the palm of his hand.

The tower came into view after hours of his upward climb, the compass leading the way. He still had miles to go but at least he had his sights set. He decided to rest for one more night before he made his final ascent in the morning before sunrise, just as Tim had suggested. Better late than never, Aaron mumbled aloud to his invisible companion. A calm had settled on Aaron as he realized that he would accomplish what he and Tim set out to do. And he would find out, finally, what a fire tower was all about.

He found an area where the trees were less populated. He could light a fire here, a small one, but one to keep him warm and heat some dried soup he had found in Tim's pack. Having gathered enough branches and some kindling, the area being surprisingly free of it, he hoped that it would be enough to start the fire. As he struggled to ignite the bit of brush he could find, he remembered. The candy and granola wrappers. Finding them wedged on one side of the pack, he placed them under the branches. Knowing they were not enough to get the fire going, he was about to search for more brush when he remembered the map. Pulling it from the pack's recesses, he opened it all the way and then proceeded to tear it into sizable pieces only to crumple each one into a ball. As he had watched Tim do with twigs and brush, he strategically placed the paper kindling under the branches to join the wrappers and put a match to one of them. Then another and then another until the flames took hold and the fire came alive in front of him. With a sense of accomplishment, he suddenly felt okay. He could do this. He had come through the worst of it. And Tim, in all his quirkiness and laissez-faire ways, had been by his side. Even in death. The thunderbolt of this realization was about to change the trajectory of his life even though Aaron was unaware of this as he watched Tim's soup come to a boil in his metal drinking cup.

Chapter 23

Willy was awake when Quin finally came to. He had not moved from his position the night before. Only his eyes, now focused on Quin, were the only sign that Willy could still function. Quin unraveled his body and stood up, Willy's eyes following his every move.

"Did you sleep okay?" Quin moved to one side of Willy to block the sunlight from Willy's face.

"I might have. I don't remember."

"Well, the important thing is that we are both awake which means we're still alive." Quin turned away from Willy and looked for a place to relieve himself.

As he came back, he was astonished to see Willy standing up, his pack on his back ready to move on. "Need to get started while it's still cool. We'll stop later to eat."

Willy sounded like he was talking to his family while on vacation, frustrated that they were losing the best part of the day while he had to wait for them all to get ready. He couldn't help but laugh as he heard Willy's statements. What world did he live in, Quin wondered?

"You sure?"

"Of course, I'm sure. Get your pack. Let's move."

The strength of Willy's voice was even more surprising than his standing upright on his own with a full pack on his back. It was uncanny and a little worrisome as Quin tried to take it all in. His decision last night to confront Willy was momentarily forgotten as he picked up his pack and joined him.

"Willy, you must have had a miracle sleep last night. What gives? I thought you were close to leaving this world."

"You don't have faith, Quin. What have I been trying to tell you all along? Faith. You've got to have faith, or you don't get up in the morning." With that, he turned away from Quin and began the day's trek through the desert's sands.

Quin followed Willy a few steps behind him. Maybe Willy was right. Maybe, with a change of attitude on his part, he could keep going away from what he knew, deep down, he shouldn't. But here he was following him once again to somewhere, and Quin didn't have the courage or the desire to put a halt to it. Whatever he had thought the night before, so sure of himself that he would change their course, faded away as one step followed another. Tonight, if they made it to tonight, he would face Willy.

Willy noticed it first but didn't point it out to Quin. He would see it and if Quin didn't, nothing lost, nothing gained. The dust cloud could easily have been mistaken for a dust devil whose life expectancy depended on the air currents. But Willy knew it was not mother nature's work but her reaction to a manmade activity. It was far enough in the distance not to be heard and barely able to be made out with the naked eye, but Willy was familiar with the cause, and it angered him. An invasion of four-wheeled vehicles crisscrossing the desert's delicate environment was the cause of numerous death tolls for all that existed naturally in and on her sands. He remembered a time when nothing existed here beyond what naturally belonged.

He knew how far away it was and he knew that the intruders would not reach them as the track ended abruptly in a dead-end. Whoever was on a joyride, unless they were absolute fools, would know not to drive farther. It wasn't allowed but there were always those who didn't follow the rules.

Without drawing attention to the moving dust cloud, he surreptitiously kept an eye on its movement. He needed to see the cloud move in the other direction. Only then could he relax. Quin followed behind him and hadn't said a word in the last hour. Willy was grateful. It gave him time to think. He wondered how much farther he would take Quin through the desert until one of them gave out. After all, it would be thirteen days by the time the sun set tonight, according to Quin. Willy was aware of Quin's count, a ritual that occurred every day since they first started, but something that Willy never remarked upon. A count, much less an accurate count, was not important to him. The passage of time had no significance, a manmade convenience that did nothing but limit a man's progress, his thinking, and his awareness of everything else. Willy understood that he had fallen prey to this contrivance many times in his life but, in doing so, he purposely avoided unnecessary conflicts with those who believed it. It was easier this way.

As he hoped, the cloud disappeared only to reform in the opposite direction until it was no longer visible. Had Quin seen it, Willy was sure that he would have said something. Thankful for this, he trudged on, his only expectation that of his certain fatigue that was not far off. Oh, and that of an accurate accounting by his companion.

Quin did not see the dust cloud in the distance. His eyes were focused on the ground in front of him. His ears took in the sound of his and Willy's footsteps crunching the hard earth as the dried salt surface gave way under their weight or the millions of sand granules shifted in their dispersal under the men's boots. Sucking in the dry, hot air that kept him going, his nose and mouth worked in tandem. There was little else to occupy his thoughts other than the sudden realization that he was in survival mode and that this could be his last day. Any thought of the strangeness of Willy's constitution, seemingly unaffected by the environment as his readiness attested to this morning, took too much energy to consider. Quin could not even remember why he wanted to confront Willy in the first place. His brain was dying. That he was sure of. It would be only a matter of time before the rest of him followed.

Willy stopped half-way through a footstep, but Quin kept going oblivious to anything but himself until he caught site of Willy's right hand gesturing him to stop his forward movement. About to say something, Willy took a step backwards and then another in slow motion. It was then that Quin saw the snake coiled tightly with its head extended beyond its body, frozen in its threatening stance. Now in the silence, Quin could hear the warning of the reptile whose rattles shot up at the opposite end of its body's coil. Its repetitive gyration was hypnotic, but only for seconds. The little his brain was functioning, Quin knew enough not to move but to follow Willy's silent instructions.

When Willy was less than a foot from him, still motioning Quin not to move, they stood frozen, their eyes on the snake's every movement. The tail's rattles suddenly silenced themselves, lowering into the coils below it. Its head pulled back as the coils began to unwrap themselves. Both men silently took in the girth and length of the snake, Willy more than Quin who had never seen a snake in the wild and had very little to compare it with besides the captive ones behind glass. Willy understood, however, how much danger they were in as he forced his breathing to slow, to regain normalcy. As the snake slowly slithered his long body across the sand, both men watched it disappear among the few desert plants that grew nearby. The trail its fluid body left on the sand was the only indication that it had been there in the first place.

Quin wanted to speak but waited for Willy to do so first. Did snakes come after you if you made too much noise? Quin, his eyes still on the snake's trail, heard Willy's sigh of relief. When Willy did turn and face him, Quin noticed the fear in Willy's eyes. However, he smiled at Quin, but said nothing right away.

"That was a rattler, right?" Quin could wait no longer.

"That was the granddaddy of all rattlers." Willy shook his head as if in disbelief that they had just witnessed it. That this moment had even occurred.

"So, is it gone? Are we okay to keep going or are we going to run into it again?" Quin was aware that he was shaking, but not enough for Willy to detect.

"I would say it's gone elsewhere. Whether we run into it again, I can't say. This is his territory, not ours. One thing I know is that he was kind enough to give us fair warning."

Quin hadn't thought of it like that. Fair warning. Something that he wished Willy had given him before they set out on faith alone not quite thirteen days ago.

Chapter 24

His fear had not left him as he continued the ascent to the tower. As much as he tried to focus on the goal of reaching it, the tower never seemed to get any closer. Aaron was not even sure he wasn't going in circles all this time. Numerous times he stopped in his tracks thinking that he heard movement just off to the side somewhere in the trees or behind the massive boulders whose outcroppings began to appear two hours into his climb. But each time, nothing came of it other than reinforcing his fear of the bear. He was convinced that it had unfinished business with him.

The early start had been the only thing that had gone right. With little sleep, he could stand it no longer and had started out before the sun rose. Still dark but not the velvet darkness that surrounded him all night, he was barely able to see where he was going, tripping here and there on exposed tree roots and partially hidden rocks. Once the morning light began to appear, he picked up his pace, anxious to make it to the tower before evening. If Tim had been right, by midafternoon. But then again, Tim knew where he was going. A flash of anger rose in Aaron as he remembered Tim's useless map of Hawaii and right behind it, regret. The guy was killed by a bear. How could he be upset about a stupid piece of paper? In an unconscious act of repentance, he hoped that Tim's body would be left unharmed until he could get back to him. Even though he knew nothing about Tim, Aaron silently promised him that he would bring his body back to civilization so that his family could say goodbye properly. And whoever was in the tower could help him make that happen.

If the situation had been different, if he had been the one attacked by the bear, he wondered if Tim would do the same for him. And if Tim did manage to bring him out, what would be the point? Who was going to care anyway? He had no one left who would. In remembering his conversations with Tim that had evaporated into the smoke of many shared campfires,

Tim's words came back to him, almost as if he were walking by his side. "I have no right to tell you that you are wrong or that you are right. I am not your conscience any more than you are mine. For us to get along, to live in harmony with the earth and all her creatures, we must accept this."

Deep in rambling thoughts, he was not paying attention to his surroundings as he slowly climbed. The terrain had grown steeper and the rock outcroppings more numerous so that Aaron depended on them for help as he grasped their surfaces for balance. He was suddenly aware of his pounding heart and the ascent's gradual difficulty. He stopped, balanced between two boulders almost waist high, unable to catch his breath until he rested. Afraid to take off his pack for fear of it falling out of sight, he leaned forward to relieve the burden, still trying to normalize his breathing. I must be getting closer, he thought, his breathing deeper now as he lifted his head and looked upwards. The sunlight was filtered with no clear opening in the trees' canopy to see much more than bits of blue sky. He slowly straightened, his over-stuffed pack almost pulling him backwards as he shifted his weight trying to find the pack's seating on his back. Taking in his surroundings, he could now see a way ahead, still maneuvering among the rocks and trees, but it gave him hope. He was farther into this ascent than he was hours ago, and this last leg would take everything he had. The temptation to give up and head back the way he had come was fleeting. He had no choice. Not really. Besides, a warm meal, companionship, and help was waiting for him.

The cloud cover had been steadily growing coming up from the south. The blue skies that accompanied Aaron as he climbed higher had not given way to any interruption. It wasn't until he felt a chill and was aware of the filtered light becoming dimmer, that he looked up. The billowing white thunder heads loomed over the top of the mountain, a sight that brought him to tears. The mountain top and the tower were so close now. For a moment, he took in the beauty of mother nature, no thought entering his mind as to the possible outcome of the rapidly moving and threatening clouds. Not until the temperature suddenly dropped and he felt the biting cold on his hands. The few trees that were outnumbered by boulders sang the growing wind's song and swayed with its rhythm. The change in the environment stunned Aaron. He understood that, like the appearance of the bear, he was no longer in control. He was at the mercy of her. Tim had told him that nature was constantly mentoring him if he understood this. Aaron realized that he had been ignoring her. He had not been thinking about anything other than his own discomfort, pain, and fears. That he had not allowed himself to comprehend that his dependency on her was more important than his worst fears.

The rains poured through the trees, onto the boulders, ricocheting into the atmosphere, slamming against his exposed body, and leaving nothing untouched. The soaking lasted no more than a few minutes, but its impact was immediately apparent to Aaron. Drenched and feeling even more weighted down, he lost his footing as he attempted to take a step forward, the soil now a slippery mud surface in a downhill trajectory carrying with it whatever was in its path. Reaching out for the rock's surface for balance, that too, did not provide a hold, its surface just as slick. He slid no more than a few feet downhill, a rock formation blocking any further descent. Unharmed but shaken, he waited before moving forward again. He was dependent on her now, more than ever, and if Tim was right, she would show him the way forward.

He scanned what was left of his ascent as far as he could see. It wouldn't be easy, not now, and he wondered if he should wait out the storm that appeared unfinished. The sky had darkened again within seconds, and he waited for the next downpour. When it came, it hurt his exposed skin. Small hail fell from the clouds. He watched from his resting place the extraordinary show that nature was performing for him. From every surface, the hail bounced and scattered in a frenzied, chaotic dance and the sound against the rocks', trees', and earth's surfaces harmonized in a cacophony of pings, pings, pings. He was spellbound as he watched and listened, wincing when struck in the face, but opening his eyes quickly so as not to miss anything. As suddenly as the drenching began, it stopped. The stillness that followed was magical to Aaron. The skies cleared so that nothing appeared above him but a crystal blue canopy free of clouds and only sunshine. He felt the warmth of her on his skin and turned his head in her direction luxuriating in her gift of heat. But she was lower in the sky, and he knew that he needed to move forward. He would not spend another night in the open even if it meant finding his way in the dark.

The flash caught his eye, just to his right and above him. He stopped and tried to make out its source. At least an hour or so before the sun set, he figured. Blinded by its intensity as the earth's rotation brought her closer to the shadows, he blinked to clear his vision. He continued to climb, now feeling that the end was within reach. The flash appeared again. A reflection, he was sure. He had seen this same thing in movies when a piece of glass served as a signal light reflecting the sun's rays. Is that what he was seeing. A signal light? If so, that meant that someone knew he was there. The tower? Someone in the tower?

Instinctively, Aaron threw his arms above his head, madly waving to the flash that had continued its presence even as the sun grew lower now. He laughed loudly, slapping his knees and clapping his hands. He had a direction. He could finally see where he needed to go. He thanked whoever was there as he moved forward, slipping, and sliding, regaining his balance, and making headway slowly to his destination. The light continued to guide him. He wanted to reach out to Tim and tell him that he had made it. And he longed to hear Tim tell him that that was cool.

He came upon the tower's base, a flattened clearing that brought Aaron to tears. Still with no one in sight, as he drew nearer, he saw the wooden staircase that zigzagged to the top of the tower onto a platform surrounded by a railing. All he had to do was climb the stairs and knock on the door. The sun's only evidence of its presence today was the rose colored whisps of clouds, remnants of the storm from earlier. "I made it before dark," he said aloud so that Tim could hear him.

He was almost to the last leg of staircase when he heard footsteps above him. They grew louder as he ascended the final steps. As he placed one boot on the platform, and then the other, he felt the muscular grasp of the man's hands, one under his left elbow while the other grabbed his right hand, steading Aaron who was surprised to feel his legs buckle under him. Embarrassed but grateful, Aaron tried to focus on the human being who stood before him. How long had it been since he or Tim had last seen anyone else? He had no energy left to consider such a thing. It was all he could do to voice a weakened, "Thank you" as he released himself to this stranger's care.

As he had imagined, the interior of the tower was warm and even warmer in the sleeping area. The stranger left him on a cot against one wall of the area across from a sturdier looking bed. He told Aaron to get off his feet, to dry off, that there was a change of clothes in the wooden trunk at the foot of his bed and to get out of his wet ones. Dinner would be up in "about fifteen." Aaron hadn't learned the man's name, nor had he told the stranger his. "First things first" were the stranger's parting words as he left Aaron to his business. It dawned on Aaron that this stranger knew that he would be here. Everything was ready for him. Had he been watching him all along?

As Aaron undressed, drying off with the towel he found neatly folded at the end of the cot, he released a massive sigh, surprising himself. The clothes in the trunk were a bit big but heavy and warm, the wool and flannel overwhelming him in luxury. He could smell the hot meal just on the other side of the wall and his stomach growled loudly as he heard the stranger moving about.

He sat on the edge of the cot, trying hard to gather his senses, his balance, his thoughts. The realization that he had reached his goal, that he was safe, warmly clothed, and soon to be fed was almost too much to comprehend. He couldn't believe his luck. "I don't believe in luck," he heard Tim say.

"…feel good words…that makes us comfortable and secure when we think about the unknown. They fill our need to always have an answer. To assume there is an answer."

As Aaron moved to the man on the other side of the wall, he couldn't hold back his grin even as he faced the stranger and was about to introduce himself. But the stranger spoke first.

"You believe in coincidences?"

Aaron was stunned. "Excuse me?"

"You finding your way right into my pathway. That's coincidence, brother. Don't ever think that luck had anything to do with it. You are here because that's just the way it goes. And if it's for some reason that we don't know now, we might figure it out down the road. Now, sit down, make yourself comfortable, and eat up. Name's Ranger Everett Logan. You can call me Everett."

Aaron thought twice before saying anything. It wasn't coincidence. He had been led most of the way by Tim. And even though Tim, and it appeared Everett, didn't believe in luck, Aaron still did. Pure luck that he hadn't died on the way up to this man.

"Thanks. Aaron Crenshaw." He reached out his hand and Everett gripped it. "Smells good."

"Good to meet you, Aaron Crenshaw. Yup, it's good but best when it's still hot. So get to it. I'll join you in just a minute."

The vegetable soup and grilled cheese sandwich were the best things he had ever tasted. Consumed with hunger, he finished the meal before Everett returned. Aaron thought he heard his footsteps somewhere above him.

"Still hungry?" Everett came around the corner, glancing in Aaron's direction, as he scooped up his share of the soup. "There's more than enough if you want more," his back turned to Aaron as he held the ladle in the air.

"Sure. Would love some more. Did you make it?"

Everett's laughter filled the room. "If you mean heated the water and stirred in the dried mix, well then, yes. I haven't seen a fresh vegetable up here in months. The new supply will be here in a couple of weeks. Might luck out then."

Aaron hid his embarrassment. "Sure. Of course. In any case, it's awfully good."

Everett sat down across from Aaron. His pace was slower than Aaron's as he sipped each spoonful. "I'm surprised you don't recognize dried soup when you see it. You're a packer, aren't you?"

Was he? Aaron had to consider his answer. He'd like to pretend that he was but considering all that he had been through recently and how he had handled it, he knew better.

"Not really. Just found myself in a situation that sounded good at the time."

"You on your own out here is a testament to either your outdoor skills and experience or your stupidity." Everett focused on the food in front of him.

On your own…Tim. How had he not said anything about Tim?

"I wasn't. I mean, alone."

Now Everett's eyes focused on his guest. "But you are now, aren't you?"

Aaron nodded.

"When did you split ways?"

Aaron tried to remember. Two nights ago? His thinking was muddled, and he felt Everett's gaze silently demanding that he be accurate.

"Maybe a couple of days ago. But it wasn't like that. He was killed by a bear." It sounded so matter of fact to Aaron, but he didn't mean it that way. He wondered why he felt detached from the event when it had been so horrific at the time.

Everett sat back, his spoon dropped into the bowl of soup. "A bear attack? Where?"

Aaron had no idea other than it was somewhere before his ascent. "I'm not sure but I can probably find my way back there. Down at the bottom of the mountain."

"My God," Everett's words but a whisper. "What did you do with the body?"

"I left him there. Covered him up with his jacket. I didn't know what to do other than get out of there. I didn't know where the bear was and if it would come back." His words rushed from him as if they had been waiting for this moment of release.

Everett listened, his face not indicating anything. "Have any idea why it attacked? Generally, they mind their own business. They want no part of us."

"We weren't thinking. Left a candy wrapper on the ground where we were going to camp for the night. I guess it smelled it or something."

Everett leaned back in his chair as if considering Aaron's words. "I'll tell you this. A bear doesn't attack unless it's being threatened. I once saw a grizzly mama with her three cubs go after a jerk with a camera. The guy kept moving closer and closer and had one of the cubs isolated from the rest so he could get the shot. He got the shot, alright. That grizzly mangled not only him but his camera. If we hadn't been there and got to him in time, that would have been his last shot. And I'll tell you this too. We didn't take down that mama. She left on her own, her cubs right next to her. She'd done nothing wrong. Just protecting her young. I heard later that the guy survived but his injuries are gonna last him the rest of his life. Don't like to see a person learn the hard way but there it is. Serves him right."

"Tim didn't threaten it. He was just trying to scare it away." Even Aaron could hear the doubt in his words. Had he threatened it?

"Let me guess. He stood tall, waving his arms like a damn bird, and yelling at the top of his lungs. Am I right?"

Aaron replayed the moment as Everett's description hit the mark. "He was just trying to make it leave."

"Well, I am sorry for...Tim, is it?"

"Right, Tim."

"Did you make it through okay?" Everett dropped his chair back on all fours.

"Yes. Just shaken, I guess. I kept thinking that the bear was coming back for me."

"Well, I can understand that but the only reason it paid you a visit in the first place was because of that damn wrapper, by the sounds of it. I'm going to assume you got rid of it and didn't make the same mistake again."

"I burned them up. In a campfire." Aaron recalled the sweetened, saliva coated ball of paper.

"Them?"

"Yeah. I had a granola bar wrapper, but the bear didn't go after it."

Everett finished off his soup. His sandwich was cold. "So can you tell me what killed Tim? I mean how severe was the attack?" Everett took a large bite out of the sandwich.

"It swiped his head. Its claws tore into his head." Aaron felt sick. He hadn't remembered this part since it happened. Self-preservation, he realized. But now he saw the moment of the strike, the wound, and Tim's lifeless body on the ground.

Everett laid what remained of his sandwich on the plate. "I'm awfully sorry to hear this. But here's what needs to be done. You've got to take me to him. I'll call for help once we get there, not knowing what we're dealing with as far as terrain is concerned. My best guess is we'll have to chopper him out. You get some good rest tonight and we'll head out in the morning."

"You mean back down the mountain?" The thought of it immediately deflated him.

"You got a better way of getting to him? If you can give me the exact location, then I could get help there without going down, but it doesn't sound like you can. Did you guys use a topo map?"

Aaron wanted to cry. How could any of this be happening to him? And now the guy wanted to know if they used a topo map. Could it get any worse?

"No. We didn't have one with us."

"That was mistake number one, as far as I can see. What were you doing out here anyway?"

That was a good question, Aaron realized. Why had they even started the trek together? Tim had no destination in mind when they started, Aaron remembered. None. And then, suddenly, he wanted to take Aaron to a fire tower because Aaron had never seen one. That's why he ended up here, sitting across from a forest ranger in a fire tower sharing a bowl of soup and a sandwich.

"Tim wanted me to see a fire tower. I'd never seen one, never even knew they existed."

"Well, sounds like Tim has been in the area before. Was it worth it?" Everett cast his arm about him as he displayed the room.

Aaron wondered if Everett was trying to be funny, sarcastic, or just fed up with the naïveté of both he and Tim. "It was worth it to get here, to be safe again. It wasn't worth losing a life."

"No, I expect it wasn't. Well, like I said, get some rest tonight. We'll start down at five. The sun will be just rising, enough light."

It didn't occur to Aaron to ask if they would have to climb up the mountain once again. Pondering this as he tried to get comfortable on the cot, Everett already under the covers, Aaron was surprised to hear Everett's voice in the dark.

"Don't fret. They'll chopper you out with Tim. You'll be back in civilization before you know it."

Aaron, about to respond, could find nothing to say. Once again, he was witness to the inexplicable. Everett's comforting words were spoken when Aaron needed to hear them. Smiling, he rolled over, his back to Everett's bed, and silently thanked Tim. It was the least he could do.

Chapter 25

Into day thirteen and still no indication from Willy of their destination. Since meeting up with the granddaddy of all rattlers and coming away unscathed, Quin considered that they were both untouchable. They had come this far with no harm done to either one of them. Although, Quin was painfully aware that his body was failing and that his mind was doing the same. The urgency that he had felt days ago about confronting Willy and putting a stop to this madness was no longer present. He couldn't call it up even if he wanted to, unable to expend any of the dwindling energy he had left. Instead, he kept Willy in his sights, walking feet behind him, no longer rushing to his side if Willy faltered. If Willy did, Quin would stop, a blessed relief, until Willy pushed himself off the desert floor. No words were shared, not until they came to rest each night wherever Willy wanted. And, even then, the words were few. There was nothing to say. At least none that came to Quin's mind.

He barely heard Willy's voice, but he was sure that he had said something. Willy was seated, his pack still on his back, using it as a support to lean against, his legs outstretched in front of him. Quin was relieved when Willy called it quits for the day, earlier than usual, but a blessing. His body had nothing left, not until it rested. Quin reached for his water bottle and gestured to Willy to do the same. But Willy just shook his head and Quin let him be. He had only a half of the last bottle of water left and he barely sipped the tepid liquid. He had no idea how much Willy had. Quin had rarely seen him drink from his supply. Another mystery as to who this man really was.

Again, Willy's voice reached him, this time a bit more forceful. Quin moved closer to him.

"What is it, Willy?"

Strangely, Quin could not take his eyes off Willy's throat which appeared to be swallowing continually. "Here, drink this." He shoved his water bottle towards him.

Willy shook his head, pushing the bottle away from him. "Listen to me," his voice now whispered but Quin detected the urgency in it.

"What is it, Willy?"

"No man should die alone without being given the chance to ask for forgiveness." Willy purposefully made eye contact with Quin.

Not sure how to respond, all Quin could do was agree. "Yes, I believe that. Why are you even saying this?"

"Will you forgive me, Quin?" Willy tried to straighten himself, but his body was unwilling.

"Forgive you for what?" He had an idea.

"I don't know if we're going to get where we always wanted to go together. Not this time." Willy's throat continued its repetitive swallowing before he spoke again. "I thought all this time that you didn't have faith, but I was wrong. Will you forgive me for doubting you?"

He wanted to tell Willy that his request wasn't necessary. That he had given Willy plenty of reasons to doubt him just as Quin doubted Willy. But he knew Willy well enough to know that a response like that would only draw out what Willy needed from Quin. It would be cruel and self-serving. This thought lingered with him as he moved even closer to his companion.

"Willy, I forgive you. And do you forgive me for being such an ass this whole time?" Quin let his face relax and smiled.

Surprised by Willy's tortured attempt to laugh, Quin laid his hand on Willy's shoulder, the physical contact they both needed but couldn't ask for.

"I forgive you, Quin. You are an ass but a good one."

Quin did not take his hand away for a long time. Willy had fallen asleep. Unwilling to lose hold of Willy, Quin scooted himself into an identical position and closed his eyes, the human contact strangely overwhelming him with an inner peace.

On the morning of day fourteen, Willy did not wake up. Neither did Quin until the heat forced him to open his eyes.

Sunrise had come hours ago as Quin shielded his eyes from the blinding light not quite overhead yet. But Quin knew enough to recognize that the morning hours were over and that ahead of them they faced the worst part of the day's heat. He reached for the last of the carefully rationed water. Allowing only two sips at a time and those intervals spread as far apart as he could manage, he was pleased that he still had some left. He wondered if Willy had done the same with his.

Slowly pushing his body up to a sitting position, he looked over at Willy who lay awkwardly on his side, his back to Quin, his backpack still attached, the only thing holding him halfway up.

"Willy. Willy, wake up."

With no indication that Willy heard him, Quin forced himself to stand but did not move right away. He knew enough now to check his surroundings. Seeing no granddaddy watching him, he moved around to Willy's frontside.

"Willy. Hey, Willy." He leaned down and gently shook his companion. Not wanting to accept that Willy wasn't going to wake up, Quin removed his companion's backpack and rolled Willy onto his back. Kneeling next to him, Quin nudged him again and again. The old man's face was pale, relaxed, and at peace.

"Oh, no you don't. Don't even think about it. I'll be damn if you're going to leave me here." Ridding himself of his own pack, Quin sat back on his haunches, struggling to understand. "Come on, Willy. You brought me this far, damn you. What am I supposed to do now?"

How long he remained kneeling alongside his companion, he didn't know. The thought that Willy would suddenly gasp for air and then sit up as if nothing had happened kept Quin by his side. But Willy never did, and the longer Quin waited, the more intense the heat became until it was too much for him to bear. What little sense he had left told him to leave. To seek safety, shelter from the heat. As he peered into the near and far distances that surrounded him, he saw no refuge. For as far as he could see, the desert stretched out in every direction. Even the Amargosa range was barely visible now. What had Willy been thinking? Where was he going? There was nothing here. There had been nothing anywhere they had been.

The sickening thought that he had been taken in by a madman enraged him but, in his weakened state, his rage died as quickly as it had appeared. "It's not Willy's fault," Quin said aloud. Surprised by the sound of his own voice, he turned back to Willy. "It's not your fault." His final words to Willy would have to do. If he somehow heard Quin, that was enough. If he didn't, at least Quin had said them aloud. And that, for him, was enough.

He searched through Willy's bag only to find empty water bottles. The essentials that he carried were of no use now any more than the ones he carried in his own pack. Once, the prospect of reaching an unknown destination was enough for Quin to acknowledge his preparedness for this adventure. He had carefully chosen what he knew to be essential from his car's trunk the day this all began. The day that Willy fell from sight off the side of the road. The day that Quin chose to go after him, only after changing his mind. But that was so long ago, according to his accurate account, thirteen days ago. And today he would be struggling to survive day fourteen but this time completely alone, lost, his body shutting down by the minute.

Trying to remember in what direction they had begun two weeks ago, he took in the area one more time. The sun, now directly overhead, gave him no direction and he would need to wait for the earth's rotation to show him. He remembered the hills they had trekked to get to the desert floor and that they always seemed to be on his right side. But he was not sure. When they disappeared from site, he could be heading in any direction as he kept up with Willy's wanderings. He wished he had paid better attention.

The reality was that, even though he was now alone, he was not. What to do about Willy consumed his thinking, shoving away any thoughts of saving himself. He had nothing to wrap his body in. The surface of the desert would not allow him to dig a grave. Besides, he had nothing with which to dig it. As he let his eyes rest upon the still face at his feet, a vivid image from a story he had read when he was a young boy, long ago forgotten, came to mind. Three men on horseback in some desert came upon the remains of a man whose leathered flesh had repelled them as well as captivated them. The man had dried up, as Quin remembered the details of the scene. There were no bones scattered on the desert floor, no dismembered body parts. Just a dried-up human being. Even his clothes were mostly intact. The riders never dismounted and finally rode off into the sunset leaving the dead man as they found him.

That was what he would do. Leave Willy as he lay. There was nothing else to be done. If he made it out of here alive, he would make sure that someone was told. That Willy's body would be removed from this temporary resting place. And if he didn't survive, everything that he was planning would be for naught.

As he said his farewell to Willy, Quin felt strangely calm. Resigned that the inevitable outcome would not be good, he had come to an understanding. Willy had gone on before him to a better place, he hoped. The man deserved it. Where Willy wanted to take him would never be known now, Quin realized. A place that he'd always wanted to go. Wasn't that what Willy had said? What place was that? How could Willy know what it was if Quin had no idea?

The sun was moving to the west, toward the mountain range that rimmed the valley. The one they drove through, the one that, without Quin's knowledge, was the starting point on this journey. The one that, if only he could, he might reach before he couldn't. As he had done for fourteen days, almost fifteen if he woke up tomorrow morning, he placed one foot in front of the other, slowly and with the determination that he could. Willy would have expected as much.

Chapter 26

In the hours before his death, Willy felt Quin's body nestled into his. The warmth of it filling his own with the last human contact he would ever know. It gave Willy peace and a sense that after being alone for so many years, he would not die alone. It was a comforting thought because he had always feared that his death would be in solitude.

Dreams came but did not stay. Fragments of his life rapidly slid by, one after another, as if in a sped-up slide show. The images never stayed in focus long enough for him to completely recognize them. As he lay in semi-consciousness, he was dimly aware that something or someone was struggling to get through the chaos of his dying mind. But the effort to recognize it was too much and it was easier to let it go.

The deepening darkness that began to creep into his partial dreaming did not frighten him. He welcomed it. Slowly but with certainty, he sensed he was not far from leaving. Had he remembered all that he was supposed to? Had he left any unfinished business behind? Was just remembering enough? The simple act of recognition? Nothing more? In the last moments of his life, Willy was suddenly aware of an urgency to remember. He could not move on unless he did so.

The velvet black stopped its movement momentarily. In the lessening space of bright light, Willy saw her as she walked away from him. He called out to her, but she did not acknowledge him as she seemed to float across the desert floor. Suddenly, he saw her climbing the rock outcroppings that he knew so well. He watched as she moved closer to the hidden danger. Again, he yelled out to her, trying to warn her, but she did not hear him. And just as suddenly, he saw her on the desert's surface once again but this time she was kneeling on all fours, her body struggling to stand up. He watched helplessly as she turned to him, her eyes pleading with him to help her. He could not hear her but saw her mouth moving, begging him. He watched in horror as he walked away from her. Still she struggled. Still begged. His steps were easy, unencumbered, as he watched himself floating farther and farther away from her. And then he turned to see her one last time. Even though he had floated so far from her, he was now standing over her body that was sprawled face down on the salt flat, its brilliant white salt sediment's light painfully piercing his vision until he could no longer stay focused on her. As he watched himself turn away from her, moving forward away from the pain and into what little of the bright light that still appeared in front of him, the darkness began its movement again. With the warmth of Quin's body still comforting him, Willy passed through the pin hole of light just as the blackness closed behind him, never having asked her to forgive him.

Chapter 27

In the year that followed Aaron's ordeal, not a day went by that he didn't think about Tim. In the first weeks following his rescue, Aaron was made painfully aware that Tim, whose last name he had not known when they were together, had no family to receive his body. That he was eventually identified as Timothy Hammond, born in Fresno, California in 1994. No living relatives. He was only two years older than Aaron. Because he was not a relative, he had no say in what happened to Tim's body, so the city morgue saw to its disposal.

There was no closure for Aaron regarding his time with Tim. Maybe that was what Tim would have wanted. Or maybe Tim couldn't care less. But for Aaron, the absence of something more important than himself, stayed with him. Maybe it was Tim's way of messaging him from some other realm that what they had experienced together and a part was not meant to fade away. Not meant to be forgotten.

Everett Logan had been true to his word. The hike down the mountain began before sunrise. He took the lead and it appeared to Aaron that he had taken the hardest way up to the tower as he followed the seasoned ranger. Aaron did not recognize any part of the mountain side and panicked at one point that he would not be able to locate Tim's body. But Everett had listened the night before and had a fairly good idea of where the attack had taken place. He knew about the grizzly that inhabited the mountain with him and of her family. He had watched as her two cubs grew into adolescents. Sometimes, he got lucky and spotted them just below the tower as they moved through the open space on their way into the forest again. He never felt threatened. Only privileged.

Tim's body remained just as Aaron had left it. His fear that the bear would come back and drag Tim away was allayed as they came upon the familiar spot. Everett wasted no time in calling in the chopper who he had alerted to be ready the night before. Aaron stood by, feeling useless, as he watched in awe the rescue effort. Everett, with the skill of a fine surgeon, prepared Tim's body for the ride up and, when secured, signaled to the chopper to begin the lift. Aaron watched as the basket holding Tim's body was lifted into the sky and growing ever nearer to the chopper's opening. Aaron wondered how many times Everett had done this before. When the basket reappeared, it was empty and was being lowered down once again. Confused, Aaron was told that that was his ride out of here. Everett laughed when he told Aaron this, as if this boy had much to learn about life. No way was the kid going to stay with Everett if that's what he thought. Everett had a job to do, and he couldn't afford any more interruptions. But he was glad to lend a hand in a time of need.

Aaron was torn as he felt himself lifted high above the terrain that had been his reality for days now. Part of him wanted to stay with Everett in the safety of the tower. It was like nothing he'd ever experienced. And he was sure that he would never come close to this moment again. As he took a seat in the chopper, he kept his eyes on Tim, now covered properly from head to toe, in the secure wrappings of the rescue team. He longed to have one more conversation with him, to hear what Tim thought about all of this. To ask him where he was now. He didn't hold back the tears. Tim wouldn't want him to.

The loss of these two men in his life had a profound impact on Aaron. Tim's loss was immediate and apparent. He had given Aaron so many gifts that he discovered with each passing day. Tim felt like the father that Aaron never knew. The silent guidance, the ever-present awareness that Tim was right by his side, guiding him, correcting him, caring about him. Aaron had never felt stronger in his life as he did after Tim's death. But he would not completely comprehend the loss of Ranger Everett Logan's brief acquaintance until five years later when he drove into Death Valley Monument, his first post as a new National Park Ranger.

Tim had made sure that Aaron had direction and Everett had unwittingly opened the doors that would take him in the right direction. Four years of study and a fifth year in the field as a ranger, Aaron could not conceive of doing anything else with his life. He only wished that he had found his way sooner. But that would mean never knowing Tim and Everett. How had he gotten so lucky?

When he was offered either one of the two openings in the park service, he did not hesitate in making his decision. The post in the mountains of northern California was enticing but the lure of the desert was more so. He had never been in a desert setting, and he was eager to learn all he could about one of earth's most desolate but intriguing places. He would be under the supervision of the senior rangers whose vast knowledge and experience would be an education in and of itself. If anyone could appreciate this, it was Aaron. He had learned the hard way to pay attention when it was important to do so. But more than that, to pay attention to the common place. There were signs everywhere if he paid attention. Tim and Everett had taught him that much.

He was off putting, a description that Aaron had never used to describe anyone, but the description fit the man. Everything about him was disturbing as Aaron saw him. His name was Hugh Reynolds, Ranger Reynolds to Aaron. When Aaron arrived at the headquarters, Ranger Reynolds was waiting for him. He stood over six feet tall, Aaron guessed, and that was without his hat fixed firmly on his head. Another four inches, maybe. He wore a beard that filled his face reaching his cheekbones and extending just below his jaw line. Speckled like granite, the grey, black, and white hairs were gaining on what must have once been a jet-black beard. His mustache hair was still mostly black. His eyes were ice blue and piercing and Aaron found it difficult to keep eye contact. He rarely smiled but the laugh lines sprouting from the outer corner of his eyes indicated that he must have once upon a time. When he spoke, his voice was strong and all business. Aaron understood that there was no crossing lines with humor when dealing with this man. He would wait until Ranger Reynolds softened, if ever.

Aaron settled into the quarters, sharing a room with Devon Bennett, a ranger who was five years ahead of Aaron. He had been under the supervision of Ranger Reynolds when he first arrived and shared stories with Aaron, a kind of mentoring in the art of avoiding making the man angry or becoming disappointed in him. Even though he thought he was well prepared to take on the job, Devon laughed as he recalled his own inexperience. Hugh Reynolds made it clear how misguided his assumptions were. But there was no animosity towards Reynolds in his voice, as Devon shared with Aaron. If anything, Aaron detected sincere admiration for him.

The work, at first, was what Aaron considered grunt work. And he was not shy about sharing his feelings with his bunk mate. It was all part of the initiation, Devon assured him. Just do it, and do it well, and it will pass. Do otherwise, and you might as well say goodbye to this opportunity. Plenty of hole in the wall places in this country he could be assigned to. If you want this, then don't blow it, Devon reminded Aaron.

"You're heading out with me this morning, Ranger Crenshaw. Get your gear. Meet you out front in five."

Aaron looked up from his breakfast. Ranger Reynolds was standing in the door, one foot on the front step while the other kept the door open enough for half of his body to appear. Before Aaron could respond, he was gone. Devon's grin was not lost on Aaron as he leisurely ate.

"That's a first." Aaron pointed to the closed door with his spoon.

"There's always a first. You better step on it. He's not kidding. You have less than five now."

The truck was running, and Aaron wasted no time getting in. The man said nothing, looking straight ahead and then gunning it out onto the paved roadway. Aaron did not speak either. Instead, he thought about the days since his arrival in the valley. It had been two months of what he still described as grunt work but now he kept it to himself. It bothered him, the irony of it. Here he was in a beautiful and awful place, surrounded by nature and her mysteries that he had yet to discover but he had spent the first sixty days cooped up behind a desk pushing paper. And when he was finished with that, he was cleaning the quarters, washing dishes after the meals, and picking up trash in the immediate area of the building.

A far cry from his time with Tim. It felt like none of that experience mattered anymore. That he was starting from ground zero having to prove himself to someone. When he was with Tim, he had no one to impress. Tim didn't care. Their long winding conversations late into the night seemed to be the most important part of their relationship. He longed for those moments knowing his longing was futile.

"Heading down to Bad Water. Got some reports about folks not paying attention to the rules."

Shaken from his own meanderings, Aaron turned to Ranger Reynolds. "Bad Water?"

"It happens more than I like. They don't read or they do and don't care. Doesn't apply to them."

The negativity in his voice was not lost on Aaron. He thanked his lucky stars that he wasn't on the other side of the badge and having to answer to this ranger.

"So, they get themselves into trouble. And when they do that, well, we get in this truck and come to their rescue."

About to offer his affirmation, the image of the chopper lowering its basket down to retrieve Tim's body and coming down a second time to rescue him, caused his face to flush in embarrassment and he looked out the passenger window instead, hoping for the reaction to pass quickly.

"Don't get me wrong. It's my job and my sworn duty to keep people safe. But it's when they not only get themselves in trouble but when they trouble the land. I've seen damage done to her that riles me to no end. Any remorse on their parts? Hell, no. I'll keep on rescuing these folks but it's a whole lot harder to rescue and repair mother earth."

Mother earth. Aaron was beginning to understand the man. Again, Tim rode with him, the middle passenger on the bench seat. His presence was overpowering. Mother earth.

"I feel the same way." Aaron ventured a comment and waited.

"Course you do, or you wouldn't be here in the first place wearing that badge."

It wasn't quite what he hoped for from Ranger Reynolds, but it was a beginning.

"What can we expect when we get to Bad Water?" Aaron shifted in his seat, his body slightly turned in Reynold's direction.

"If they're still out there, it was reported that a small group had walked beyond the area they're allowed to, out on the salt flats that are running at 101 degrees…," he looked at his watch, "at eight in the morning. Fools."

Aaron was adapting to the excessive heat but even in the airconditioned quarters, it seemed to seep through the concrete walls. Still not used to stepping outside each morning only to be slammed in the face with the early heating of the valley, Aaron wondered if the decision to post here was the best one. But like everything else he had experienced in his life, he would adapt. He was sure of it.

"What they don't understand is the 101 degrees on the desert floor, especially on the salt flats, is not the same 101 degrees they experienced back home. Everything in this valley and its surrounding mountains is intensified. That's just the way she wants it and if you want to survive, you better damn well respect her."

He was right. Aaron and Tim had tried but had not succeeded. Their nonchalance, momentary as it was, took Tim's life and almost took his own had it not been for Everett. As they pulled into the parking area packed with cars and tour buses, Aaron was surprised to see so many people in one spot. The area was developed so that concrete walkways led the visitor down to the desert floor, to the spot indicating Bad Water. For a moment, he felt like he was in Disneyland about to experience a magical ride created by someone's imagination. But this was no Disneyland and the only imagination at work here was his own.

The stark reality that at the end of the concrete walk, passing by the last information signs, passing the few who had ventured a few steps off the concrete to take photos, lay an expansive surface of dull whites and greys that went on for nearly two hundred square miles in all directions. Reynolds was right. The heat was searing, and it hurt to breathe. Even the expensive sunglasses he thought to buy before coming here were not enough to ease the offensive glare that surrounded him. If there was a hell on earth, this must be it, he thought, as he followed Reynolds farther into the desert.

Aaron didn't see the group, but Reynolds had set his sights on them as he scanned the terrain with his high intensity binoculars. Aaron did the same, but his lenses weren't as powerful. Besides, he was having trouble focusing on anything but his body's depleting strength and overheating.

"Got 'em." Reynolds pointed but Aaron still could not make anyone out. "Let's head back. I'm calling it in. Get a chopper out here. They'll get them off her."

Before Aaron could respond, Reynolds was walking back to the truck. On his way, he made sure to tell the few still wandering off the concrete walk to get back on it and stay on it. And they did.

Chapter 28

The terrain gradually changed so that Quin wasn't aware that he had made some progress. His mind was on Willy and nothing else. His legs, barely moving forward, were not considered as they mechanically went through the motions of movement. His whole body, for that matter, no longer felt a part of him, the only real sensation the burden of his backpack that he had no strength to remove.

When he stumbled, his body fell to the desert floor like a ragdoll. No resistance given because his brain did not tell him that he was falling. The impact, however, was enough to draw him briefly out of his stupor, enough to understand that the ground beneath his feet had changed. No longer never-ending expanses of salt crusted surface but scattered rocks, small ones with others no bigger than the width of his boot. Somewhere, his brain was working overtime so that these rock sightings were starting to mean something to him. Where there were rocks, there must be more of them, and they must come from hills that become mountains. A fleeting image came to mind. He recalled the rocky descent to Willy, the rescue two weeks ago that was the reason for his predicament now. How close was he to finding his way out of here? Was it just a matter of following the rocks until he was forced to climb?

Pushing himself awkwardly to his feet, he reached out to balance himself, a dizziness taking him by surprise. He was going to be sick. The nausea was simmering somewhere in his gut, slowly rising, threatening, but refusing to act on it. He had never felt such misery. The dry heaves that followed forced him to his knees. Now, on all fours, he silently cried as the heaves subsided. The last of his water waited for him to reach for it. A matter of lifting his arm from the surface, stretching it back to the side pocket of the pack, a move that he had made numerous times before with no thought given but that now seemed impossible.

"You don't have faith, Quin." Willy's voice rolled across the desert floor and Quin heard it as clear as day. He looked up certain to see Willy towering over him. From all fours, he knelt and searched the expanse of desert all around him. He was completely alone. But he had heard him. He was sure of it.

"I do, you old bastard." Quin thought he had spoken aloud but his words stayed within.

"If you do, then prove it." Again, as clear as day.

Quin forced himself to stand, once again, and this time he felt no dizziness.

"Think before you move." Willy's voice was louder now.

His water bottle. He needed to drink. He focused on his right arm as it reached behind him for the bottle. He didn't remember it to be so light in his grip so that it slid from its side pocket with ease. Without opening it, he gently slushed it back and forth, his ears listening for the water's trapped movement. Instead, he felt it. Not much but it was enough.

"Sips. Only take sips. One or two." Willy's voice was encouraging now.

"One or two," Quin repeated, this time spoken aloud. Tipping the bottle carefully back against his lips, he managed two sips. Lowering it, he felt the remaining water settle to the bottom of the bottle. He had very few sips remaining.

He waited for Willy's direction, but no further help came. His bottle placed safely again, he had no choice but to move into the rocks. Was that what Willy had in mind? Slowly, Quin moved forward, the sun now lower as he moved west. He hadn't gone far when he looked up and beyond the increasingly treacherous surface, the placement of his feet his only recent concern. He guessed the terrain in front of him no more than a mile or so away, looked to be rising in elevation. A gentle rise but one, nonetheless. He wanted to pick up his pace, but he knew better. Slowly and carefully, he continued to move toward to what he prayed would be the beginning of the end of his ordeal.

When he stopped again, he had gone less than a mile. His body refused to go any farther. As he gave in to his weakened state, he realized that he was somewhere in between the deathly expanse of the desert floor behind him and the life-giving mountain range rising in the diminishing distance before him. A limbo land, he considered, where he could die or live. Too exhausted to entertain this idea any further, he lowered himself to the ground and maneuvered his pack off his back. A rock that protruded from the earth's surface served as a back rest as he pushed himself against it. Desperately wanting to drink, he thought better of it. Instead, he closed his eyes, his fourteenth day in this place almost to an end, and he dreamed of The In Between Time.

Chapter 29

As the weeks passed, Aaron found his grunt work, as he still referred to it but never in hearing range of Hugh, as routine. His days were full but rarely with the unexpected. The consistency was comforting. He had gone out with Hugh on a couple of runs since his introduction to Bad Water. One for a hiker stuck in a ravine with a broken ankle. "Must have thought he was a mountain goat," Hugh had commented, as he recounted the rescue to the other rangers over dinner that night. "Leaped from one side of the ravine to the other and missed. Real bright." The second rescue was more serious. A rattle snake bite. The young girl, just turned twelve, wanted to climb the rock formation and did so until she disturbed the creature that had every right to be there. However, she did not, having left the trail while her parents stood by taking a video, the posted warning to stay on the trail right in front of them. There was no mistaking Hugh's opinion when it came to foolish folks visiting his park. He had no patience and certainly no room in his heart for their own stupidity. But Aaron had to give him credit. Hugh never let his true feelings be known to the rescued other than to remind them to follow the park rules and guidelines.

The call came over his walkie talkie as he was picking up the last of the day's trash. It was Hugh and he wanted Aaron back at the station pronto. Another rescue operation, this time taking both Aaron and Devon with him. Farther out than either of the younger rangers had been before, almost to the border with Nevada. Hugh explained that he had gotten a call from a chopper pilot out of Beatty who said he spotted someone in distress or possibly deceased almost at the base of the Funeral Mountains, southwest and on the California side. Hugh had the coordinates from the pilot and already had a chopper waiting for them.

Devon was not new to helicopters, his father once owning one, until he was too old to fly it anymore. At least, safely.

Devon gave Aaron some guidance once inside when Aaron told him that he had only been in a chopper once before. Aaron's nervousness was obvious. And when he asked where the doors were, Devon had a good laugh explaining that this was a rescue vehicle and that the doors were slid back. "Just grab on to the handhold and keep your eyes peeled," Devon yelled over the noise of the chopper as it lifted them off the desert floor.

Aaron did as he was told as he and Devon sat behind the pilot and Hugh. His headset in place, he was beginning to get the hang of it. Hold on, keep eyes in search mode on your side of the chopper, listen, and respond when one of the guys says something. And if you see something, say something. The whole experience was exciting and the more he relaxed into it, the more exciting it became. He almost forgot that they were going after someone in distress, that they might be accompanied by a grievously injured person or worse, a body, on their way back home.

"There. Straight ahead." The pilot's voice was clear and strong.

Aaron felt his stomach leap as the helicopter began to descend, level out, and then descend again. He couldn't see anything from his position. The sands kicked up and swirled around the chopper as the pilot gently put her down. Slowly the whop, whop, whop of the blades lessoned until they were almost still.

"Keep your head down!" Devon yelled to Aaron as they each exited and jumped to the desert floor.

"It's too rocky to land any closer. Grab the stretcher!" The pilot pointed to Devon. "You get the med kit," he directed Aaron.

When they cleared the chopper and came together, the four men lost no time in heading in the direction where the victim was spotted. Gingerly keeping their foothold on the uneven surface, they made good time. Aaron could tell that this was not the first time for at least two of them to have done this before. He wondered about Devon but snapped out of his daydreaming when he tripped on a rock, almost losing his balance and the med kit.

"Eyes open!" he heard Hugh yell back at him.

Quin could not identify the sound. Still smothered by the muck that had almost taken him completely under, he lay in the dark, his eyes unable to open. He wondered if the darkness above him had changed. Had he missed the sliver of light that he longed for? Its warmth? And the tiny creatures who were frantically making their way to the surface? Had they made it? He felt nothing. His senses dulled, maybe dead already. He had no memory of his recent efforts to reach the mountains. No memory of his desperation to do so and his departure from Willy. His brain was fixated on his dream and the longer he lay in semi consciousness, the more he remembered. The bridge. The redwoods. The mountains and then the ocean. A fishing boat. He traveled alone but was haunted by those he had left behind. He tried to recall who they were, but nothing came to mind.

Another sound but not as loud as the first. A rhythmic rattling that stopped and then started. Quin was unaware of his body's movements as he unconsciously reached out, quick, jerky, uncontrolled movements to hold on to something, anything. Anything to keep his head above the surface of the muck. And each time he did, the rattling grew louder.

Quin was unaware that the rattling had stopped. And he was unaware of the snake's weight on his chest having found a place to rest, to coil its body, to wait. It would not threaten now. It knew it did not need to. No harm would come to it. Besides, the warmth of the human's body felt good.

Hugh saw Quin first. When they came within clear sight of him, Hugh froze. His gestures to the other three were unmistakably clear. Don't move! No one questioned him for they saw it too. It was almost too much to believe. There was a silent assumption on all their parts that this was no longer a rescue but a retrieval mission. How could it possibly be anything else?

As the men stood in place, the snake lifted its head in their direction, but only for a moment. It searched the air with its tongue, a flickering in and out, in and out, until it was satisfied that it and its resting place were no longer alone. The snake turned its head towards Quin's face. They watched in horror as the snake lifted its head higher stretching it closer to Quin. They could not see, from their vantage point, the snake's final movements before leaving Quin. So close to Quin's face was the snake that its tongue reached Quin's right cheek and then his closed eyelid, its flickering tongue sensing all that it needed to know. Gentle kisses of departure. As it slowly uncoiled finding its way off Quin's chest, over his right arm, and onto the ground, the three men were captivated by what they were witnessing. The snake did not head away from Quin's body but slowly moved along Quin's side up and around to his shoulder, brushing his neck, and rounding the contours of his head. It was only then that the snake moved off, out of sight, among the many rock outcroppings that it called home.

No one spoke, each man attempting to rationalize what he had just witnessed. The improbability of the incident had the greatest impact on Hugh who had seen his share of snakes out here, especially rattlers. A predator only when it comes to sustenance and only that which it can handle. It understands its limitations. The instinct of this reptile is to steer clear of humans or anything that might harm it and, in most cases, to warn the intruder of the imminent danger it is in if the intruder chooses to disregard the warning. Had it done that with this human who appeared to be dead? And had this person ignored, surprised, or aggravated the snake who struck the deathly blow? Most likely, was Hugh's thinking. But there was no way he could explain the snake's behavior after the attack. It went against everything he knew, everything that made sense. But he had seen it with his own eyes as had Devon and Aaron. He had witnesses to back up his story.

"Let's get to it." Devon was the first to speak, his mind clearing first.

"Right. Watch yourself, though, just in case." Hugh moved forward, Devon by his side and Aaron followed with the med kit.

"He's alive. Barely." Hugh had not forgotten the snake, but his only focus was getting this man out safely. Aaron watched as Hugh and Devon prepared him for rescue. They found no snake bite, even more baffling considering what they had witnessed. He was placed in the stretcher and then lifted by them while Aaron followed still carrying the med kit and now the victim's backpack. Neither man remarked on the weightlessness they felt as they grasped the stretcher's frame. It was as if they had added nothing to it. This was the first time that Aaron had seen a starved human, the little of him remaining but a frame covered with skin. His face was sunken, the contours of his skull and facial structure striking. He wondered how close to death this poor soul was, unimaginable in his limited knowledge, that he would survive at all.

The pilot assisted in getting the stretcher on board and the three men followed.

"Check his pack for any identification," Hugh yelled at Aaron who had forgotten to put on his headset. Hugh gestured for him to do so.

In a zippered inside compartment, Aaron found a worn leather wallet and handed it to Hugh. It contained little other than his driver's license, a bank card, one credit card, and two hundred dollars in cash. No contact or health care information.

"Anything else?"

Aaron dug through the pack and its pockets finding nothing unusual.

"Doesn't look like it," Aaron yelled into his headset. "Maybe he's got something on him."

Hugh nodded but Aaron knew that was not their job. Not now. Once at the hospital, someone would do it. Aaron glanced in Quin's direction but quickly averted his gaze. He felt like he was invading the man's privacy.

Upon returning to the ranger station after leaving Quin under the care of the ER doctors at the hospital, Hugh wasted no time in preparing the report on the recovery mission. Aaron was surprised when Hugh asked him to go over it before he sent it in. Devon had already reviewed it. He found no inaccuracies in Hugh's account of the mission and its outcome. He did learn that the man's name was Quin Leet, age seventy-three, and little else. He wondered if Mr. Leet had people who should know about his circumstances. He was sure they'd be anxious about him. He had no idea how long the man had been out there but based on what he saw, he figured it had to be for some time. His mind wandered as he and everyone else returned to their daily responsibilities almost as if nothing out of the ordinary had just occurred. But he knew better than to assume that the incident didn't have any impact on Hugh or Devon and maybe even the chopper pilot. He couldn't see how it wouldn't. This wasn't a broken bone or snake bite. The man was knocking at death's door. For all Aaron knew, he might already be dead.

"Anything you want to talk about?" Hugh came up behind him as Aaron was starting his rounds.

Startled, still deep in thought, Aaron turned. Hugh stood in front of him, hands resting on his belt.

"You mean about today?"

"Right. Your first time seeing someone in that condition?"

"Yeah."

"Hopefully, you won't see that again, but never can tell. I can count on one hand how many times I've seen it and I've been at it a lot longer than you, Aaron. So it's hard. You think you're prepared but you never are."

Aaron detected compassion in Hugh's words, and it touched him.

"Any word on his condition?"

"No, not yet. Probably won't release it to me anyway, but I'll try though. I know the ER doc up there and he and I have an understanding. So, I ask again. Are you okay?"

"Sure. I'm fine." Knowing that Hugh had struggled with it provided relief for Aaron. He was not alone. "Thanks for asking though."

"Good." Hugh turned to head back to the station but stopped and turned back to Aaron. "The day's pretty well shot. Call it a day in an hour. This will all be here tomorrow."

Aaron checked his watch. It was only two. His regular hour for quitting time was six. "Are you sure?"

Hugh was already walking away. "Don't make me rethink this. You might regret it," his words flung back over his shoulder.

One more hour and then three hours all to himself. A small gift considering everything that had taken place so far in the day. He hadn't whistled in a very long time but now he accompanied himself as he worked, his spirit lifted.

Chapter 30

Almost three weeks later, after rescuing Quin, Hugh took Aaron aside to let him know that Mr. Leet was to be released from the hospital by the end of the week, three days from now. That Mr. Leet had fully recovered. The doctor informed Hugh that Mr. Leet was one lucky man to be found when he was. Another day, maybe less, it would have been a different story.

"Wondered if you want to go visit him before his release? Maybe get some information from him about how he got into that circumstance to begin with." Hugh sat behind his desk as Aaron sat across from him. "I'd be curious to know if he was traveling on his own or if there was someone with him. Hate to learn there's another body out there."

"Don't you think you should send Devon? He's got more experience at this than I do." Aaron was not comfortable with Hugh's suggestion.

"Well, that's why I want you to do it. How else are you going to get the experience? Like I said to you before, this situation is a rarity. Make use of it while you can." Hugh kept his eyes on Aaron.

He knew he was not being given a choice. Hugh had made up his mind before bringing him in to his office. And he knew Hugh was right. If he was serious about his career, then he better jump at any opportunity that presented itself.

"Okay. When do you want me to go?"

"Head up there tomorrow. Early. And stay as long as you need to. I need every detail you can pull out of him, you understand? There could be someone whose life depends on it."

"Understood. Is there anything else?"

Hugh leaned back in his chair. "If I think of something, I'll let you know."

The drive to the hospital in Lone Pine gave Aaron time to compose his thoughts. As he imagined his conversation with Mr. Leet, he struggled to forget the man's appearance when rescued and he wondered what he really looked like. Strangers to one another, Aaron wasn't sure how he would begin. What do you say to someone who has come back from the dead or close to it? Welcome home? His thoughts scattering from the ridiculous to the reality of the next hours of his life, Aaron tried to concentrate. Two questions that Hugh wanted answers to. What was he doing out there and was there anyone else with him? Simple enough. Just stick to those and, hopefully, Mr. Leet would fill him in.

Fully expecting to interview Mr. Leet at his bedside, Aaron was pleasantly surprised as he was directed to the "sunroom" where Mr. Leet had recently spent an hour or two each day as part of his recovery. The irony of the room's name was not lost on Aaron as he tried not to comment on it to the nurse's aide who was more than happy to show him the way.

"Mr. Leet. Excuse me, but you have a visitor." The young girl placed her hand on his shoulder as she spoke to him. "One of the park rangers who rescued you. Ranger Crenshaw."

That was Aaron's cue to come to her side. Quin was seated facing the large window that rose from the base of the floor right up to the ceiling, a view of the manicured succulent garden stretching out in front of him. The heat from the window's surface was not overpowering but comfortable and Aaron could see why a place like this would help in recovery even though the irony of it all lingered with him.

"Mr. Leet? I'm Ranger Aaron Crenshaw and it's really good to meet you." Aaron wasn't sure if he should reach out his hand, but Quin did not hesitate.

"The pleasure is all mine, sir." Quin's voice was not as strong as it once had been before his journey into the desert. He was painfully aware of this, hoping that the young man standing in front of him had heard in his voice his gratitude.

"Do you mind if I visit with you for a bit?"

"Of course. I'm just glad to be able to visit with anyone." Quin stopped short. "No offense meant by that."

"None taken." Aaron laughed and it felt good. This might be easier than he thought. He pulled over a chair and sat across from Quin.

"So, you rescued me? Am I understanding that right?"

"Not just me, Mr. Leet. Ranger Hugh Reynolds and Ranger Devon Bennett from the park service, we found you. Oh, and Steve Lenox, the life flight pilot. Couldn't have done it without him. You were spotted by a chopper pilot out of Las Vegas heading to Palm Springs. Lucky he sighted you."

"I don't remember anything about the rescue." It wasn't as if he hadn't tried. Ever since recovering, he had that and one other question on his mind.

"You were in pretty bad shape. I can tell you that you came awfully close to never waking up."

"That's what the doc told me."

"Can I ask you a couple of questions?"

"Sure. What's on your mind?"

"Were you out there on your own? Was someone else with you?" Aaron pulled out his notepad and pen. "Just want to make sure I get your information right. For my boss. Is that okay with you?"

"I've got no problem with that." Quin was struggling. This was the first time since leaving Willy that he was forced to remember him and to speak his name aloud. "No. I was traveling with a friend."

This was not what Aaron wanted to hear. The idea that someone else was stranded out there was almost unbearable to think about. A sudden urgency to tell Hugh overwhelmed him.

"Is this friend still out there?"

"I expect so. I hope so." The image of a dried-up Willy still where he had left him was bigger than life.

"Who is your friend?"

"His name was Willy. That's all I know. He didn't go by anything else. At least that's what he told me."

"And where is he? Do you know?"

Quin had no idea how to tell the young man eager to record his every word. In the desert.

"I have no idea. I was barely able to keep alive myself."

Aaron focused on his next questions. One step at a time. Maybe.

"Do you remember where you started?"

Quin pushed his body into the cushions of the chair. "We started up off the roadway that takes you out to Beatty. I remember because that's where I wanted to take Willy. But he wanted to be dropped off alongside the road up there. When I looked back, he was gone. Just like that. So I went back for him. I couldn't leave him out there on his own."

"You mean Daylight Pass out of Death Valley?"

"Sounds familiar but not sure. I just know we were up in the mountains when we started."

Aaron, confused, sat quietly for a moment before continuing. He tried to imagine just where Mr. Leet was describing. It could be just about anywhere on that pass.

"Okay. That's okay. So what happened then?"

"Well, I found him, and we just started walking."

"Did you have a destination in mind?" his pen poised on the notepad.

"Funny you should ask that. That's exactly what I kept asking Willy. You know what he told me?"

"Can't say that I do, Mr. Leet."

"He told me we were going to a place that I had always wanted to go to. A place I had always wanted to see." Quin was lost in the memory, and he looked around the room to see if Willy was right there with him.

Aaron finished writing before he spoke again. "And did he tell you where this place was, its name?"

Now it was Quin's turn to pause. Willy was not in the room with them. He could see that, but he couldn't shake his presence anyway.

"You're going to think me a real fool when I tell you that he never did say, and I never pursued it with him. Just kept walking with him until…well, until he couldn't. That's when I was on my own."

Aaron, intrigued by Quin's revelations, refocused his questions. "While you were walking with Willy, did you happen to notice anything about the terrain? Maybe how far out into the desert you walked? Was it all flat and desert sands or did you see any sand dunes? What about mountains? Did you see any off in the distance?"

Quin could see how serious this young ranger was about locating Willy. For a moment, he wondered if he should tell him what he remembered. Maybe Willy should be left in peace. After all, it was his choice to be out there. Maybe even his choice to end his life out there. Maybe that was what Willy had in mind all along, even if he didn't believe the word "suicide" meant anything.

"Mr. Leet? Can you remember anything that will help us?"

"There were mountains in the west. I know that because I watched the sun set behind them. And I know that on the other side of them is where Willy and I spent time in the valley before heading out of it."

"That's good. Really good. So how close were you to those mountains do you think?"

"At first, they were a long way off but when Willy started heading away from the south and towards the west, we got closer each day."

Aaron now had something to work with. The terrain and its changes. "Did you leave Willy in the desert sand or maybe in more rocky terrain?"

Quin's memory was becoming more detailed, its images clearer. "There were some rocks, yes. I remember now. Willy sat down one afternoon, all of a sudden, earlier than usual, and pushed himself up against a rock. I remember that now. I did too. That was when he closed his eyes and never opened them again." His throat tightened and his eyes stung. Poor Willy.

Aaron was writing as fast as he could not wanting to miss a single detail. "That's really helpful, Mr. Leet. That means you were somewhere close to the rise in the mountain range. Like the foothills. So, Willy died there, is that right?"

"Yes." Quin fought to gain control.

"And you said it was earlier than usual. Does that mean earlier than you usually settled for the night?"

"Yes. I figured we had a few hours of daylight left but Willy couldn't go any farther. Maybe I couldn't either. Not until we rested."

"This is a long shot, but can you remember exactly where the sun set?"

"Nope. I fell asleep right alongside of Willy and the next thing I knew, it was morning. But I do remember that the sun was directly behind us making long shadows of those rocks."

Aaron's mind was in overdrive. Maybe this was enough information to get a chopper out there and make runs along the edge of the valley. He had no idea if Hugh would agree or even if he was on the right track. Had he asked the right questions? Would Hugh be angry that he hadn't?

"Does any of this help you out?" Quin leaned forward, his forearms resting on the chair's arms.

"It does, Mr. Leet. It sure does." What harm was there in reassuring the man? And maybe it did. He would have to wait for Hugh's approval. "One more thing. Your car? You left it in a turnout, right?"

"Yes. But it wasn't mine. A rental out of Lone Pine." Quin made a quick calculation. "Only rented it for a week. Maybe it's still up there where I left it?"

Aaron knew better, but he wished it was still there. A place to start. "I doubt it. Probably towed into Beatty. Highway Patrol doesn't let abandoned cars sit around for long. Expect it's already been reported to the rental company."

Quin did not respond. He was not worried about what that would mean for him. Water under the bridge, as far as he was concerned. After all, they would need to find him first and he had made sure that would never happen.

"So, you're going out there to get Willy?"

"I believe so but can't say for sure. It's not up to me to make the decision."

"Well, if it helps any, he won't mind one way or the other."

Aaron caught the glint of a twinkle in Mr. Leet's eye as he smiled for the first time since his rescue.

Chapter 31

He knew what Hugh was going to say before he said it. He could hear him as clear as day. There wasn't enough to go on. Did Aaron have any idea how much territory he was talking about? The full length of the Amargosa range? All they had to go on was some rocks near the mountain's ascent. The sunset was of no help.

Aaron watched as Hugh read over his notes. "Are you confident that he was speaking clear headed?"

"Well, as far as I could tell, yes. He warmed up as time went on, remembering more, I mean."

"Okay. I'll call it in and get a chopper out there. You want to go with?"

Aaron was stunned. "Sure. Of course."

"Good. I'll let you know as soon as I hear back. Remember, though. This one is recovery, not rescue."

"Right."

Everything was happening quickly. Aaron had only gotten back from Lone Pine an hour ago and already the chopper was lined up to fly out in two hours with him on board. When Hugh wanted something done, it got done. Aaron reflected on his mentor and how lucky he was to be under his wing.

The same pilot, Steve Lenox, was waiting for Aaron and waved him on to the chopper. Feeling confident, Aaron sat next to Steve, buckled up and put on the headset. He had seen the cockpit from the back but never right in it and was in awe of the aircraft's capabilities and those of Steve's. The 180 degrees view in front of him was a far cry from his last experience in this aircraft. He felt guilty for being excited about the flight as if he was on a ride at an amusement park, the awful reason quickly taking hold.

He directed Steve using Quin's words. As he did, even he could hear how futile they were. How on earth would they find a tiny human being down there. Even though Hugh had never said it, Aaron was sure that his original thoughts about what

Hugh would say were true. Hugh had just held back, maybe wanting Aaron to learn another lesson. He had to admit that Hugh was a good teacher.

They flew close to the mountain range and low enough, at times, to see the rocks that Quin had referred to. But there were so many of them and they went on for miles that Aaron was the first to voice his doubts.

"There's nothing down there."

"Don't be so sure. We'll take one more swing. This time look where you didn't the first time." Steve's voice was dead serious and committed to the task before him.

The chopper rose above the rocks, turned, and headed back north, having followed the range south. Steve brought the aircraft as low as he dared without disturbing the land beneath it. If anyone was anywhere where Steve flew, he should be seen. How could he not, Aaron wondered?

When they arrived at the heliport, both men were silent. They had been since leaving the search area. Aaron took off his headset, unbuckled, and waited for Steve to do the same. The props were still rotating above them casting odd, long shadows across the tarmac as the sun set behind them.

"Thanks for trying, Steve."

"No need to thank me, Aaron. It's my job. Just sorry that we didn't find him. Sometimes, that's how it goes. Doesn't mean we'll stop trying. It will be Hugh's call how he wants to proceed. Don't beat yourself up over it."

That evening over dinner, Hugh, Devon, and Aaron discussed options for recovery but no decision was made. Hugh wanted to sleep on it. Probably a good idea, Aaron thought, considering Hugh had jumped on Aaron's input with no success. Better to let the expert among them decide.

As promised, the next morning Hugh called Devon and Aaron into his office. "I've given it a lot of thought. Considering how much time has gone by since we rescued Mr. Leet, three weeks ago, and considering the chopper search with no sign of the man, I'm calling it off. If he's out there, I can guarantee there's not much left of him. That is if he was ever out there to begin with." Hugh cast his glance in Aaron's way and then looked back down at the paperwork on his desk.

The idea that Willy did not exist at all never entered Aaron's mind, not until now. Could it be that Mr. Leet never had a companion? Was he lying or imagining it? Maybe Mr. Leet had not fully recovered mentally? Aaron was taken aback and suddenly confused.

"I didn't even think about that," Aaron mumbled.

Hugh picked up on it right away. "You haven't dealt with enough. Not your fault. No accounting for some people and how they move through life. And it's worse out here. The desert can play bad games with the mind. Enough so that you don't know who you are anymore. I wouldn't be so sure that Mr. Leet isn't a victim of her game."

"But if he's not and he's telling the truth, how are we supposed to live with that?"

"Look, Aaron. We'll never know, not unless by some miracle someone stumbles over his body out there. And I can pretty much tell you that's not going to happen. So in order to live with this decision, you have to put it behind you and concentrate on the ones you can save from themselves. Every day, they're out there doing stupid things that we tell them not to do. The best thing you can do with this recent business is not to let it get in the way of your job right now. If you do, you'll have more to regret than losing this one poor fellow. Am I making myself clear here?" Hugh's eyes moved from Devon and then to Aaron.

"Yes, sir." Devon spoke up.

"Aaron? You clear?"

"I understand, sir," even though he didn't. Hugh had not listened to Mr. Leet's recollections. Had not caught the sadness in Mr. Leet's voice. Had not met his eyes, seen the recovered skeleton of a man, the human being now in a recognizable form. And Hugh had not seen the twinkle in Mr. Leet's eyes. There was a connection between Mr. Leet and this Willy person. It was as clear as day to Aaron as he spent his time with

Mr. Leet. There was a Willy who was most likely dead by now. But there was a Willy.

"Yes, sir. Understood." There was no more to be said. Not now and not here.

A week later, Quin made his way back to Death Valley. It was a difficult decision to make but he had no choice. Since meeting Willy in the soup kitchen in Eugene in what seemed ages ago now, as he reentered the park, fully recovered, Quin felt the unidentifiable tug to keep Willy in his life. He understood that now it was Willy's spirit that had its hold on him. The only other person who might understand was the young ranger who visited with him in the hospital. He seemed to be genuinely concerned not only for Quin's outcome but also for Willy's. Quin had written his name down with the intent of finding him again. Once found, he wasn't sure what would come of it but, like Willy's influence on him, so it seemed to be with Aaron Crenshaw's.

Quin drove straight to the information center where Willy had egged on the ranger behind the counter. As he recalled the moment, he smiled. What a character he had let enter his life. The information center was just as busy as he remembered it to be. Making his way to the counter, he looked for the ranger, but he was not there. A young female ranger greeted him.

"I'm looking for the older one?"

The young woman's laugh relaxed him. "Well, I doubt if he wants to be referred to that way. That's Ranger Hugh Reynolds, I believe you mean. He doesn't do the desk unless we have a shortage of folks up here. He advanced beyond this counter long ago." Again, she laughed.

"So, where can I find him?" Quin didn't see the humor in any of this.

"He's the head ranger here so you can contact him at the rangers' headquarters. If he's out, just leave a message with the other rangers there and someone will get back to you. Are you staying in the park?"

The memory of a familiar question and a familiar answer suddenly appeared. "No, I don't think so. Haven't looked into it yet."

"Not a problem. You might want to try the ranch. Probably booked but no harm in asking. That is if you plan to stay the night or longer."

"Right. Might just do that after I see…what did you say his name was?"

"I'll write it down for you. Ranger Hugh Reynolds. There you go." She handed Quin her card with Hugh's name written on the backside. "Hope you make contact."

Quin made his way through the crowds to the exit of the center all the while battered by slivered memories of Willy. It was almost too much to bear.

His mind, now set on meeting up with Hugh Reynolds, he wondered why the name sounded familiar. He was certain that neither he nor Willy had been told. If they had, he did not remember. As he pulled into the small parking area in front of the headquarters, it suddenly came to him. The ranger who visited him in the hospital, Crenshaw. Was that how he knew the name? Had Crenshaw mentioned it? Angry that his brain was still fuzzy, he sat back in the driver's seat, and took long, slow breaths before getting out. He needed to be ready for whoever was on the other side of the door. He needed to be clear headed and appear rational in his request. He needed to close this chapter of his life and here was the place to start. As he came to the door, he paused before going in. What was he waiting for? Waiting for someone else to take the lead? Not this time. This was his alone to accomplish. Quin's imperceptible shaking of his head in disbelief that he would even entertain the thought, made him smile. Willy would get a kick out of it. Quin was sure of it.

Aaron looked up from his desk when he heard the door open. It took him a minute to recognize Quin who looked healthier than when Aaron last saw him in the hospital.

"Well, this is a surprise!" Aaron came over to greet him. "It's good to see you again, Mr. Leet," reaching his hand out to the older man.

"Same here." Quin looked around the room only to find just the two of them in it, surprised to see Ranger Crenshaw.

"What brings you back here, Mr. Leet?" Aaron led him back to his desk and pulled up a chair next to it. "Here. Have a seat."

"I was looking for Ranger…the head?" Quin pulled out the business card and turned it over. "Ranger Hugh Reynolds. That's the name."

"He's not back here for a few more hours. Meeting with some big wigs from the county and state up in Lone Pine. Is there something I can help you with?"

It occurred to Quin that the man in front of him was the one who had drawn him back here, not Hugh Reynolds. He was only a starting point. The way was just made easier for him.

"I actually came back to meet up with you. I mean, I have a question for you and a request. Thought about this after you left or would have maybe asked you then."

"Okay. No problem. Go ahead, then."

"Have you looked for Willy?" Such a simple question but one that was so hard to produce.

Aaron shifted forward in his chair. His suspicions about Mr. Leet's sudden appearance were playing out. Why else would the man come back here? The truth was what Mr. Leet was requesting without having to say it.

"We did a search, Mr. Leet. In the terrain you recalled as the last place you saw Willy. We didn't find him or any sign of him. I'm truly sorry."

"What do you mean?"

"The search was called off. The reality is that his body may never be found. It could have been taken by predators. Maybe the reason we couldn't locate him." He had said enough. The image was disturbing, even to him.

Quin knew that the young ranger was probably right. That all logic pointed to the fact that Willy was lost to the desert. He could find no reason to believe otherwise unless he allowed himself to believe beyond all rational thought.

"I see."

"I really am sorry, Mr. Leet."

What harm could it do? Quin's second request had not been presented. His first question was answered but the truth of the matter was that it was an assumption that Willy was dead. A search had been conducted and an assumption made. But still no definitive answer. Willy was still here, somewhere, in some form or another. Quin felt it but needed to be certain. That's all he needed and that's all he would request. Willy was worth the effort.

"Will you go with me to find him?"

Stunned by the question, Aaron was confused by Mr. Leet's obvious inability to grasp the situation. He thought he had made himself clear.

"No. I mean, I'm afraid that isn't possible. Mr. Leet, you need to understand that the desert and the surrounding environment do not allow for mistakes and are unforgiving. You were lucky to be found and even luckier to be found alive." Had anyone told him about the rattler on his chest, Aaron wondered? He thought better of bringing it up.

"I don't believe in luck." Quin smiled as he welcomed Willy into the conversation. "There's a reason you found me just as there is a reason you didn't find Willy. At both those points in each of our lives, Willy's and mine, they were part of our life journey. Luck has had nothing to do with any of it. For all I know, Willy is still wandering around out there. It wouldn't be the first time that I thought he was dying or close to it. But he got up each time and continued. I've got to tell you what I believe. He's still out there and I don't mean drying up in place or something's dinner. He's going to the place he always wanted to go to. Just as I was until you found me. But that's okay, too, because that was supposed to happen. You understand?"

Aaron, struggling to understand, to listen with compassion to this man's ramblings, could find nothing to say. The reality was that no matter what he said, it would be wrong. If he agreed with Mr. Leet, he would be playing into the poor man's delusions, giving him false hope. And if he disagreed, it might just send Mr. Leet right back out there. He appeared to be stubborn enough to go it alone and Aaron wasn't sure he could bear the guilt, even though Hugh had advised him to move on. No, he had warned him. If he didn't, he was not fit for the job. That much had been communicated clearly to him, not like this conversation with Mr. Leet.

"I know it's a different way of looking at it, and I never saw it that way before I met Willy." Quin could see the confusion and the silent indecision on the young man's face. He didn't hide his emotions very well, Quin noted. "But one way or the other, for my life to have any further direction, I need to proceed with this closure. It's very simple." Quin broke into laughter, surprising Aaron even more. "I learned that from Willy too."

The door opened and Hugh Reynolds walked in. Hanging his hat on the rack next to the door, he waited patiently for Aaron to introduce him to the visitor whose back was to Hugh.

"Ranger Reynolds! You're back so soon?" The relief in Aaron's voice did not hide his surprise.

"It appears I am. The meeting was called off on account of two of the participants got held up elsewhere. It's been rescheduled which doesn't sit all that well with me, but what can you do?" Hugh's eyes were on Quin as he spoke to Aaron. "Sorry to interrupt."

"No, it's okay. Ranger Reynolds, this is Mr. Leet, the gentleman we rescued."

Quin turned in his seat and then stood, moving to Hugh, his hand outstretched. "It's mighty good to see you again, Ranger Reynolds."

Hugh did the same all the while trying to place the man's face. He knew he had seen him before and not just on the desert floor waiting for rescue.

"Yes, it's good to see you, Mr. Leet. How are you feeling?"

"Just fine. Docs tell me I'm out of the woods and back to normal. Best I could hope for, but I wouldn't be here if it wasn't for you and Ranger Crenshaw. I am mighty grateful that you found me."

"We like stories that end like this. What brings you back to us?" Hugh moved over to his desk and sat down.

"I was just telling Ranger Crenshaw my thoughts on my friend, Willy. I'm up to date on what has taken place from your end of the business and I thank you for your efforts."

"Never like it to turn out this way, Mr. Leet. I'm sorry about your friend."

Aaron, about to clear the air so that Hugh could be caught up, was not fast enough.

Quin moved over to Hugh's desk. He leaned on it with both hands.

"You see, I am sure that Willy is still out there, and I was just asking Ranger Crenshaw to help me find him."

It was obvious to two of the men in the room that they were dealing with less than a full deck. Hugh did not look at Aaron but kept his eyes on Mr. Leet.

"That's not going to happen, Mr. Leet. We have closed this search. None of my rangers will be involved any longer. And I advise you not to even entertain the thought of doing this on your own."

Aaron's admiration of Hugh grew with each passing day, but this last communication rose him to the top of Aaron's admiration scale. There was definitely something to be said for experience. Relieved that Hugh had finally cleared the air, Aaron felt off the hook. Mr. Leet was officially on his own. Aaron's boss had said so.

Quin listened patiently, straightened his body, and took a few steps backwards. Now standing between the two desks, he took both men in with his gaze, moving from one to the other and repeating the movement. Both men waited, not a word spoken.

"I see. I appreciate the clarity, Ranger Reynolds. At least I now know where I stand." He looked in Aaron's direction and then back again to Hugh. "You don't remember me from before, do you? I wouldn't expect you would."

"From before?" Hugh was curious.

"When my friend and I asked you about the trails?"

"Sorry. Can't say that I do. I talk to a lot of people in a day about this place." Hugh was eager for the conversation to be over.

"It's been a while, almost two months since Willy and I talked with you. You don't remember him asking about going out on our own outside of the park? Telling him that he could get shot if we found ourselves on private land?"

A vague memory came to mind as Hugh listened. "You know, I do remember something like that. I hope I took the time to warn you both of heading out on your own. It appears I wasn't all that convincing, unfortunately."

Quin ignored Hugh's reference. If he was being truthful with himself, Quin knew that what Ranger Reynolds said was accurate. It wasn't worth the effort to tell him that he had listened, had been unwilling to follow Willy who didn't care about the advice, that he had done what any reasonably caring person would have done unwilling to leave a friend in jeopardy. He had no argument with either ranger sitting in front of him. He just wanted help and if it wasn't coming from them then this effort was done. He would find another way.

"Well, I have wasted enough of your time, both of you, so I'll be on my way. My thanks again for saving my life. And I appreciate what you tried to do for Willy." His let his words sink in. "And I am sure that Willy will tell you the same when you see us next."

Hugh and Aaron, speechless, watched as Quin turned, opened the door, and closed it behind him.

When they were finally alone, Hugh could not hold back. "Well, I'll be damn. That guy is going to do what he wants no matter what anyone says. The fool. That's what got them into trouble in the first place. Why the hell did he even bother to ask us?"

Not sure that the answer to Hugh's question would fly with him, Aaron spoke it anyway. "Because he really believes that Willy is still out there and alive. It's as simple as that."

Chapter 32

He took a chance. A Quin Leet was registered at the Ranch for two nights. Throwing all caution to the wind, Aaron was compelled to follow up with Mr. Leet, if nothing else than to make one more attempt to convince him not to go out there again. And if he was unsuccessful, at least not to go on his own. Aaron knew perfectly well what the consequences of his actions would be. Neither one was acceptable, nor was the decision to do nothing. The possibility that he would lose his job for disobeying his superior while putting others in jeopardy if a search was activated, weighed heavily on him. Was Quin Leet and his friend worth it? Even if Willy was dead, could he live with not helping Mr. Leet and his inevitable demise? What was it about the man that Aaron could not walk away from, his hold on him that was about to change the trajectory of his own life? It was obvious to Aaron that he would never know the answers, not until he had the courage to find them.

Quin had just settled in for the night when he heard someone at his door. When he opened it, he was not surprised to see Aaron.

"Well, well. Seems your timing is just a bit off. Just heading to bed but now that you are here, come on in." Quin held the door wide open and Aaron, removing his hat, stepped inside. "What's on your mind, Ranger Crenshaw?"

"May I?" Aaron pointed to the one chair in the room while Quin sat on the edge of the bed.

"Make yourself comfortable."

"I've come to try and convince you not to do what I know you must do."

Quin was touched by the ranger's candid appeal. It appeared that the ranger did understand him. He just didn't agree with the solo effort. A good place to start with him.

"It seems to me that you have defeated your purpose in coming then. I mean, you know I have no choice in the matter.

Are you telling me that your only worry is that I am doing this on my own?"

Aaron was taken aback momentarily. Mr. Leet was right. What was he thinking? Why had he come to see him? Nothing was as clear in his mind as it had been just before knocking on the door.

"Yes. I guess so. It's suicide to go out there, Mr. Leet, on your own."

Quin saw himself in his car with Willy, pleading for the man to listen to reason. He heard the same words he had spoken to Willy now spoken by the ranger. Only this time, he was the unreasonable one.

"And if I don't go on my own? Would I avoid my own suicide?" Quin was beginning to enjoy this and suddenly understood Willy's infatuation with the word games he'd play with Quin.

"I guess not but that's not the point, Mr. Leet. If we can't locate him, what's to say that you can? Do you have any idea how much land is out there? How much of it is inaccessible? What the dangers are besides the terrain?" Aaron tried to hold back his frustration, knowing that anything he said was useless.

"I have some idea. All I know is that I need to find Willy one way or another. With your help or without it. I don't hold you responsible for me and what happens to me out there. And you don't need to feel responsible for me. I know you do, but you need to free yourself of that. It's just a matter of finding what's the best path for you. I can't and won't try to persuade you, if that's what you're waiting for. It was a simple question to begin with. Will you go with me to help me find him? A simple yes or no is all that's needed from you."

If he had ever faced a greater dilemma in his lifetime, he could not recall it. Every part of his being was screaming at him to simply say, "No." A simple answer to the man's question that would end this whole thing. So simple, so final.

"If I go with you, will you listen to me? Let me take the lead for both of our sakes?"

Aaron heard the words spoken aloud but wasn't sure that he had produced them. Had he or was it a part of his muddled thinking in front of this man? Once again, he sat with Mr. Leet completely confused by his own actions.

"I will, of course. I owe you my life. It is expected of me. A way of expressing my gratitude for all that you have done and will do for Willy and me. I am very pleased."

The flash of heat radiating from somewhere in his being surged up his chest and into his head causing Aaron to break out in a sweat, his heart working overtime. What had he done?

"I didn't say I would. I didn't say that." A childish attempt to correct his error.

"Well, it appears to me that you are considering it and I am responding to your request with heartfelt thanks." Quin knew he had the upper hand and a fragment of remorse surfaced then disappeared as he watched the ranger slowly succumb.

"I could lose my job." A last-ditch effort to save himself.

"Yes. I am sure that's possible."

"Why are you putting me in this impossible situation?" his raised voice startling him.

"I don't know what to say that will help you, Ranger Crenshaw. Try to understand that no one is putting you in any situation that you are unwilling to accept. You make the decision, not me. I will abide by whatever you say. It's as simple as that."

"It's not simple. Stop saying that! Nothing's simple." The tears fell as he recalled his parents, a father he had never known, his mother's death, and his struggle to find stability, even now what he thought he had with Hugh and Devon, with his job and his future. It felt like he was no longer on terra firma but sinking rapidly with no one to come to his rescue. He heaved great sobs, unaware of Quin's arm around his shoulders, silently sharing in the young man's grieving but knowing full well that it would pass in time. The worst was over for him but not for this young man. He had only dipped his toe in the sludge, a first step, but a step to be sure.

"So, will you help me?" One final request as Aaron's sobs subsided. "Yes or no?"

Chapter 33

He tried not to think about it as he readied himself to meet Quin at the ranch. He understood that the consequences for saying yes to Quin were dismal. Another starting over, this time as a disgraced and fired National Park Ranger. It would happen as soon as he returned with the borrowed four-wheel drive truck taken without permission. He considered that it might happen sooner if anyone caught up with them.

With Quin in the passenger seat, Aaron headed out of the park out to Daylight Pass heading east. With no sign of the rental car, not surprising and confirmation that Aaron was probably right about it being towed, Quin was trying to recall the exact spot where he had dropped Willy off before going back to catch up with him the first day of their wanderings. Less than half a mile past the spot, Quin remembered and told Aaron to turn around.

"Right here is where I made my way down to him. Found him at the bottom of an eight-foot drop. Not a scratch on him. Yes," Quin took in the area again, "this is the spot."

"Which way did you head after that?" Aaron knew the area but not well enough to trust himself out there.

"I can't say for sure. Out into the desert as I recall. I don't think Willy had any idea where he was going, and it wasn't like I didn't try to get him to turn around and head back to safety."

"Well, that's too bad. Not being able to convince him, I mean. Turned out not so good for the man. Or for you." Based on Quin's repeating basically what he had told Aaron in the hospital, the mistake he made in saying yes to Quin hit home and hard. What was he doing? A crazy wild goose chase whose only outcome was nothing good.

"Well, we're not going down there from here. And we're not going on foot anywhere. Get back in. I have an idea."

Aaron checked his watch. They had been gone for less than two hours. It was still early, not even eight in the morning. If what he was planning was successful, he could be back at headquarters well before dinner. At some point he would radio in his location, make up some story, or maybe even tell the truth.

As Aaron pulled out of the area back onto the pass, he briefly turned to Quin. "You told me that you walked through a rocky area along the western side of the desert. Right?" Quin returned his eyes to the road that wound itself out of the pass.

"That's right."

The flat expanse of the desert was now all around them on either side of the road. To Quin's surprise, Aaron pulled off the pavement but did not slow down. Before he could say anything, Aaron was driving onto the desert floor heading south across the immensity of flat land. It was exciting, a part of Quin wanting it never to stop. Such freedom. So much space. The environment that had been so threatening to Willy and him was now a thrill to experience from the vehicle that Aaron was commandeering.

Quin said nothing as Aaron crossed the landscape. When they came upon what looked like a break in the surface of the desert, Aaron turned right and drove the rugged trail toward the west. It was apparent to Quin that they were not the first to take this trek. In some places, deep ruts in the road made by vehicles like theirs and possibly larger, heavier ones, had become permanent, dried by the heat. Quin reached up for the handhold above his right shoulder while gripping the edge of his seat cushion with the other. Aaron did not slow down nor try to avoid the ruts. For a minute, Quin wondered if he was going survive the ride. He glanced over at Aaron about to say something but thought better of it. The ranger's face was nothing but dead serious and fully focused on what lay ahead of them.

Another junction and Aaron took a sharp right turn, his foot off the accelerator only enough to get them into the turn and then he gunned it. Another trail, this time smoother and not well used. Quin started to relax but not enough to release his handholds. Now they were heading directly west, the morning sun still at their backs, the heat of the day only just beginning to build.

The mountains that Quin had noted on his right since starting out rose in front of them as Aaron drove closer to their beginnings. He left the trail and was driving on the virgin desert surface by the looks of it, the best Quin could tell. Slower now, in less of a hurry, Aaron continued to move closer to what was beginning to look familiar to Quin. The desert floor's uninterrupted expanse was now littered with rocks, none so big as to stop Aaron's forward movement. Not yet.

When the first of the rocks appeared, it was Quin who spoke first. "Here! Somewhere around here. I'm sure of it."

Aaron slowly came to a stop, turned off the engine, and turned to Quin. "Are you sure?"

"No. How can I really be sure, but this place is familiar. I feel it."

Without responding, Aaron got out of the truck and waited for Quin to come around to him.

"We go the rest of the way on foot." Aaron shifted his hat, the sun slowly crawling up their backs. "And when I say this is where we turn around, I mean it. We'll do our best to find Willy, but we're not going to repeat what's already played out for you. Am I clear?"

"Perfectly."

The going was slower than Aaron would have liked but considering his companion's age and his failing recollection, Aaron remained patient as he kept track of the time. If Willy did exist and was somewhere in the area, it would not be hard to find him. None of the rock outcroppings were big enough to obscure from view anything but small animals and snakes.

"Watch where you're going. Rattlers love this terrain." Aaron looked back at Quin whose pace was slow.

"Well aware but thanks for the reminder." He didn't feel like telling Aaron about the granddaddy of all rattlers as Willy had called it. One of those encounters that had to be experienced to be believed.

"Let's move southwest a bit and then reverse it." Aaron waited for Quin to catch up with him. "You doing okay?"

"I'm fine. Just wish I knew exactly where I left him. I can see it so clearly."

"I expect you can. Not something anyone forgets, I imagine." Aaron felt sorry for the old man and what he must have gone through before they found him. "Let's keep going. Tell me if you see anything that looks familiar. I just don't want to wander around here all afternoon."

Quin understood and a small part of him tried to convince him to give up now. It was like finding a needle in a haystack, just a lot more uncomfortable. The heat was getting to him as he followed behind Aaron.

They hadn't gone very far when Quin let Aaron know that they were going in the wrong direction. Nothing looked right the farther south they walked. "I'm sure it's behind us and closer to the mountain."

"Okay. Let's head back then," Aaron sighed. "Drink before we do, though." He held his water bottle out to Quin before he drank.

"Thanks." Quin took small sips but this time more than one or two.

By the time they returned to where they started still with no success, Aaron was ready to call it off. Quin appeared to be failing in the heat and his pace had grown even slower. The last thing Aaron needed was a near fatality on his watch especially since he wasn't supposed to be out here in the first place.

"Could we try over there?" Quin pointed to the west. "Not far but I think that might be the area."

"Be honest with me." Aaron placed his hand on Quin's shoulder. "Are you feeling okay or is it time to stop? I can't have you pushing yourself for you to collapse out here."

"I can go some more. You'll just have to trust me. But if it makes you feel any better, I'll stop before it's too late. I won't put you in a difficult situation. You've done more than enough for me already."

Aaron didn't know what to believe but he was willing to give Quin one more chance. Checking his watch, he noted there was still time.

"Okay. Another drink and then we'll head in your direction this time."

Quin knew they were going in the right direction as they moved closer to the mountains. He recalled the relief he felt as he moved off the flat desert surface and further into the rocks. The same feeling came to him now. One or two rocks were the sizes of the ones he remembered. But his memory told him that there were more than a few large rocks in the area where they had stopped to rest.

Aaron kept ahead of him but not by much. Quin noticed that Aaron had slowed his pace, enough so that Quin could almost walk next to him. However, the terrain did not allow it. Each man for himself.

The thought shot through him so suddenly and vividly that Quin came to a stop almost losing his balance as he did.

"My God! What am I doing?" His voice reached Aaron.

"What? What is it?" Aaron came to Quin's side. "What's the matter?"

"This is not where I left Willy. I remember now. This is where you found me. All this time I've been remembering where I stopped, not where Willy did. Oh, my God. I'm sorry." This time Quin reached out to Aaron, his hand catching Aaron's. "I'm such a fool."

If Aaron felt any frustration as he listened to Quin's confession, he did not make it known. The old guy was doing his best. Aaron understood this even before he made the decision to say yes to him. He fully expected nothing to come of it but had been willing to help him. And if they had found Willy, for both men there would be closure.

"It's okay, Mr. Leet. It's easy to get confused out here. The desert can do that to a man." Aaron took in the landscape. "You know. This is not where we found you. More to the north than this far south. Don't blame yourself. I should have considered that myself before we started. If anyone's to blame, it's me."

"So, we've been wandering around here for nothing?" Quin was disappointed, his exhaustion evident in his voice.

Aaron felt like a fool. What had he been thinking to drive this far south? Why hadn't he been smarter? Worse yet, how would Hugh and Devon react? He knew and he wished that he didn't. He had made a greater mess of things, not only for Mr. Leet but also for himself.

"I'm afraid so. Come on. Let's get in the truck and head back north. If it's not too late, we'll give it one more try." Again, he checked his watch. Two hours and counting before he had to face the music.

Quin was painfully aware that he was not going to find Willy. He could barely make it back to the truck much less begin another search. Aaron helped him up to the passenger seat.

"Buckle up."

If he had not left Willy in the rocks, where had he left him? As before, neither man spoke allowing Quin to recall uninterrupted any detail that might, in a last-ditch effort, locate Willy. As the truck moved back along the desert floor, Quin suddenly visualized the spot where Willy dropped, pack still on his back, legs stretched out in front of him. It was nowhere near any rocks. It was desert floor all around them, as he remembered the sinking feeling of seeing the vast surface in every direction he looked. He remembered the fatigue he felt as he fell into unconsciousness only to wake hours later with Willy by his side, the heat of the day already making itself known. And Willy, who would not wake up.

"I remember," his words mumbled unheard by Quin. "I remember," this time loud enough to be heard over the laboring engine.

Aaron turned to Quin. "You remember what?" Aaron yelled.

"I left him in the desert. There were no mountains in sight. I only saw desert everywhere I looked."

Aaron stopped the truck and let it idle. "That's a far cry from where we were. And it makes it harder to find him. Any idea at all where you might have been?" Aaron knew this was completely futile to pursue.

"I have no idea. I just don't know." Quin felt his throat tighten, the profound sadness he carried just below the surface.

"One last thing. Did you see, maybe even walk on the trails like I've been driving? Anything that would give us a place to start?"

All Quin had seen was the sand and salt beds beneath his feet. Day after day. He couldn't remember ever purposely trying to take in his surroundings, not until he had to. And if he and Willy had come anywhere near these trails that Aaron had driven on, he was sure Willy would have said something.

"No. There was nothing like this anywhere we went."

Both men knew that it was over. Willy would not be found, not today, and not by them. If he were to be discovered, it would be by a stranger or an animal, or maybe never. Quin felt a strange mixture of regret and relief. He had tried. He had told his dead friend that he would come back for him, and he had. But Willy had other plans. He was never meant to be found by Quin. It was his parting gift, Quin realized. A separation that was permanent and, as Willy had always intended, with no strings attached.

"Let's go back. I want to go home."

"Are you sure?" Aaron turned to Quin.

"Haven't been this sure about anything in my life. Yes, I'm sure. Take me back, please."

Aaron left Quin at the ranch but not before making sure he had walked him to his room. Once Quin was inside, he assured Aaron that he needed nothing. Just some rest. He'd be sure to say goodbye tomorrow before he left. Would Aaron be at the headquarters in the morning? They set a time to meet before Quin's departure.

Both satisfied that this wasn't the end of their relationship, Aaron closed Quin's door and drove back to the station. If he could have, he would have gone anywhere else but there. It was time for him to face up to what he had done. He laughed out loud as it crossed his mind that, more likely than not, both Mr. Leet and he would be saying goodbye not only to each other but also to the valley if Ranger Hugh Reynolds had anything to say about it. There were no ifs, Aaron reminded himself.

Hugh was at his desk and didn't look up when Aaron walked in.

"Did you have any success?" Hugh's fingers flying over his keyboard.

Aaron stopped short. "Sorry?" He was suddenly aware of his racing heartbeat.

"Out there with the truck and, I suspect, Mr. Leet. Did you find him?" This time, Hugh looked up, his fingers resting on the keyboard.

"No, sir." Aaron was afraid to say more. Not until Hugh had his say. Aaron braced himself.

"That's too bad. Sorry to hear that. I expect Mr. Leet is feeling pretty low."

"He's okay. I left him in his room. He just needs to rest."

"I expect so." Hugh returned to his keyboard, his fingers tapping away.

Aaron didn't know what to think as he stood in place, hat in hand, his desk only a few feet away. He waited. He looked for Devon, but no one was in the room except the two of them. Aware that the typing had stopped again, Aaron focused on his desk. He probably should sit down and get to work. Obviously, Hugh had a plan for Aaron but his silence on the matter was making everything worse. Aaron walked over to his desk and pulled out the chair.

"Not so fast." Hugh's voice stopped Aaron in his tracks.

"Sir?"

"Take the truck, gas her up, calculate the mileage you put on her, and meet me back here."

"Yes, sir." Aaron put on his hat and started toward the door. The tenseness between the two men was unbearable. "Sir, I apologize. I deserve whatever you plan to dish out."

Hugh pushed his chair away from his desk and stood up. Shifting his belt, he walked over to Aaron.

"Let me tell you something, son." He was within inches of Aaron's face. "When I have someone working for me who doesn't have the balls to disagree with me out in the open, who just says yes sir, when he and I both know that's not what he means, then I have to question who I have working for me. That you took property that doesn't belong to you, that you took a civilian out there, the last place that civilian needs to be ever again, and that you didn't communicate any of this nor your location at any point, is enough for me to dismiss you from ever working for the service again. You can't be trusted. You see my point?"

Aaron could not speak, his mouth dry and his throat constricted. All he could manage was a nod.

"Not good enough. Say it so I can hear it. And, by God, say it only if you mean it."

"Yes, sir." He was so close to tears and was sure that he would break down any moment.

"All right, then. You made some poor decisions, young man. And the report I just finished says as much. My recommendation is for you to be dismissed from the service. It's written on that computer over there."

Aaron was shaking as he watched Hugh go over to his desk, sit down, and hover his right hand over the keyboard.

"Got anything to say to me?"

"I'm sorry, Ranger Reynolds. I know I blew it. It's just that I couldn't say no to him. I can't tell you why. I just couldn't, not if there was a chance his friend was still out there."

"We have rules. We have protocols. We have structure. If we didn't, we would be worthless. We have an order to follow, and we depend on each other for our survival. You signed on knowing this. You understand?" His hand still above the keyboard.

"I do. I don't know how to make this right with you, sir. I guess I can't. Just hope you can forgive me."

Hugh allowed Aaron's words to linger between them, purposely not responding but letting the young ranger suffer a little longer. Hugh audibly sighed as his index finger dramatically tapped a key. "You just did. Between you and me, that's the first time I've ever done that."

"Done what, sir?"

"Deleted it."

Suddenly understanding, Aaron felt his knees buckling under him and reached out to catch himself. Hugh got to him before he fell to the floor.

"You deserve one more chance, as I see it. Your heart was in the right place but in our business that can get you into trouble. Follow the rules. It's simple."

Aaron let his weight fall into Hugh's body as the older ranger did not let go but huddled on the floor, the two of them breathing long slow breaths of relief.

"So simple. Just remember that. So simple." Hugh's words floated around them like feathers released to the winds.

Chapter 34

Aaron did not join the others for dinner. Even at Hugh's urging, Aaron begged off unable to face any of the other rangers, especially Hugh. Not yet. Hugh knew not to push it. Aaron had a lot to sort out. In Hugh's almost forty-five years of service, this wasn't the first time he'd come down hard on a young ranger. And most times, he was successful. Some of his best rangers were the ones who went through the fire first. There were a few he tried not to remember but who were hard to forget. Their actions warranted their permanent dismissal. Hugh was not one to ignore the facts when presented to him but when he found those facts to be outright lies, his patience was nonexistent. "A man who lies to save himself is not worth it," Hugh had commented many times to those who listened. "That man will never be a team player, never think about anyone but himself." There was no way Hugh would ever keep someone like that on the team. Too much was at stake to risk a second chance.

Aaron wasn't the only one shaken by the day's outcome. As Hugh sat with Devon and the others over dinner, he told them the truth, to a point, when they asked the whereabouts of Aaron.

"He's had a rough day and it's best he keeps to himself right now."

That was the extent of it, but Hugh knew that his rangers were good people and that they could handle their association with Aaron in their own way. It wasn't his place to speak for him. He must speak for himself, part of the healing process that Hugh knew needed to happen. Nothing would be right until it had.

Sleep evaded Aaron. Not surprisingly, his mind would not shut down, the underlying realization he had come so close to destroying the career he loved. Worse than that, he had disappointed the one man he truly admired who would now never see Aaron in any other light than his worst. It made little difference to Aaron that Hugh had given him one more chance. Of course, he was grateful and relieved but those were surface reactions that didn't begin to reach the depths of his soul. That's where he felt the injury that he had caused Hugh. It was lodged there, now a permanent part of who he was. A disappointment. Much as he must have been to his biological father who never bothered to know his son. To Tim? Could he have done more to scare the bear so that Tim would still be alive? To Quin Leet? Had he given up on finding Willy too soon? Was Quin disappointed that the one person who had given him hope had failed him?

Unable to stay in bed, sleep the last thing that would visit him this night, he quietly gathered his gear and backpack in the dark and closed the door behind him. He had no idea what he was doing, where he was going. The only thing he was sure of was that he needed to get away from here. Maybe he could clear his head, see everything in a different light. One that he could live with.

He set out on foot towards the ranch where Quin was staying. The halfmoon illuminated the valley floor enough so that he thought twice about using his flashlight. Its harsh glare would be offensive under the moon's natural light. The warmth of the early morning hours surprised him. He had become used to the airconditioned quarters he shared with the other rangers. Too exhausted every night from a full day's work always resulted in a solid eight hours of sleep, undisturbed by the desert heat. Three-thirty in the morning, still as can be, the only sounds the few insects up early to greet the eventual dawn, Aaron's senses were heightened, and his earlier disruptive thoughts were dissolving with each step he took. He was aware of the sound of his boots on the dried surface, the movement of sand beneath his soles, the crunch on harder salt flats. The hint of a dawn breeze momentarily brushed his face until he moved out of the air current and then back into it. He knew that in the distance, the great mountain ranges of the Amargosa and the Panamint rose from the desert floor and enclosed it on its east and west sides, but they were mere shadows of themselves in the night's darkness, the moon's light not enough to make them real.

He let his mind wander. He tried to imagine what it must have been like for Willy and Quin out here, much farther away from civilization than he was now, but even so, the desert's immensity struck him as he walked alone. He knew his way to the ranch from the rangers' quarters, but he could understand how quickly someone could lose their way in this place as had Willy and Quin. For that matter, as he had but in a different environment. And he had a destination unlike Willy and Quin as far as he could tell. He reached back to his pack, to a side pocket in which he had placed his compass. Feeling the hard object reassured him, and he left it there.

He came upon the roadway that led visitors into Furnace Creek where the ranch was located. Crossing it, he walked along the side of the road until he came to its entrance. The amber lighting of the scattered lamp posts cast an eerie hue on the buildings and walkways. He made his way to Quin's room moving quietly past darkened guest rooms. He hadn't thought far enough ahead. What was he going to do once there? It was much too early to disturb him, and he couldn't sit outside his door. His uniform would attract attention from the early risers heading to the restaurant or out for an early walk.

Thinking better of it, he turned around and headed back out to the roadway. Less than an hour had passed, the darkness not yet giving way to any hint of sunrise. It wouldn't be for another hour or so, but the moon was lower in the sky, slowing slipping behind the Panamint range in the west while, in the east, the outline of the Amargosa Range remained indistinguishable. Heading east, it occurred to him that he was entirely alone out here. As he ventured into the desert away from the population in Furnace Creek, he was aware of little else than a welcomed sense of peace. He knew it was not to last. That, just as he did day after day, before the sun rose, he and others began their workdays. But at this time, the in between time, in which the valley's human inhabitants were still asleep, Aaron knew enough to appreciate it. When the first headlights appeared on the roadway or the first lights of the now distant dwellings filled window spaces, the in between time would be over.

He had no destination in mind as he continued east. Finding a spot where he could take in the sunrise was not difficult. A matter of staying on the desert's surface or climbing any outcropping of sandstone that rose in soft, undulating edges all leading into alluvial canyons that met the desert floor. He chose to climb.

Purchased on the cool surface of stone, he took off his pack and, using it to prop his back, leaned against it and waited for the day to officially begin. He was tired, he realized, as he struggled to keep his eyes open. With no sleep and the early rise, he gave into his fatigue, sleep dragging him under. He was oblivious to anything else but welcomed darkness and rest.

In the darkness, he saw his mother. Her face floated in and out of his dream but always left something of her behind. He felt the comfort and safety of her embrace or detected her scent or listened to the soft, rhythmic pattern of her voice. But never did she appear in her entirety to him. His sleep was disturbed by this.

The compass, suspended in air in his dream, was larger than life. He reached for it, but it was so large that he could barely hold onto it. When he no longer could, it fell from his hands into two much larger masculine hands below his that held onto it with ease. The compass lay in the open palms of these hands as if an offering to him, but he was unable to reach it.

He felt himself waking up and fought to stay asleep. The unfinished effort would not leave him. If he just tried harder, he could stretch far enough to take it back. The darkness pulled him back under so that he was aware of his mother again but only part of her, her hands, which appeared between his and the larger ones. He watched as her hands gently lifted the compass from the open palms and brought it back to him. In her hands, it appeared weightless, with no apparent effort on her part to hold on to it. He reached out his hands and she gave it to him, its weight now heavier than before. As he dreamed, he felt the cumbersome weight grow but he struggled to hold on, the muscles in his hands and lower arms burning with fatigue. His straining body now worked in concert to keep the compass in his possession, the heat of his body burning his skin. But he would not let go. He could not let go.

His eyes opened to the offensive daylight. Shocked by the brightness, it only took moments for Aaron to realize that he had blown it. Checking his watch, it was almost eight and his first thought went to Quin. The sickening realization that he had probably missed saying goodbye to him shot him to a standing position as he grabbed his pack and climbed down the rock's surface.

It was a long shot, Aaron knew, but he knocked on the hotel door anticipating no response. Now almost eight thirty, he was convinced that Quin had gotten an early start.

"Ranger Crenshaw. I thought I'd catch you at the headquarters." Quin stood in the doorway.

Aaron could see that his luck was holding as he saw behind Quin his backpack ready to go. Another few minutes and he probably would have missed him.

"Thought I'd save you the trip."

"That's kind of you.

"Wondered if we could talk over a cup of coffee? Don't want to keep you."

"Well, I could do with one. Been a hard night. Glad to see the morning. And I'm in no rush to leave." Quin turned and picked up his bag. "I hope that what you want to talk to me about will not make me wish I had kept this door shut. I thought we were just going to say goodbye." Quin stepped forward, Aaron backing up, as Quin closed the door behind him.

Why had he come back to see him? Aaron searched his mind, still not fully recovered from the last few hours of sleep.

"It's just that with everything that's happened, I guess I needed to make sure you were okay. I mean with not finding Willy."

"Let's get that cup of coffee." Quin took the lead as they headed toward the restaurant.

The place was not packed. Not tourist season yet, the whole ranch was breathing a sigh of relief. It was temporary and the ranch's employees knew this. The atmosphere was not as hectic, the servers were relaxed and didn't mind staying at a table and chatting with their customers, and the restaurant was filled with smiles and laughter. A truly welcoming atmosphere that Quin and Aaron settled into, steaming hot mugs of coffee placed in front of them.

"So, you had a bad night too?" Aaron sipped the hot liquid, the jolt enough to waken him further.

"I did. Sounds like you did too." Quin did the same.

"Yeah. Not completely unexpected, though." He was uncomfortable about telling Quin about his confrontation with Hugh.

"I suppose that's right."

"Look, Quin. I am really sorry that we didn't find Willy."

"No need to apologize. None. I wish we had but it's not meant to be. You need to put it out of your mind. Move on. We both do." Quin drank.

"Is that what Willy would have wanted?"

Quin stopped mid-sip, his cup held just below his mouth. "I believe so."

"Are you headed home, then?"

"Headed somewhere." Another drink.

"Any idea where?" Aaron tried to hide his concern for the seventy-three-year-old man seated across from him.

"Haven't given it too much thought. I think Willy has rubbed off on me that way."

"You mean, heading out with no direction in mind? I don't want to belabor it, but isn't that how you ran into trouble in the first place?" Aaron tried to keep it light.

Quin laughed loudly, throwing his head back as he did so. The few customers in the place did not hesitate to look his way.

"I suppose it is."

"Will you be alright?" It was a simple question, but Aaron felt a pang of regret and loss that caught him by surprise. Was he going to break down in front of this man? Why?

Quin drained his cup before answering. Running his index finger around its rim, he searched for the right words, the ones that would comfort the young man.

"If I tell you I will be, I expect you won't believe me. And if I tell you I won't be, then that's just plain foolish on my part. This is supposed to be a parting cup of coffee, remember?"

Now it was Aaron's turn to laugh. "You do have a way with words. But I'm serious. I just don't feel right saying goodbye to you without knowing you'll be okay. So, I guess you can make something up and I'll have to accept it."

"Can't do that. Can't say what isn't true. And I'm sorry if that leaves you unsettled. But that's the nature of truth, sometimes, isn't it? It's hard to hear."

It was apparent to Aaron that he was not going to win this one. He had done his part, rescued the old man and set him on the next part of his journey. But he had no hold on him beyond that.

"I understand. And, yes, the truth is hard to hear sometimes." He remembered his mother telling him that she was dying. His heart was breaking then as it was now.

"Walk me out, will you?" Quin pushed his way out of the booth and waited for Aaron to do the same.

As they stood together just at the entrance of the ranch ready to part ways, Aaron reached into the side pocket of his backpack and worked the compass out of its secured space. He did not hesitate but handed it to Quin.

"For keeping you going in the right direction, Quin." Aaron waited for Quin to take it, but Quin made no effort to do so. "It's okay. I think you need it more than I do."

Minutes seemed to pass before Quin reached for it. He held it in the palm of his hand and gently opened the heavy lid of the compass. Aaron thought that he saw Quin's hand trembling as he traced the contours of the object with his index finger.

"I can't accept this," but he did not offer it to Aaron.

"Sure you can. Think of it as my parting gift to you. It's the least I can do. If nothing else, it will make me feel better to know that you have a direction to go in and that you won't veer from it. Selfish, I know. Please, keep it."

Quin recognized the compass as soon as he felt the weight of the lid as he lifted it. It was unmistakable. He suddenly felt the earth shift beneath him, and it was all he could do to stay standing, so sure was he that he knew this compass.

"I need to sit." Quin turned back to the area where benches lined both sides of the restaurant's entrance. Aaron, unsure of how to help, caught up with him, ready to extend his arm as support.

"What is it, Quin?" He helped Quin take off his pack as Quin lowered himself onto the bench.

"Give me a minute, would you?" Quin still held the compass.

Aaron watched as Quin's focus was on nothing else but the compass. In all the time that Aaron had had it in his possession, he only remembered using it a few times in his early teens, and even then, he was not sure he was using it correctly. He had found it in his mother's belongings after she died, and it was one more way he felt closer to her in her absence. A remembrance. In giving it to Quin, something that his mother would have wanted him to do, Aaron felt closure.

"If you really don't want it, that's okay. Here. Give it to me and we'll forget it." Aaron reached his hand out to Quin. "No harm done."

Instead of giving it back, Quin sat up straighter, keeping the compass balanced in his palm. Aaron watched as Quin maneuvered the lid gently squeezing its sides until a second lid popped away from the first, hanging by the minute hinges of the outer lid. He was amazed that he hadn't discovered this himself and finally understood why the lid was unnaturally heavy. A double lid. Who would have thought?

Quin felt the familiar release, a movement he had done hundreds of times before to read the words inscribed inside the outer cover long protected by the second lid. The script appeared as though it had only been engraved yesterday in contrast to the tarnished outer shell of the compass. He knew the words by heart and mouthed them silently as he read them once again after so many years apart.

"Always seek true North"

Unable to comprehend why he now had it in his possession once again, it was all he could do to keep his composure. How had it come back to him? A stranger until recently had given it to him. A young man who was responsible for saving his life. The reason he woke up this morning. And now the reason he questioned what he had been so sure of just a short time ago.

"What is it, Quin?" Aaron's curiosity was getting the better of him. He leaned closer to Quin trying to see what Quin was seeing.

Quin handed the open compass to Aaron. He said nothing still struggling to understand what had just taken place.

"Always seek true north," Aaron read aloud. "Good reminder. I had no idea this was in here."

"Where did you get this?" Quin's voice was stronger now, but he didn't feel on solid ground. He wouldn't, not until he was sure.

Aaron was taken aback by the question. It was the last thing he expected to hear. What did it matter? "It was my mother's. I guess she inherited it from her parents or maybe it was hers. I never saw it until the day I found it. Why do you ask?"

"Can I ask you who your mother is?"

"My mother? You mean her name?" Aaron did not hide his confusion.

"Yes, her name."

"Amelia Crenshaw."

It was not the name Quin had known her by, realizing that she had moved on from him.

"And your father?"

"Damian Crenshaw."

Aaron had been asked this question many times before, his answer always immediate. Damian Crenshaw. But it wasn't until he was twelve that he was told by his mother that Damian had not been his real father. That she didn't know who his real father had been, a lie spoken in retaliation against Quin even after the twelve years since she had last seen him. A lie that was Aaron's truth and that rested comfortably with Aaron until he was old enough to understand the implications of his mother's revelation. Even so, he thought no less of her. And as time went on, who his real father had been held no importance to him. Unknown. Always had been unknown. But suddenly, as he felt Quin's eyes upon him, questioning, fear drove its spear right through his heart, an uncomfortable and inevitable outcome for years of never knowing.

"But I don't know." Aaron was aware that his whispered response went unheard. He tried again, this time louder. "I don't know who my biological father was. I've never known. Why?"

Everything that had led up to this moment for Quin came crashing down on him. Fragments of memories cascading, colliding, and shattering as he struggled to come to grips with the truth that had finally caught up with him. A truth, he realized in the chaos of his state of mind, that he never knew. He was not to blame. He never knew.

"What you are holding in your hand, Aaron, belonged to your grandfather." Quin paused, letting his words settle.

"How do you know that?" Aaron asked incredulously. It wasn't that he hadn't considered that it could have belonged to his mother's father but why would Quin, a perfect stranger, make such a statement?

"Because your grandfather gave it to me, Aaron. It was a gift from his father, your great grandfather."

"I don't understand. So why did my mother have it in her belongings if you had it?"

Neither man spoke. The answer to his question was impossible for Aaron to comprehend. Not without Quin's help. And even then, he feared that Aaron would not accept the truth.

"Aaron, your mother and I were married but it didn't work out. It was over before I gave it a decent effort. I am to blame for it ending." Quin parceled out his thoughts, one revelation at a time.

Aaron was dumbfounded.

"How old are you?"

"Why?"

"Would you just answer my question, please?" Quin struggled to remain gentle in his prodding.

"I'm turning forty next month."

Quin knew the answer before he asked it. The ramifications of it, however, struck him dumb. It meant that Amelia had been pregnant when he left her, and she had said nothing. She let him walk away without knowing the only reason he would have stayed. His anger lay deep and stayed there. He saw no reason to disturb it. What good would it do? It was all he could do right now to get through the next moments with his son.

"I left your mother forty years ago, Aaron. I never knew that she was pregnant. She never let me know about you." As he spoke, he remembered. He did walk out on her. He never gave her the chance to say anything. The most cowardly act he had ever committed, he realized now.

Now it was Aaron's turn to make sense of Quin's words. Was he saying that he was his real father?

"I don't believe you. This is crazy."

"I know. I know it sounds crazy, but that compass? When I left your mother, I took very little with me. I left it behind. It didn't occur to me to grab mementos. The last thing on my mind. And that little compass was just that. A memento from my father, your grandfather, that held no real significance to me until now." His last words begged him to consider further their meaning, but Aaron interrupted his thoughts.

"Are you trying to tell me that you're my father? Just because I told you her name? My father was Damian

Crenshaw. The only father I ever knew. And this compass doesn't prove a thing, by the way." He was so confused that even he wanted to take back his own words and start over.

"I can prove it to you, Aaron." Quin pulled out his worn wallet. Delicately separating an almost time sealed compartment, he gently pulled from it a small photograph. It appeared to have been cut away from a larger one, its uneven borders hastily created. He handed it to Aaron.

His mother's smile spoke loudly to him as he gazed upon her face. She looked just the way he remembered her before her illness robbed her of her smile. A beautiful bride, it had been taken on their wedding day with Quin standing by her side.

"My God."

"Your mother was beautiful in every way, Aaron. She deserved better than me."

"You kept this? Even though you left her?"

"She was my first love, Aaron. Her place in my heart will always remain. Yes, I kept this with me. She gave me strength, I think, even though I didn't realize it at the time. Even in the desert when I was so close to dying, I think she helped keep me alive so that I could finally meet you."

Aaron desperately tried to catch up with Quin's words, his summation of three lives that once were intertwined.

"How is your mother, Aaron?"

"She's dead." Suddenly, mental fatigue muddied his thinking so that the only reality he absolutely knew to be true was uttered without emotion.

Now it was Quin who could find no words that would have any significance to his son. Any he produced would sound hollow, insincere, and a lie.

"She died when I was twelve. She was sick, cancer."

"I'm sorry, Aaron. That must have been hard on you and … your father." Quin struggled to hide his emotions.

"My father died when I was six. My mother never remarried. So when she passed, I went into foster care and other people took care of me until I aged out." Aaron wanted his words to hurt, to be ripe with blame towards Quin but they fell flat. Statements of fact, nothing more.

"And after that?"

It was like filling out an application for a job, Aaron thought. Just keep filling in the blanks with facts while hiding behind so much more that needed to be said. An odd thought but it lingered with him as he responded to Quin.

"I made my way, met people who helped me, and ended up here. That's about it." He had no energy left. No desire to speak further.

"And you saved my life, Aaron."

Chapter 35

Quin did not leave that morning. Nor did he leave the following. As the days passed, he and Aaron spent hours in the evenings talking to each other about their lives. Quin knew it would be difficult, at first, for Aaron. It was difficult for him, but he had a collection of difficult life experiences that he had survived to fall back on. Aaron was too fresh in the world, even at forty.

When Aaron told his father about Tim and the bear attack, Quin listened with rapt attention. It was a miracle that his son survived it and a tragedy that his friend had not. He was gripped by Aaron's retelling of his ascent to the fire tower and about Ranger Everett Logan who had been waiting for him to arrive, had watched Aaron's struggles to reach him but had never leant a hand, not until Aaron succeeded in his journey. That it was because of Everett Logan that Aaron made his decision to go back to school and become a ranger. But even more intriguing to Quin was Aaron's description of Tim, another wanderer with no direction. It was not lost on Quin that Tim and Willy seemed to play the same roles in both his and his son's lives. An unsettling but intriguing thought.

Quin could find little comfort in the fact that he had not been there for his son, had not been the one to guide him, when he could, on his son's life journey. But as he listened to Aaron relate his relationships with those who did play their part as guides and mentors, Quin was grateful and in awe. His son had always been protected, not from the losses he endured, that of his mother and father and that of an unknown father, but from having to find his way alone.

On the fourth night, Quin returned to his time in the desert with Willy. Every part of his life leading up to stepping off the side of the road to go with Willy had already been shared. And of course, the rescue. But he had not told his son about the in between time. He had purposely steered his account away from what had been and still was the most disturbing and life altering moments of his journey. At one point, he decided there was no need for Aaron to know. What would be the point? But now, he understood that there was something else at work here between the two of them that could no longer be ignored.

"Did you dream when you were with Tim?" It seemed the easiest inroad to take with Aaron without pushing him away.

"I don't remember." That time seemed so long ago. So much had happened since.

"It doesn't matter."

"Then why did you ask?"

"I dreamed, Aaron. Such moments in my dreams that I was convinced were real."

Quin remembered now, the end of the in between time dream that had found him back on the open ocean in his father's boat not far from Conical Island. He remembered it clearly and felt the water's strength under the hull of their small fishing boat. It was almost full circle, his return to the water, and he wondered if he wasn't meant to complete his journey by returning to the island. But not alone. With his son so that Aaron could complete this part of his own journey. One half of his heritage made known to him. The inscription on the compass whose source was a grandfather whom Aaron would never know, would carry more meaning if Aaron could walk in the footsteps of his grandfather and father. Quin was sure of this.

"Aren't most dreams like that until you wake up?" Aaron had no idea where Quin was going with this.

"I suppose so, but these dreams were more than just real to me. They were predilections. I see that now."

"You've lost me."

Quin knew he had until he provided explanation.

"I met Willy after I experienced one of these dreams. And I think that I wasn't supposed to meet him until I went through the in between time in my dream." He watched Aaron's face and saw little evidence that Aaron was sharing any interest in his words. "I know this sounds nuts, but I know that there is something to it."

"How about we walk." Aaron stood up, stiff from sitting and eager to get out of the small hotel room.

Taken by surprise, Quin did not object.

The desert evening air was still warm but comfortable. They walked beyond the ranch's entrance and headed toward the desert on the other side of the roadway. A familiar route for Aaron.

"This is nice out here. So quiet." Quin needed this.

"Yeah. Kind of crazy to be hunkered down inside when we have all this to enjoy." Aaron did not turn in Quin's direction but kept his eyes straight ahead. "So, tell me about your dream."

"Yes, my dream. Parts of it I don't recall but other parts won't leave me alone, Aaron. Those are the parts I need to share with you. When I asked you if you dreamt when you were with Tim, I was remembering Willy. I dreamt just before meeting him for the first time and during my time with him. They were dreams that I had never experienced before and haven't since Willy's death. When you told me about Tim, all I could think about was how much alike Willy and Tim were. That they each came into our lives when we needed them the most." He paused, hoping that Aaron was listening and starting to understand.

"Interesting. Go on."

"Willy seemed to have no direction just as you described Tim. But I followed him even though everything told me to reconsider. I went back for him, trekked all over the desert with him, never with a spoken destination in mind. The only hint he gave me was that it was a place that I had always wanted to go to. A place that I wanted to see. And I couldn't figure out why I was doing that. We were risking our lives, but it never bothered him. He wasn't doing this for himself. He was doing it for me, Aaron. Just like Tim was leading you to the fire tower even though you questioned where it was and why you had to climb a volcano, of all things, to get there. You had your doubts, but you stayed with him. And only when you couldn't stay with him anymore because he was dead, just as Willy was, you and I were left on our own to make our own way. I made my way off the desert floor to the rocks for the same reason. You made it up the mountain to the tower for the same reason. And in both places, we were saved. Don't you see?"

Quin was exhausted. The words poured from him as if he was suddenly aware of the clarity of the events, the significance of them, and the connection that bound father and son together. He couldn't speak fast enough to empty himself completely of his revelation.

Aaron, even though not completely following Quin's train of thought, was intrigued by the common thread. It was, he had to admit, strange and an interesting coincidence.

"I see what you're saying. We both came through a rough patch and survived it."

Quin was shocked. Was that what Aaron heard? Had he not listened?

"No, no. That's not my point." Frustration crept into his voice. "You're not listening."

Aaron had had enough. The man who claimed to be his father was off his rocker. He had given Quin enough of his time, four nights' worth, and it was apparent to Aaron that he needed to cut him off. Send him on his way.

"Look. I am listening and have been listening to your ramblings for nights now. If you are who you say you are, then it's good to know you exist. But everything you have been through in your life up to the moment we met has nothing to do with me. Any more than my life has to do with you. For whatever reason, we were brought together after a forty-year absence. That's basically half of my life, so far. I've done okay without you and no matter how much you think there's some mystical thing going on between us and Willy and Tim, I don't believe it." Aaron took a deep breath, audible to Quin who was reeling as Aaron continued. "It's time you go your own way, like you were supposed to days ago. Finding me does not give you the right to enter my life any more than you already have."

Aaron was aware that his words were hurtful, but he didn't care. The people who counted in his life knew him and even though he had disappointed them, they still had faith in him. Hugh and Devon and the rest of the guys knew him and would be there for him. The last thing he needed was an old man making unproven claims of kinship and going on about some mystical event that supposedly brought them together. He couldn't believe he had wasted so much time on him and was beginning to regret that he had found the guy in the first place.

"Willy told me he was taking me to a place I had always wanted to go. To a place that I had always wanted to see. I thought he had done that when I saw your compass. I thought that, finally, I had made it to that place even though I was never able to articulate what that place was. But you. You, Aaron. You are the place. Can't you understand that?"

Aaron almost felt sorry for the man. If he let himself, he might give in. But even if Quin was his father and even if what he said had an ounce of sense and truth to it, it still made no difference. There was no connection, no feeling, no longing for Quin to be a part of his life. Nothing.

"I'm sorry, Quin. It's not going to happen. Whatever it is that you want, whatever you think I want, it's not going to happen." Aaron reached into his shirt pocket and handed the compass to Quin. "This isn't mine. It never was."

Aaron turned away from Quin and started back to the roadway. He knew Quin was not following him. Instead of waiting for him at the entrance to the ranch, Aaron turned right, crossed the roadway, and headed back to headquarters. The closer he came, the more at ease he felt, the reassurance of Hugh's presence somewhere nearby, of Devon's humor striking when least expected, and of those who wore the same uniform and who knew him, faults and all. As he thought about them, he picked up his pace with no thought of Quin. He was no more present now than he had ever been before meeting him. Aaron's conscience was clear, he realized, as he remembered Tim's words. "I see it as simply existing while understanding and accepting that as an individual I am solely responsible for my actions, my thought, my beliefs, my understanding of my own existence. …I cannot presume or project any of these on another individual. It is so simple, in my thinking." And Hugh? His words of comfort? "Follow the rules. It's simple. …So simple. Just remember that. So simple."

None of the rangers were at the station when he arrived. He checked his watch and was surprised to see that it was past midnight. Hugh knew where he had gone after dinner but never said a word about it. Tonight had been like the last three nights. Aaron was off duty and Hugh understood what Aaron needed to do. At least Aaron had been up front with him as to his whereabouts. A lesson well learned and now practiced was how Hugh viewed it.

Aaron sat behind his desk. His paperwork for the day was completed and in the outbox. No messages were left on his desk. Everything was in order ready for the new day that was only six hours away. He felt tired and let his body relax in the space that was reassuring to him. Everything had its place and was in it. Looking up and scanning the office, he saw that the same was true for the entire room. A sense of order permeated the room and it felt good.

Sleep came quickly, its darkness enveloping Aaron. He didn't dream, his mind a blank slate. When he awoke at the sound of his alarm, the sunrise filled the small window above his bunk and cast hues of a new day's light against the opposite wall of his room. The rose hues were warm and welcoming, full of promise. He lay still, breathing deeply, taking it all in, with no thought of Quin. He smelled breakfast before he got out of bed and smiled knowing that Hugh was just on the other side of the wall, frying bacon, scrambling eggs, and toasting bread. Aaron had never felt so alive as he did on this morning. Luck and good people. That's all it took. It was so simple.

Chapter 36

As Quin watched Aaron walk away from him, he understood that he would never see his son again. Aaron's words had made that clear. Quin was deleted from his son's life in a matter of minutes. He knew there was no use in following him, all the while desperately trying to explain to Aaron what Quin thought to be true. He believed Willy. Willy had led him to Aaron. There had been a reason for Quin not to give up on Willy. But Aaron would never understand and as Quin made his way back to his room, he found peace in that. It was not Aaron's path, Quin considered. It was only his and Willy's. He had no right to impose himself on Aaron, given that he had never been there for him to begin with. Never been a part of his journey. And he did not blame Aaron.

He left Death Valley a different man. He knew now what he was meant to do before he died. It was as clear as the brilliant sun that flooded this valley in the daylight hours and as astonishing as the infinite number of stars and their galaxies that filled the velvet black desert sky at night. As close to death as he had been only a short time ago, he now felt the farthest from it. He tried to recall when he had felt this way before. When he had direction in his life. It had been so long ago. Slipping his hand into his coat pocket, he felt the small round object, his fingertips running over the cold smooth surface. But he left the compass safely tucked away. He didn't need to open it to navigate his next journey. He knew the way. And he didn't need to read his father's words. Just their presence again was enough. He was closer now to arriving at the place he had always wanted to go, had always wanted to see. He now understood that he had been seeking true north his entire life.

The bus pulled away and headed south into the valley before turning north. Two people waited on the side of the roadway and when it stopped for them, they boarded. Less than two hundred yards farther, the bus slowed and made a U-turn. Quin took in the last views he would ever have of Death

Valley from the airconditioned confines of the bus. It was enough for him as he said goodbye to what would have been his final resting place as it was for Willy. As the bus headed north out of the valley, he did not allow himself to weep. Instead, he closed his eyes, shutting out the daylight, his imaginings of what might have been seeping into the darkness that he allowed to consume him.

His decision to go to Yosemite and from there into the northern California forests was made not to avoid his final destination; rather, to prepare himself for it. No matter how long it would take, when he was ready, and only then, would he finish what he had started so long ago.

≈ ≈ ≈

Word came midmorning while Aaron was on duty. The radio call was from Hugh who had just been notified that three hikers had come across a body just west of the California border in the Amargosa Desert not far from Indian Pass. It appeared to have been out there for a while. He wanted Aaron and Devon to be there when the chopper landed. Hugh didn't say it, but Aaron understood that they were both thinking the same thing. This body might be that of Quin Leet's companion, Willy.

Aaron had never seen anything like it. Once, when younger, he flipped through a National Geographic Magazine and stopped cold when the colored image of an unwrapped mummy filled the page, the latest finding in a pyramid's tomb in Egypt. He never forgot staring into the leathered eyes of someone who once lived and breathed just like he did. Lifeless but, in a way, full of life, the mummified eyes staring right back at him. As he stood over whom he assumed must be Willy, the same chill ran through him.

The men worked quickly but carefully and respectfully as Willy disappeared into a body bag and then into the waiting basket. Aaron watched, once again as he had for Quin and Tim, as the basket rose to the opening of the hovering chopper. As he turned back to the spot where Willy was found, he felt Devon's arm hold him back. There, on the spot where Willy had perished, the granddaddy of all rattlers rested, its massive body coiling, its tail rattling a familiar rhythm, its large head rearing above its body, and its tongue investigating the air.

≈ ≈ ≈

"He's been identified as Paul Redmond. Age seventy-five. Went by Willy." Hugh laid the copy of the autopsy report on Aaron's desk. "Died of what we already know. Starvation, dehydration. Bottom line, his body shut down little by little. Terrible way to go."

Aaron read for himself, it finally sinking in that Quin had been telling him the truth all along. Willy did exist and had been out there with Quin.

"I'll leave it to you to connect with Mr. Leet and give him the news seeing as how you spent some time with him. I'm sure he'll want to know. Take care of it." Hugh walked back to his desk, one less chore to deal with today.

"Right. Of course."

Considering how he left everything when he walked away from Quin, Aaron wasn't at all sure that he could do what Hugh commanded. He didn't want to try crossing a burned bridge. Too much was at stake. Besides, the way Quin had described Willy, it made little difference in Quin's life. That's the way Willy wanted it. Quin accepted this. Why stir it all up again? Why? Because he had told Hugh that he would carry through with his order. That's why. Quin was long gone from the valley. Four months had passed since they parted ways. Even so, Aaron felt the unspoken pressure Hugh was placing on him, expecting him to "take care of it" now.

Able to get a cell number and address from the ranch's hotel record of Quin's stay, Aaron had no excuse not to make the call. However, the number was no good. He tried a few times just to be sure. If Quin had a cell, which Aaron was beginning to believe he never did, then he purposely gave a fake number. He looked up the "home" address on Google maps and it didn't exist. Just as he wondered if Willy ever existed, he now wondered the same about Quin. A foolish thought, but it nagged at him. Just a foolish thought. And then it hit him. If Quin was really his father, he had never wanted to be found. It was fate that connected them and, even then, only for a moment in time. It was enough to jolt Aaron and, he guessed Quin, out of their perceived realities that were now permanently altered.

"There's no way to contact him. I've tried. He's given everyone fake information." Aaron stood in front of Hugh's desk.

"As long as you've tried, I expect that's about all we can do. Besides, if there is any next of kin, someone higher up would have made the call. I expect we've done all that we can. Put this one to bed, Ranger Crenshaw. You clear on this?" Hugh refocused on his computer.

"Okay. Very clear." He did not try to hide the relief he felt, and Hugh glanced up at him.

"Anything I'm missing here?"

Aaron was about to say that there was so much that Hugh was missing here but it would remain unspoken. He couldn't help but smile as he responded to Hugh.

"Not a thing, sir. Not one single thing."

Chapter 37

His journey had been long. It had been five months since Quin left Death Valley and his son. His travels alone to the mountains and deep into the forests of northern California supplied him with the needed peace and balance in his life he knew would prepare him for what was to come. He arrived in Crosswood in the early afternoon in time to find a place to stay. Only one night, then he would be on his way. Plenty of time for what he needed to do.

The cemetery was not far from the motel, a good walk that he welcomed after sitting on the bus for so long. Little in the town where he walked had changed since his last stay here. A new strip mall replaced homes, as he remembered them. He wondered where those people were now. As he came closer to the cemetery's entrance, he remembered the slow ascent to the gates. Someone had had the forethought to establish this place on the top of a rise that overlooked most of Crosswood.

He had no idea where or if Amelia was buried here. He never got the chance to ask Aaron. The office was located just to the left of the entrance gates, a small stucco building whose only identification was that of angel statuary on either side of the door. In one angel's hand, a small wooden sign said, "Office" and above the door, "Welcome" was chiseled into the wall.

With Amelia's grave site circled numerous times on a "map" of the grounds, as the woman behind the small desk insisted on doing, Quin made his way along the narrow roadways until he came to the area where Amelia lay. He gently walked among the stones, some only inches above ground while others' heights and masses dominated the lesser ones. The thought crossed his mind that he might be treading on the sacred spaces of the dead who lay below his feet. He hoped not.

Amelia's head stone was no more than a small wedge of granite no higher than a few inches; perhaps twelve inches in length and 6 inches wide. Her name was clearly engraved, her dates, and the simple statement, "Mother". Quin tried to feel something. Anything for the woman he once loved and for the mother of their son who wanted nothing to do with him. His words were silent at first but soon became a repeated whispering to the granite stone at his feet. "Please forgive me for leaving you and our son." He reached down and placed a single rose on the stone and left.

He knew where the next stone lay. It was far from Amelia's almost on the other side of the grounds. He realized that he was descending the small rise to reach his brother. It was an easier attempt than reaching Amelia. He noticed that the grounds were well cared for and he recalled the grounds-keeper he had spoken to after Edward's burial. He wondered if, after all this time, he was still employed or was one of the dead beneath his feet.

There was nothing but the stone. Unlike the other stones that surrounded his brother's, whose adornment of fake flowers gave false comfort to those who no longer cared, Edward's was sterile. As Quin came closer, he remembered the last time he had spoken to his brother. The dismissiveness that they had both engaged in, the eagerness that they both felt to move on beyond that moment. It was painful to Quin as he saw it so clearly. Laying his hand on the headstone, he silently spoke with his brother. He told him all about his travels, where he had gone, whom he had met, and how close he had come to joining him. He told him that he was a father, but in name only. He spoke Aaron's name aloud to Edward. "Aaron. His name is Aaron." Before he left Edward's grave, he asked his brother to forgive him for leaving Conical Island and him behind, accepting that Edward was dead because of him. He had nothing to leave with Edward but his words. He took one last look at the gravestone before leaving, not wanting to forget this final time with his brother. Quin knew he would never return.

He followed the roadway to the entrance. It felt familiar to him, not the road leading out of the cemetery but another moment in time. He stopped and looked around sensing that he was missing something. Looking back in the direction of Edward's grave, he remembered the groundskeeper. Their brief conversation about newly dug graves. Quin walked a bit farther until he recognized the plot. It was not hard to miss. Seven individual stones placed one next to the other and one very large stone centered behind them. When he saw it so long ago, no one occupied the freshly dug sites. But now, they were well established, and the individual stones showed the climate's impact. How many years? Edward was twenty-two when Quin buried him. Quin was a year older. Fifty years!

Curious, he walked over to the plot and stood close enough to read the large stone first. The family name was Redmond. An unusual marker, Quin thought, as he read the brief history of the Redmond family. The last sentence was the most intriguing to him. "Now we all sleep together in our final rest." Yes, he remembered now. The groundskeeper's hesitancy in revealing what he knew but doing so anyway. Members were being exhumed from sites elsewhere to be buried in the family plot. The reason for so many in one spot.

Stepping back, Quin began to read each of the seven stones. He followed the progression of dates beginning with the early 1800s. When he came to the sixth stone, he stopped, staring at the name. "Jeremy Redmond". It sounded familiar, and he searched his memory as to why. Reading on, he remembered. "He left us too soon. Age 25". The man who killed Edward. It all came flooding back to him. At the time, he was convinced that he'd never forget the name. That was all he had to blame because he never saw the person behind the name. Not even a picture of him in the local paper at the time. Quin fought to keep standing, the deep-seated anger rising in him as if the accident had just happened. He looked back up the rise in the direction of Edward's grave as his vision blurred through his tears. The realization that his brother and his murderer were buried within days of each other here froze him in place. The strangest of thoughts consumed Quin. Had Edward and Jeremy made peace somewhere beyond the here and now? Occupying the same ground so close in proximity in death and, for a tragic second, in life? Did forgiveness exist there?

Wiping his eyes, he felt a calmness settle around him, centering him, and allowing him to move on. It was an inexplicable feeling, one he had experienced before when he was in the desert with Willy. It did not frighten him as he accepted its presence.

As he turned to leave, he realized he had not read the seventh stone. He approached it and saw that the burial site, the ground beneath the stone, and the stone itself seemed fresher than all the others. If his shock at reading Jeremy's stone was almost debilitating, as he began to read the seventh stone his shock should have killed him on the spot. He could not breathe, could not slow his heart's pounding in his head, could not feel the rest of his body. He was paralyzed as he read the final stone's wording. "Paul 'Willy' Redmond". It couldn't be. He read on. "Age 75. Born 1935 Crosswood, CA. Died 2010 Death Valley, CA. Beloved son of Jonathon & Beatrice. Beloved brother of Jeremy. No man should die alone without given the chance to ask for forgiveness. A wanderer who finally came home."

Quin read and reread the stone's words, not believing what he was seeing. He gave in to his body's urging to collapse, to fall upon the earth so that she would hold onto him just as she had done in the desert. She would not abandon him. He would not be submerged into the sludge that once held him under during the in between time.

He felt arms lifting him, heard the concerned voice, and tried to open his eyes. Someone was speaking to him, but he couldn't respond. Slowly, he felt his body readjusting until the fresh cool water touched his lips and they parted allowing the liquid to enter his mouth and slide down his throat.

"Careful. One or two sips."

Someone had applied a damp cloth to his face, his forehead and behind his neck. His breathing came easier, and the pounding subsided. He slowly opened his eyes and tried to focus them. Kneeling in front of him was a young man, one hand holding a water bottle, and in his other the damp cloth.

"How are you feeling?"

Quin tried to sit up straight and realized that he was on the grass at the foot of Willy's grave. The pounding had stopped but the swirling confusion in his brain would not let him think clearly.

"Who are you?"

"I was just about to visit my grandfather's grave and saw you collapse. Glad I was here to help. Name's Bernett but most everyone calls me Bernie. Bernie Redmond." He pointed to Willy's stone. "That's my grandfather's grave."

"You're Willy's grandson?" Quin was slowly grasping all that had taken place in the last few minutes.

"Yeah, but I only saw him twice when I was kid. He never stayed around very long, and I hardly remember what he looked like. Heard plenty of stories, though, from my dad. Sounds like he had a mind of his own. Wish I could have talked to him myself."

"Willy had a son?" It was incredulous the idea that Willy was ever attached to anyone as Quin remembered his companion.

"Did you know my grandfather?" The young man sat down on the grass next to Quin.

Quin wanted to say that he did. Of course, he did. He had shared the most mysterious and meaningful part of his life with the man. But it occurred to him, as he turned to Bernie, that he had never known the Willy whom Bernie called grandfather. The Willy whom Quin knew for such a short time during the man's seventy-five years on this earth was only meant to be known to Quin. He was now very sure of it. Their relationship was formed for a reason. The sixth and seventh stones tied them together just as Quin and Edward had been. Brothers. Brothers whose fates permanently separated them from one another. Unrelated brothers whose paths crossed unexpectedly and tragically. Brothers in memory only whose names chiseled in cold hard stones were the final reminders of what could have been. Willy had promised to take Quin to a place he'd always wanted to go. A place he'd always wanted to see. If only he had faith, kept up with him, and asked nothing of him, Quin would get there.

Bernie Redmond waited patiently for Quin's response. For a moment, Quin recognized Willy's presence in the young man, and it made him smile.

"Yes, I knew your grandfather. He was a fine human being."

"How did you know him?"

"We spent the last month of his life together, Bernie." Quin sensed Bernie's growing interest and wasn't sure he could say much more to him. He had said enough.

"Where?"

Quin turned to him and sighed. "In the desert, Bernie. Your grandfather and I were in the desert for fourteen days."

"My dad told me that my grandfather loved the desert. Went to Death Valley and the Amargosa Desert just about every year since he was a kid. Knew them like the back of his hand."

Stunned, Quin held back. He let Bernie continue.

"My grandmother only went with him a few times and, according to my dad, she hated it. But he kept going. And she was happy staying home. When she got sick, he stopped going for a while. It wasn't until a year or so after my grandmother's death that my grandfather finally returned to the desert. Dad figured it was his way of mourning her loss because he stayed out there for longer periods of time. But as a family, we were worried that he wasn't thinking clearly. Heading out on his own and never telling anyone where he was going other than to the desert didn't sit well with my dad. But my grandfather was his own man and dad understood this." Bernie paused, realizing that he was taking over the conversation. "I'm sorry. I tend to babble on. How are you feeling?"

"I'm feeling better. Thanks. Please, go on."

"You sure?"

"Very sure. Please." Quin sensed that Willy wanted him to hear what his grandson had to say.

"Okay. So, as I was saying, my dad couldn't do much about my grandfather. He was going to do what he wanted to do no matter what anyone thought."

Quin remembered and smiled. "Yes, indeed."

"Then, one day many years later, he announced that he would never go back to the desert. He told my dad that the desert had taken the love of his life from him. It seems my grandfather had met a woman on one of his earlier trips whose love for the desert was even greater than his own. Her name was Isabella and my dad said that she was my grandfather's soulmate. We aren't sure if he was with her while my grandmother was still alive or not, but in any case, it came as a complete shock to my dad. My grandfather would not tell my dad all the details of her death other than to say that he was to blame for it. That he should never have taken her to his favorite spot. He knew the dangers of doing so. A snake's strike that, had he been with her, he would have been able to save her, but she had wanted to climb on her own that day while my grandfather stayed at their campsite. My grandfather never spoke about it after that."

Quin struggled to understand. In a matter of minutes, a perfect stranger had filled in the blanks for him, as tragic and disturbing as they were. He released a sigh that shuddered his whole body.

"I had no idea," was all he could manage.

"The family was surprised to learn that he died in the place that he insisted he'd never return to. Not after Isabella's death. One of life's surprises, I guess. And my dad believes that he was not alone when he died. He believes that he purposely went back there to the spot where Isabella perished so that he could die with her spirit present. Were you there when they found him?"

"No. They found him after I left. We tried to find him. Went back to where I thought I left him, but we had no luck." He put his hand on Bernie's thigh. "I'm ashamed to say that at one point I thought that I imagined him. I began to question my own sanity. Right up until a little while ago, I thought that if Willy had been real, he was still out there on the desert floor where I left him when I went to find help. Instead, I was the one rescued and poor Willy was lost out there."

"Gee, I didn't know. What were you doing out there with him in the first place? Exploring?"

Quin could not hold back. His laughter penetrated the stillness and took Bernie by surprise. It was just too wonderful, Quin thought, the irony of it all.

"That's exactly what we were doing, Bernie. Exactly."

≈ ≈ ≈

Quin stayed behind long after Bernie said goodbye. He never told Bernie his name. It never came up. And it didn't matter, not really. Now, in a different state of mind, he wanted to visit with Willy a little longer. Even though Bernie's revelations struck Quin deeply, he would not speak of it to his friend. Instead, he would speak with him as he had always done. He didn't expect any response. Not because Willy was dead but because Willy probably wouldn't have anyway even if he was sitting right next to Quin. And if he did, it would be a practical response as Willy saw it. A simple response to a complicated question, always setting Quin back a few steps.

"I bet you don't even know how long we were out there, do you? It didn't matter to you. You had other things on your mind. I get it now."

Quin unbuckled his belt and pulled it through the waistband's loops. He laid it on the ground in front of him, flattening it as well as it would allow him to. Slowly, he traced each one of the fourteen marks scratched into the worn leather, counting out loud as he did. When he finished, he wound the belt tightly and laid it at the foot of Willy's gravestone.

"Just something to remember me by, old friend. Sleep well.

Chapter 38

The last time he traveled the waters between the island and the mainland, he stood at the railing of the small working vessel, anticipating all that awaited him on the mainland. He wanted to remember each moment as he watched the sea churn under the hull that bore its way to its destination. He wanted to experience what freedom felt like to those unencumbered by any restraints. He was young, naïve, and cursed. The first he knew. The second never entered his mind. The third was never known to him.

He stood on the deck of a car ferry, one of three that transported residents of both places, Conical Island having become a tourist destination and the mainland now easier to get to and to explore. Time had moved on without his consent, without his observance, without his input. The shock was almost too much for Quin; the unfamiliar was off-putting, and the expectations he had when he made the decision to return home for the last time now questionable. But he bought the ticket, boarded the ferry, and made his way to the upper deck where he once again held onto the railing, his eyes focused on the water beneath the ferry's hull. It occurred to him that the sea was much farther below him than he remembered it to be in the small working vessel. He longed to feel the spray of salt water against his skin, to clearly hear the slapping of the sea's disturbed surface against the hull, and to ride with the undulating motion of her unceasing movements, her reminder that she was being violated with the vessel's passing. A deep sadness followed as Quin remembered another time on her waters.

He tried to remember the small fishing harbor at Whittlestone. He could not see it clearly, much of it lost in his memory. He watched, still from the upper deck, as the ferry came closer. Nothing looked familiar as the ferry made its way into its mooring against a long concrete pier. A canvas canopy covered half of the pier where people were waiting in line to board her back to the mainland. So many people. Where had they all come from? He did not see it until he disembarked, the paved roadway that ended at the ferry's stern. Eager to drive into her belly, two rows of parked cars waited for the signal to move forward. Quin watched, fascinated by what he was seeing. Was this the Conical Island he left so many years ago? Was there any of it left as he had known it?

He made his way toward the village from the ferry depot. Once away from it, he began to remember. The houses along the ocean front were still the same. A few had been turned into bed and breakfast businesses but whoever owned them now had not disturbed their original appearances. A new paint job, perhaps, but that was it, putting him at ease. He knew his way to the pub. Even after all this time, he could find his way there with his eyes closed, he mused, so sure that it was still as he remembered it. When he arrived, it took a moment for him to recognize it. Not that the building had changed any more than the houses, but it was surrounded by shops that he knew had not been there before. Boutiques. Tourists flowing in and out of each one as if on a moving sidewalk. Some bypassing the pub while others entered it.

He suddenly felt crowded with no space in which to move. He wanted to enter the pub, to sit among the fishermen and the outliers once again. He wanted nothing more than to listen to the rising heat of arguments, the raucous laughter, and to feel the slaps on his back from fellow Whittlestonians. A confirmation that they owned this part of the island and not the outliers. It was a time when he was allowed to accompany his father to the pub, his father's way of introducing him to what he expected would become a part of Quin's life. Even though too young to drink, his father would pass him his mug admonishing him to take only one or two sips. No more. It was a special time between father and son, his father told him. And it was to be kept between them, never for his mother to find out. As Quin stood on the other side of the roadway, he chose not to cross it and enter the pub. It was better to leave it as he once knew it. As he once knew his father. It was enough for him.

The house in which he was born had weathered over fifty years without much change. The exterior of the building was evidence to the damage of winter storms and the wooden shutters of the summer sun. Faded from the emerald green he remembered, they needed a good sanding and repainting. One or two slats hung on for dear life. The front door was in no better shape. Quin remembered the brass knocker, a fox head, that his mother cherished. Every morning she would clean it and, when needed, give it a good polish. After all, it was the entry way into their home. First impressions counted she would remind him when he was old enough to do the chore well. Where the knocker had rested for years, there now appeared only a faded shading of its original shape. Even the brass doorknob was gone only to be replaced by a metal handle. The house appeared lived in, but no longer the Leet residence. He knew where his parents were, one of the reasons he came back to Whittlestone.

Behind the one Catholic church in Whittlestone a small cemetery was hidden from the roadway. To enter it, one had to walk up to the church as if entering it only to take the narrow path around the right side of the building that led to the cemetery's entrance gate. Like his birthplace, the wooden gate needed repair. He wondered why it had been ignored as he carefully lifted the latch and pushed it open. With the same care, he shut it behind him. The fence that surrounded the area was in better condition but not by much. He recalled that this was the oldest graveyard in the area and, he thought, maybe the only one. But he soon came to realize that most of the stones were at least a century old or older. It crossed his mind that perhaps his parents weren't buried here after all. With no death date to go on, he relied on the fact that they passed sometime in the last fifty years. Rather recently compared to the stones he gazed upon. But as he moved slowly through the stones, he remembered. There was a Leet family plot, the one that his parents had denied Edward entering for his final resting place. A surge of anger rose in Quin, but he needed to let it go. What was done was done. Besides, he was not here to blame his parents.

The plot contained only six headstones, the most recent being his parents. His mother died one month after his father's death thirty-one years ago in 1974. He quickly calculated that he had been forty-two. Around his time with Amelia, if he remembered correctly. Happily married if for only a short time before he deserted her and their unborn child. It was a time, he realized as he stared at his parents' stones, that he was beginning his journey without any direction in mind. A lost soul who, at the time, relished the freedom. A naïve and selfish man who had paid the price. He silently began an accurate account all those whom he had known and lost along the way. The ones who had been placed in his path to guide him if he allowed it. His thoughts tangled as he stood in front of his parents, and he struggled to clear his mind. To focus on the reason he was here, after all this time, in this cemetery on Conical Island.

"Excuse me?"

A gentle voice broke through his meanderings. He turned to see an older woman standing just to his left. She leaned heavily on a wooden walking stick, her back bent so that her upper torso leaned painfully forward. Her white hair was sparse, a whisp falling forward over her right eye. She slowly reached up to place it behind her ear before she spoke again.

"Did you know them?"

Quin barely heard her, a whispered used up voice. "Yes. They were my parents."

The woman took a step closer, her walking stick stabilizing her.

"You must be Quin Leet." She was smiling, a cockeyed sliver among the deep wrinkles that were her face.

"Yes, I am." Quin did not try to hide his surprise as he struggled to identify her. It was impossible.

"I knew your parents. Good people, they were. It was terrible to see them go but the good Lord made sure that they were not parted for long. I'm sorry you weren't able to come home for them, but they understood." She did not look at Quin but kept her eyes on the stones.

"May I ask who you are?"

"Oh, that doesn't matter anymore. I was just a friend."

Quin was sure it did matter but he wasn't sure why. "Did I know you? I'm sorry, but I don't recall."

"No. I never knew you or your brother. Edward?"

"Yes, Edward. Forgive my confusion, but how did you know them, my parents?"

"I was their doctor until the day they died. I saw your mother through her misery and despair, and I was the one to examine your father's body when they brought him back home. It was a terrible time." She slowly shook her head back and forth as she remembered.

What Quin had expected to be a simple visit with his parents was rapidly evolving into much more and he toyed with the idea of ending it now. This was not what he came to do, what he needed to do, what he needed to know. Before he could respond, the old woman continued.

"I don't know what you know about what happened. I expect nothing as your mother's despair was caused by her separation from her sons. It was a terrible time when young Edward passed and that wounded your parents to their core. They were never the same after that, I can tell you. But when your father died, I was damn sure your mother would do the same and, not long after, I was right. Ever hear of heartbroken? When the heart no longer works, well…you understand."

For one who appeared aged and infirm, Quin was taken by her ability to chat. Maybe she was lonely. He remembered Willy.

"How did my father die?" He hadn't wanted to know but she was compelling him to ask.

"He drowned at sea. The crew retrieved his body after he fell overboard but it was too late."

"Oh, my God." It was a whisper, but it carried the heavy weight of Quin's seventy-three years.

"Yes. It was to be his last fishing trip going out on that boat. He promised your mother that after this one, he was done. Ready to retire, ready to be with her and enjoy life. Terrible time."

Quin slowly digested the information. What his mother had feared everyday of her life with his father had become her reality. However, what he and Edward had fled from was not the possibility of that same reality for each of them. They had fled for other reasons, too young to consider their own mortality.

"I expect you want to visit without my interference. So I'll be on my way. My Winston is just over there." She lifted her stick a few inches off the ground as if to point out her husband's grave but immediately placed it firmly on the earth. Quin reached out to steady her but pulled his hand back as she grounded herself.

"I come to see him almost every day. It's getting harder though. But I try. Another good man."

"Thank you."

The woman looked puzzled. "Why do you say that?"

"I didn't know. I mean, about my parents. I never knew." His words weighed heavily on him.

"Don't blame yourself. What's done is done. They understood about you boys. It wasn't what they had hoped for, and they were never right with it. But I can tell you that in the end they didn't blame either one of you for leaving. It came hard for them to get to that place. I would be lying if I told you otherwise. But the important thing you got to remember is they got there. Your father told me once that his boys couldn't live his life. It was impossible. He told me…," the old woman began coughing, waving her hand at Quin not to worry, before she continued, "he told me that he had no right to tell either one of you what you can and cannot do." Another spasm. "Sorry. Ninety-four years of sea air has finally caught up with me."

"Are you okay?" His concern was sincere, and he was surprised by it.

"I am as fine as I'm meant to be. Don't you worry. Poor Winston is probably wondering what's keeping me." She looked in his direction as did Quin.

"Please, don't let me keep you. I just appreciate that you stopped to talk with me."

The old woman slowly lifted the same strand of white hair that had fallen again during her coughing fits. Her cockeyed smile reappeared, and she reached out for Quin's hand. He met hers and held on feeling the fragility of her aged body in his palm.

"Winston will understand. I am glad that we met. I think your parents are too. It's really very simple, you know. Life is simple when you get right down to it. We're just mighty good at making it harder than it needs to be. Something that I've learned over these last few years. You don't mind if I pass it on to you, do you?" Her eyes met Quin's.

Willy appeared, standing behind her, his smile as broad and warm as Quin remembered it. The moment was profound. He wanted to tell her about him, but the words remained unspoken. It wasn't necessary. She already knew. He was sure of it. What he could produce came easily.

"I don't mind at all."

A look of satisfaction crossed her aged face and Quin understood that he must remember this encounter.

"Now you have a good visit with your parents. They have been more than patient with you." She turned to his parents' headstones and spoke to them.

"It's my fault, keeping him from you. I'll be on my way now."

Her words struck him and the guilt he had submerged for so long was revealed but not by him. He was staggered by her insight or was it mere coincidence? Was she referring to the last few minutes or his entire life? Had she identified one of his many faults? The one that did not allow him to rest and find peace? Patience.

He wasn't aware of her leaving his side, his thoughts racing trying to understand. When he turned to say goodbye to her, she was halfway to Winston's headstone. A gentle rise from where Quin stood. He watched her slowly and deliberately take one small step at a time as she purposely placed her walking stick ahead of her steps. He wondered how far ahead of herself she could see, her back so stooped. A flash of memory surprised him as he recalled walking for miles in the desert following Willy, always steps behind him, always keeping his eyes only on the ground in front of him. How much of that experience had he missed? Quin kept her in sight until she turned a corner, no longer visible as she disappeared behind a great stand of trees.

He suddenly felt very alone. In the old woman's absence, Quin was aware of how comforting she had been, how much he needed to have someone tell him about his parents. A perfect stranger who knew so much more than their own son did about them. It occurred to him that he did want to know, that he had always wanted to know and that he did care about them. But, instead, he had spent almost his whole life finding diversions so as not to have to care. And each one of those diversions, he realized, had led him right back to them.

It had not been the easiest path to find his way home. He reflected on the complications that he thought he had overcome with each encounter. The list of people he had hurt along the way, none intentionally. But that last thought gave him no peace. He knew better. He heard Willy speak to him as he stood in front of his parents' graves. "Don't assume you are right, Quin, and that I am wrong." Willy's words were meant to wake him up. He understood that now as he, once again, strongly felt Willy's presence.

Quin looked around him, knowing Willy was not standing by his side but he needed to be sure. He knelt next to his mother's grave and placed his hand on the earth where he thought her heart lay. "I'm sorry, mom. I'm sorry I didn't stay with you, that I was the reason Edward left you. Please forgive me, mom." His whispered words fell from his mouth, and he did not hold back his tears. "Please, mom. Please."

When he moved to his father's grave, all regret that he expended over his mother's grave was gone. In its place, a familiar dislike began to rise from within and Quin hesitated to kneel as he had done for his mother. Instead, he stood at the foot of his father's grave and struggled to clear his mind of negative thoughts. The old woman's words had meant something to him. His father admitted that he was wrong to expect his sons to follow him to sea. At least that was how Quin interpreted them. Words, that had he heard his father say them to him before embarking on the working vessel for the mainland so long ago, might have changed everything. Might have changed Edward's and his direction. Edward would be alive now and this thought instigated a walk back in time from the old woman only minutes ago, to the moment he walked away from his father. An unraveling of his life that revealed only "what ifs". A frustrating exercise that led him nowhere. He was too old now to look forward instead of backwards, he told himself, but he knew that he had no choice. He would go forward until he couldn't, just like Willy had done. Just like the old woman now aged and physically struggling was doing and had done every day since Winston's death. And Aaron? He was going forward, making something of himself, despite being abandoned so long ago. Quin understood clearly that he had no place in his son's life and he cast no blame.

He would go forward but not as he had done so long ago with no direction and completely lost. This time he would keep in mind Willy's words. He should never have doubted him in the first place. He should have had faith. That was all Willy was asking of him. It was so simple.

"What if I tell you I know where we are and where we are going, and not in the direction you have in mind? What if I tell you that not far from here, there's a place that you've always wanted to go to?"

This time he accepted Willy's "what ifs" for they were all that mattered. Quin reached into his coat pocket. Holding the compass in his hand, he took one last look at it. He didn't need to open the lid and release the second lid to see his grandfather's inscription to his own son, Quin's father. He knew it by heart. A simple statement that gave him comfort and strength to continue. He stepped to the side of his father's grave and leaned down. Gently, he placed the compass on the earth in front of the headstone. As he did so, he remembered Aaron's words. "It never belonged to me." At the time, a hurtful comment that stung Quin, but now he understood that his son had been right. He was tempted to tell his own father the same thing but did not. Instead, he whispered once again over a parent's grave his words intended for only his father this time.

"Keep this with you, dad. It belongs to you. It's been on a long journey, and I wish I could have told you all about it before you died. But I want you to know that grandpa's words have led me right back here without me ever understanding my journey until now. Right here with you and mom. Please forgive me for what I did to you. Somehow, I've got to believe that I was always seeking true north. Maybe that was what Willy was talking about. Faith. It's taken me too long to realize it. So, you rest easy knowing that you did nothing wrong, and that grandpa's words brought me back to you."

Quin shed no more tears. He knew he wouldn't as he turned and walked away from his father and mother. He thought to look up the rise hoping to see the old woman one last time before he left Whittlestone. She was nowhere in sight. However, he knew she would stay with him. For how long, he couldn't say. But that didn't matter, did it? What mattered was that she had been in his life, as brief an encounter as it was. For that, he was grateful. And he was grateful for all who shared his journey. His footsteps were lighter, he stood straighter, and his mind was clearer than it had been in years as he walked out of the cemetery to his final destination.

Once again, Willy was present, this time walking by his side. Quin welcomed him as he heard Willy's words for the last time.

"You don't have faith, Quin. What have I been trying to tell you all along? You've got to have faith, or you don't wake up in the morning."

Quin smiled, fully certain that he would wake up tomorrow morning.

Chapter 39

There was an absence of breakfast smells, a silence in the station that was eerily disturbing as Aaron struggled to wake up. His alarm had gone off, but he hadn't heard it. As he came into the common area, Devon met him, distraught and teary eyed.

"He's gone, Aaron. Hugh's gone."

Aaron learned that Hugh Reynolds had suffered a massive heart attack, a shock to everyone at headquarters and those who knew him in the valley. He had lived each day without complaint when it came to his physical wellbeing. As a matter of fact, the subject never came up, not by him and certainly not by any of the rangers. They accepted that Hugh was a very private man when it came to anything personal, but his death left them wondering if he had been suffering while still doing his job. There was no one like Hugh Reynolds in the rangers' opinions. He was the perfect man for the job. He never let his personal life interfere with his professional one. He had made sure that no one knew anything about his life outside of the job.

He died in his sleep after a night of celebration. Two new rangers were on board and to welcome them, Hugh wanted to do it properly. Devon and Aaron were directed to make the celebration happen. Everyone was invited. All the employees at the ranch and inn facilities and every member of the Timbisha Shoshone Tribe who lived just south of the ranch on their tribal lands. The celebration went late into the warm desert night, and no one wanted it to end. It slowly wound down until just the rangers and a few employees at the ranch remained. Hugh was the one to close it completely down, citing the late hour now into the next day. Aaron and Devon cleaned up not getting to bed until almost four in the morning. Wake up was at six.

Rangers came and went in the duration of Aaron's tenure in Death Valley. When Hugh Reynolds died, Aaron mourned for a long time. The one man who filled the absent father figure role was no longer in his life. But Hugh had not departed without mentoring Aaron in the most important aspects of being human. Hugh had never really known Aaron but as time went on, Aaron realized that Hugh had understood him much more than Aaron knew himself.

In the years following Hugh's death, Aaron's new position as second in command to Head Ranger Devon Bennett demanded everything of him, and he gladly welcomed the challenge. He worked every day to be the best he could be. To be the person Hugh would expect him to be. Not a day went by without Aaron taking a moment to remember Hugh and to thank him. It became a ritual that Aaron committed to. It was the least he could do for the man. Aaron never allowed himself to think beyond the strong connection he felt for Hugh, that of respect, admiration, mentorship, and gratitude. But there would always be something missing between Hugh and him that would complete an unsatisfied need to be loved by a real father.

Aaron never heard from Quin Leet again. As the years passed, Aaron did not forget his encounter with Quin. It was not for lack of trying. In the months immediately following Quin's revelation, Aaron had moments of regret and doubt. If Quin Leet was really his father, should he have turned him away as he had? Was Quin telling the truth that he never knew about the pregnancy? Had he reacted too quickly giving in to his disgust for the man who did not follow the rules. It was so simple, in Aaron's thinking. If you commit to someone whom you love, then you stay with that person. If children come along, you stay committed to them to see them through no matter how long it takes. One thing was certain for Aaron. No one had the right to come back into his life as Quin had done and expect all to be forgiven. To pick up where nothing had ever started. It was all too much for Aaron to deal with and so he unsuccessfully struggled to forget.

The day began as most in the height of summer in the desert. The sun scorched the earth earlier in the day so that by midmorning the heat was unbearable. These were not the days that Aaron enjoyed. Not like the early spring days that filled the valley and its surrounding hills with wildflowers, especially if the rains of the previous season had been plentiful. Everywhere he looked, evidence of new beginnings greeted him as he welcomed another season. On days like today, however, he never gave into the temptation to stay in the airconditioned building. He had a job to do no matter what mother earth's status was.

"We've got another one." Devon stood in the doorway of Aaron's office.

Aaron did not look up from his computer right away. He was one sentence away from completing the monthly report. He held his hand up signaling to Devon to hold on.

"Okay. Got that one off my back. Sorry, sir. Say again."

"We're going to need a chopper for this one. Out in the southeastern end. It was just reported to the information center."

"Any more details than that?"

"Just that it's one deceased person a couple of hikers came upon."

Aaron wasted no time calling the incident in and getting the chopper in the air. In recovery mode, he acted almost by instinct, following protocol and not letting emotions interfere. No one on staff ever wanted to hear what was just reported to him. His humanity would have to wait for him to allow it entry. All business now and nothing else.

"Get Karen and Dave on it."

"You and me, we're not heading out?" Aaron was surprised by Devon's decision.

"No. It's a good one for them. If it was a rescue, well, that's a different story. Recovery's a good place to start. Besides, Steve Lenox is flying, right?

"Right. I just confirmed it with him."

"He'll make sure they don't mess up. Time for the chicks to leave the nest."

Aaron recalled his first time, but he had had Hugh with him. About to question's Devon's decision, he thought better of it. Devon was not Hugh. Besides, Devon was in charge, not him.

The area where the body was found was off the beaten track. The deceased had to have hiked in purposely, the terrain unforgiving and desolate. There was no easy entrance that the rangers could see. Not like the alluvial plains that invited one to explore. The area in front of them was rough rock formations that rose from the valley floor well above any of their heads. They wondered if the deceased had found its way to its final resting place by a different route. One from the east instead of from the valley floor. Had the deceased's destination been the valley?

The chopper hovered over the body, releasing its basket to the rangers below. Karen and Dave, both a bit shaken that, for the first time, they were putting into play the protocols for recovering a body, watched as the basket rose into the bowels of the chopper and then flew off. There was nothing more to be done. The report from the medical examiner would follow.

Aaron tried to stay calm but his frustration with incidences like this one always got the best of him. He knew why. Hugh. How many times had he listened to Hugh express his feelings regarding people who didn't follow the rules. Who thought that nothing applied to them that applied to everyone else. Who were stupid enough to risk their lives as well as those of the ones who had to rescue them. Possibly recover them, as was the case this morning. As much as Aaron tried to sympathize, he could not. They had not followed the rules. It was just that simple.

The report was sent down almost a full week later. Pending DNA results, the deceased was listed as "John Doe". Aaron learned that the victim's death was initially the result of multiple rattle snake strikes. Unusual for multiple strikes, Aaron thought, but the report stated that the victim suffered from seven strikes on different parts of the body. The amount of venom in the deceased's body was enough to kill a large animal or two. Stunned by this information, Aaron tried to imagine what could have taken place for such a death to occur. The only explanation he could come up with was that the deceased had to have disturbed a nest of rattlers. He shuddered to imagine the actual attack. And for a moment, he detected something like sympathy for the poor soul. He would not wish that kind of death on his worst enemy.

A separate mailing arrived the following week from the coroner's office addressed to Aaron. The outer envelope contained a formal letter stating that the personal possessions of "John Doe" were now in Aaron's possession, as requested by the deceased in a written request found on the deceased's body. It was a small package in which a new compass in a silver case had been placed in a small plastic bag along with a note. Not putting two and two together at first, Aaron's curiosity was peaked. It wasn't until he unfolded the note paper and read the signature that he almost lost it. He closed his office door and pulled down the shade. Visibly shaking, he sat down behind his desk and let the paper fall to its surface. The compass lay underneath it.

After all this time, every emotion Aaron had felt when Quin was in front of him trying to explain himself, rose to the surface and Aaron sat paralyzed, unable to take the next step. He didn't want to, but he knew he had no choice. Quin was not done with him any more than Aaron was done with Quin. Aaron reached for the note praying that what he was about to do would not change anything in his life, not then and not now. Quin's intrusion was not welcomed but Aaron could not ignore it.

"*Dear Aaron,*

If I don't reach you to give this to you in person, I hope that whoever finds me will get it to you. I know you didn't want what was rightfully yours, so I got you your very own. No strings attached. You see, it carries no history until you make it. Let it guide you on the rest of your journey.

Quin"

Aaron held the compass in his palm and felt a familiar weight to it. Suspecting what he was sure to be true, he squeezed the sides of the lid until the second was revealed. And, as he suspected, the underside of the first revealed an inscription. "*To my son, with my love.*"

Aaron did not cry. In fact, he did not react at all. He was suddenly devoid of feeling anything. Instead, he tucked the compass into his pants pocket, folded the note and slipped it into his desk drawer. He left the office and headed out to where Quin's body had been recovered. The heat of the day was intense, but he didn't care. He knew what he had to do.

He parked and walked in as far as he could. The next leg would involve climbing and he had come prepared. When he reached the top of the rock formation, he headed farther into it, wary of hidden dangers like those that had greeted Quin. It never occurred to him to question the sanity of what he was doing. It never occurred to him that he was going against everything he knew was wrong, everything that he had mentored the younger rangers never to do. To go it alone. Not to tell anyone where he was going. Not until Hugh's voice rang in his ears as he maneuvered his body through the narrow openings in the rocks, slender gateways to the unseen other side. The farther he made his way back into the formations, the less he comprehended anything but what lay immediately in front of him. One careful step at a time. One hand placement for balance only after observing no hidden dangers. One deep breath at a time as he struggled in the intensified heat radiating from the rocks' surfaces that surrounded him now. He stopped and drank, small portions, enough to keep his head clear.

Referring to the rangers' report, he came to the spot where Quin's body had been found and stopped his forward movement. He stood frozen. He knew he needed to back up, but his body would not obey his brain's command. He didn't dare turn to look around him. If others were there, they would make their presence known. He waited, keeping his eyes on it.

The rattler was enormous even in its coiled state. Aaron could gather that much as he mentally judged its girth by the height of the coils. The snake's head was as big as his hand and Aaron was mesmerized by its gentle swaying back and forth as its forked tongue searched the air. Its tail positioned vertically above the top coil displayed a series of rattles that extended down its tail at least three inches. It was an incredible specimen and Aaron, his fear mounting by the second, could not help but appreciate it and comprehend that he was in the presence of the inexplicable.

Time stood still. He had lost count of it. None of that mattered as he listened for others. But silence filled the rock formation. It had not rattled. It had done nothing but set its eyes on Aaron, its tongue still searching the air, its tail still vertical, its rattles silent. How long he had been standing there, Aaron could not tell. It was a matter of who would retreat first, he was beginning to realize. The law of nature was not on his side. He had trespassed into their territory, and they were cordial enough to allow him to admit his mistake and depart. He knew all this as he imagined a conversation with the only one he could see. The one who must be trying to communicate this to him. But still, he could not bring himself to leave.

"You must be the elder of your family. The wisest of them all." Aaron heard his words whispered to the snake surprising himself. Was he losing his mind in the heat? What was he doing? But he continued. "What do you want from me? Will you let me leave you unharmed? Will you leave me unharmed?"

Aaron waited. The snake's eyes never leaving Aaron as he spoke, and they stayed on his when he stopped speaking. Still no warnings were heard. The snake withdrew its tongue and lowered its head but did not uncoil nor lower its tail. Instead, Aaron watched in horror as its head touched the surface of the rock and begin to move towards him, the rest of its body slowly following.

If he could just hold still long enough, could hide his fear, all the while trying to comprehend what was taking place, he might survive. Now within two feet of him, the snake continued its advance. As it did so, Aaron could finally see what he had suspected. This was the largest rattler he had ever seen, and he wondered if he was in the presence of one of a kind. No one would believe this.

Aaron was aware that there was no escape that wouldn't set the snake off. Any movement would be clumsy and dangerous if he tried. The snake's body, now half exposed while the other half remained coiled, was less than a foot away from Aaron's boots. And it came even closer so that Aaron, in disbelief, imagined that it would continue its crawl onto his boot and up his leg. The sweat dripped from his forehead and his face prickled from the dampness that he could not wipe clear.

Indeed, his worst fear was taking place as the snake's head made its way on top of his boot and then continued over the other. Statuesque, he dared not lower his head to witness his inevitable demise. Instead, he kept his head upright while his eyes strained to watch its movements below him.

The rattler moved across his boot tops and, just before completely crossing them stopped. Aaron watched as it raised its head and turned as if to take one last look at Aaron. Its tongue continued to search the air, its flickers rapid and intense, until it turned its head away. Its long body moved over Aaron's boot tops slowly as the snake's full body continued to uncoil.

When it was gone, Aaron still could not move. Afraid of its whereabouts, he tried to breathe deeply and slowly, conscious of his rapid pulse. Fear and excessive heat were his enemies now and he longed to be off the rocks and in the safety of his truck. But he would need to wait it out, until he was sure it had gone on its way.

The climb down the rocks was the most harrowing he had ever experienced and, if he made it out safely, it dawned on him that it would make a great story at dinner that night with everyone. A passing thought that he quickly shut down as he focused on the terrain in front of him and underfoot. The final drop-off of the rock formation landed him safely on the desert surface once again. His mind on nothing else other than getting in the truck and heading back to headquarters, Aaron wasted no time as he turned onto to the roadway.

It wasn't until he was in the safety of his bedroom that it all hit him. Behind a closed door, Aaron sat on the edge of his bed and recalled the last few hours. His reason for going out there in the first place? To see where Quin had perished. He struggled to find the answer as to why he needed to be there. Perhaps there wasn't one, other than he needed closure. Something that never entered his mind before. He had been done with Quin. That was until the compass came to him from his father.

In the quiet of his room, what should have concerned him well before now, suddenly overwhelmed him. If Quin wanted to give the compass to him, why hadn't he? He knew where to find him. Why had Quin returned to the desert? And at his age? Aaron figured he must have been in his eighties by now. He must have known that he would not survive this time. The note inferred that he did. Why had he taken her on one last time when he didn't need to? He had no answers for he knew there were none. Quin had seen to that.

And the snake? Why had there been the biggest rattler he had ever seen resting on Quin's deathbed? And why had the encounter played out as it had? Unbelievable in every aspect but a story, nonetheless. If he were superstitious, Aaron could imagine why he had experienced a near death moment. Had been witness to one of mother nature's prized gifts. Had been spared his life, unlike Quin. He wondered if this same snake had led in the attack on Quin. And then he wondered if the snake was trying to tell him something. Not a warning as much as a communication that Aaron had, at one time, specifically chosen not to hear. As foolish as it sounded in his head, he could not ignore the thought. Had Quin only been an idea, a place holder for the real thing, a passing thought without any permanency? Not a companion, mentor, and certainly never a father. Quin had walked out of Aaron's life before it ever began and just recently had walked out of his life once again midway through Aaron's journey. And now, finally out of his son's life forever because the desert had not been merciful.

Suddenly, he recalled what he had purposely submerged. He felt Hugh's arm against his chest, holding him back as they came upon Quin. He saw the snake resting on Quin's chest. And he saw it crawl away from Quin as if its responsibility to protect Quin was now left up to someone else. Had this same snake found Quin's final resting place again, once again staying with him even in Quin's absence? And if it had, what did it all mean? Had it purposely waited for Aaron to come upon it, to finally come to his father's last place on earth? And had it left Aaron, slowly crossing over his boots with no intention of harming him other than to remind him of why he needed to come there in the first place?

Aaron's thoughts collided and shattered the more he tried to understand. He was exhausted both physically and mentally. It was all he could do to get up, shower, and calm himself. He would be able to think better once he had. Forgetting that the compass was in his pants pocket, he threw his clothes into the hamper along with a week's worth of laundry.

During dinner that night, he kept all that had transpired to himself, still not fully understanding its significance, if any. He realized that he had no way of explaining any of this to anyone else if he couldn't explain it to himself. As Hugh had taught him, keep personal business to yourself. Eyes on the job. When he recalled Hugh, the rest fell into place easily.

"Excuse me, sir?" Karen came up behind Aaron as he was getting into his truck to start his morning rounds. "Dave found this in one of the washing machines. He gave it to me to give to you. Figured you could mention it at dinner tonight?" Karen handed Aaron the compass.

It hit him squarely and soundly as if Tim, Everett, Hugh, and Quin were lined up in front of him, each with the self-assurance that eventually Aaron Crenshaw would finally understand. Aaron smiled, the first time in days, as he took the compass from Karen's hand and held it tightly in his own. It couldn't be more obvious as Aaron said a silent thank you and then said aloud the same to Karen.

"Right. No need. I'll take care of it. I know who it belongs to."

Acknowledgements

The first time I traveled to the desert, I held an unspoken fear of it. I had only my imaginings of what I would experience once there. Intolerable heat, desolation, poisonous things, void of all that I knew to be beautiful. However, nothing prepared me for the indelible impression it left upon me. Yes, it was hot and yes, it was desolate and yes, poisonous things existed but so did an indescribable beauty that changed from moment to moment in every direction I turned. But more than this, the sacredness of this land made itself known to me, and my initial fear of the desert no longer existed. In its place and deeply seated in my soul, resides a reverence for this land's profound existence.

I offer my thanks to the National Park Service Rangers who introduced me to Death Valley and its surroundings. As one of millions of visitors to the valley, I was made to feel that I was important enough for them to spend time with me as they regaled me with their experiences and knowledge of this magical place. My questions were answered and those that weren't, were not supposed to be. Better to leave to the imagination.

My deepest thanks, however, is to one that will not read this, nor understand my words of gratitude spoken aloud. In fact, even if it could, it would not care one way or the other. But even so, I will continue to thank the desert for its gifts. This story begins in the desert and ends there. Its influence on the characters who appeared on these pages was not of my doing. They were subject to her just as I had been the first time we met. This story could not have developed as it did without her.

Finally, my thanks always to my dear husband, John. Without his wanderlust, the desert might still be a stranger to me, my imaginings continuing to get the better of me.

About the Author

Born in Massachusetts but raised in California, Linda M. Mutty knew the Santa Clara Valley before it was Silicon Valley. Her explorations of the state have covered miles of its diverse topography, leaving indelible imprints that find their way into her novels. In her most recent book, *An Accurate Account*, the mystique of Death Valley takes center stage. In *Cadences*, her debut novel, as in her second novel, *A Stone's Throw Away*, she draws on her memories and experiences while exploring the power of the unknown and it inevitable impact on human interaction. Her stories create a playground where fact, fiction, and the unknown collide.

Linda M. Mutty lives in Carmel, California with her wise and loving husband.